The Edge of the Water

Michael McNabb

Writers Club Press
San Jose • New York • Lincoln • Shanghai

The Edge of the Water

All Rights Reserved © 2000 by Michael McNabb

No part of this book may be reproduced or
transmitted in any form or by any means, graphic, electronic,
or mechanical, including photocopying, recording, taping, or by any
information storage or retrieval system,
without the permission in writing
from the publisher.

Published by Writers Club Press
an imprint of iUniverse.com, Inc.

For information address:
iUniverse.com, Inc.
620 North 48th Street
Suite 201
Lincoln, NE 68504-3467
www.iuniverse.com

This is a work of fiction. Any resemblence to any persons, living or dead, is merely coincidental.

ISBN: 0-595-09845-2

Printed in the United States of America

To my loving wife, Kay.

Thanks for hanging in there.

Acknowledgements

I want to thank two wonderful writers, Helen Adams Ingram and Marcia Pugh, for their encouragement and support. I especially want to thank Mrs. Sharon W. Putman, my editor, for her excellent work in turning my manuscript into a book. May God bless all of you.

Chapter One

My name is Doug Wallace, and I have a story to tell you that occurred during the summer of 1963. One of the nice things about my tale is that you don't have to know anything about the sixties to be able to relate to the changes I encountered. If there are any qualities that would be helpful in enjoying this story, being a baby-boomer is one of them. For the rest of you, even those born after the sixties, the ability to remember your life as a sixteen-year-old will be more than enough.

The summer of 1963 was a time of subtle and dramatic change for many of us. We were right on the cusp of a societal revolution that would affect an entire generation. Most of us still had fresh memories of our childhood of the fifties such as "I Love Lucy," "The Lone Ranger" and "Sky King." One of the most popular movies of 1963 was "The Birds" by Alfred Hitchcock. "Lawrence of Arabia won the academy award that year for the best movie of 1962, and "How the West was Won" got a big award for a great concept in film making called Cinemascope. Chevy Impalas and Buick Riveras ruled the roads.

Our music was The Beach Boys, Elvis, Bobby Vinton, Little Richard, Ray Charles, Roy Orbison. A group called the Kingsmen got a lot of airplay for "Louie Louie." Neil Sedaka sang about breaking up being so hard to do. Ben E. King sang "Stand by Me," and the Marcels belted out "Blue Moon." I can still remember the Isley Brothers who came out with "Shout" and "Twist and Shout." Both songs were classics. In the meantime, Dion was "Wandering."

This is also a story about my summer of awakening to a new beginning. The setting of this journey is in a small mountain resort town named Gatlinburg. Nestled in the Great Smoky Mountains in east Tennessee, I stood at the edge of the cold and turbulent stream of life and dipped my toe into the water. This was my first startling contact with adulthood, and my life was forever changed for years to come.

Quite often, I got in over my head, but it was a real rush. Like that summer of your own, you may of gotten in slowly or dived in head first. Either way, you'll remember how it felt.

You have your stories and I have mine. In order for you to gain a better perspective on my journey, I want to introduce you to my family. It has been said that sometimes people get mixed up with a tough crowd. Well, I think that happened to me at birth.

My mother was the oldest of three children, the others being boys. A taciturn and demanding father had raised them on a farm. He was a tall, raw-boned man who rarely smiled and believed that hard work was the reason for one's existence on earth. Never one to show much affection, the primary attention he gave his children was a beating with a razor strop. My grandmother, who had been orphaned at an early age, always stood by in deference to Granddaddy, because she, too, had been put in her place several times over the years. She would read her Bible and pray silently to herself until she could reach some level of serenity.

What goes around, comes around. Mother learned a lot of lessons from her father and carried them with her all of her life.

My father had a little different childhood. His mother and two older sisters had been the primary influences in his development. His father, a railroad worker, had had a stroke when my father was about ten. The stroke had been severe enough to render him homebound and in a constant state of confusion. He often told my father that he was bound to die in the electric chair every time Dad's mother or sisters told my grandfather of some minor offense he had committed. The greatest lesson my father learned from all of this was to be submissive.

Are you beginning to get the picture? My mother and father were made for each other. Not exactly a marriage made in heaven but more like a union that produced material that keeps psychologists and psychiatrists with crowded waiting rooms and large houses. Their heavy caseload is based upon the premise that there are people who actually seek help for their problems. That is much truer today than it was in the fifties and sixties.

You may be asking yourself the validity of this retrospection without some examples? That is certainly justifiable and worthy of a few examples. However, I must preface these examples by telling you that I never had any doubt about my mother's love for us. She was a big proponent of tough love way before it became a popular bit of psycho-babble. My experience with tough love is that it may be due to the absence of a "compassion gene" or an "ability-to-express-love gene." Either way, tough is a good descriptive word, and my mother loved the absolute hell out of us.

Mother taught me how to fight dirty. As a child, I was always on the heavy side. Let me rephrase that. I was always the fattest kid in my class. Start with "fatso," move on to "lard ass" and develop you own list of cruel names for someone overweight. I hated being picked on and hated fighting more, until my mother gave me some tips on the old sucker punch.

"Hit 'em first, hit 'em fast and hit 'em hard," my mother screamed at me after I had once come home crying. She grabbed me by the shoulders and shook me, her fingers digging into my skin.

"The element of surprise and sudden pain will work wonders on those sons-of-bitches. You need to learn how to hit somebody squarely in the nose so fast and hard that they never see it coming. Especially if you put all **your** weight behind it."

I looked into her ice blue eyes. Her teeth were clenched and the veins in her temples were throbbing. A strand of her blonde hair fell across her forehead. She was almost drooling. For a moment, I was sure that she could've whipped anybody that crossed her. I included those boxers I used to watch with my dad on the Gillette Friday night fights.

I knew my mother meant business, so I had a couple of choices. I could start kicking some ass or get all my crying out of the way before I came home. I chose to try it in my mother's way at the next opportunity which I was sure would be in the very near future.

My chance to prove myself occurred a couple of weeks later on the ride home on the school bus. One of the kids in my neighborhood had been tormenting me loudly to the amusement of everyone on the bus. I just sat there and let my rage build, trying to think of a way to get back at the little red-headed, freckle-faced bastard.

I had a reputation in my class for being a pretty good artist. Even the kids who made fun of me gave me high praise for my accurate drawings, so I decided to use that as a lure. When Ricky and I got off at our stop, I asked him if he wanted to look at my latest spaceship drawing. I guess he was so accustomed to my never fighting back, he said sure and strolled over to me as I lay my notebook on the ground and squatted to turn the pages. I was almost shaking with anticipation as I planned my move.

Keeping my head down in serious concentration, I said to him when I saw his tennis shoes next to my notebook, "You'll have to lean over to look at it. Its kinda small."

I looked up at him as he began leaning over. I balled my fist as tightly as I could and swung for his mouth. There was a look of utter shock on his face as he fell back on his ass. His lip was bleeding and one of his front teeth dangled from his mouth. As he began to realize what had happened, he began to bawl loudly. I was shaking so terribly, I didn't think I would be able to pick up my notebook, but I did. Just before I left him, I leaned over, spat in his face and turned away toward home. I never noticed that my knuckles were bleeding.

When I got home, my mother's face was flushed a bright red and her eyes were as big as saucers. I had no idea what to expect when she grabbed me and hugged me so hard that I could barely breathe.

"I saw the whole thing from the front window. Honey, I'm so proud of you. You really nailed that little shit. Look at your hand. Is that his blood or yours?"

As I look back on how I felt at the time, I was sure that the gold medal winners in the Olympics had nothing on me.

After washing up and putting a bandage on my hand, she fixed me a large glass of chocolate milk and a small plate of cookies. Her face was glowing with pride.

In a few minutes, our phone rang and Mother answered it. I wasn't paying any attention until I heard my mother say, "Yes, I'm his mother."

I looked in her direction, and she smiled at me and winked. I kept my attention on her side of the conversation.

"Is that right?" She asked.

"Hmmm."

"Pay for the dental work? When hell freezes over, you bitch. Your son is lucky my boy didn't knock all of his goddamn teeth out. You come over here and I'll knock out a few of your teeth, too."

With that she slammed the phone down and laughed gleefully.

"Stupid bitch," she said to no one in particular.

A few years later, my mother taught me about the quick kick in the nuts. This, she pointed out, was a very effective method of putting someone on the ground. Once they were on the ground, you should keep kicking your victim until your legs were worn out.

I learned my lessons well. That of a person who was unpredictable and viscous replaced my reputation as an artist. I became the protector of my younger brother and gained the admiration of the school thugs.

During all of this time, my dad pretty much left the pugilistic training up to my mother. He knew that she was the expert in physical contact. As I look back, I really believe that Mother and Mike Tyson shared a similar psychological profile.

The unfortunate thing about Mother was that if someone had not offended her, she often took it out on my dad, my brother and me. Sometimes she even imagined some sort of insult by another person that would fire her temper into high gear. The thing was that you never saw it coming.

Chapter Two

Right on time. Ever since I had gotten my driver's license in March, my dad had imposed a midnight curfew on me. He once told me that he could set his watch by the noise of the garage door being raised as I returned home. I always figured that if I obeyed the small rules I could break the big ones. Funny how you can believe it works that way.

    I had just spent four hours cruising back and forth between the Dwarf drive-in and the A&W drive-in, waving to my friends, eyeballing girls and occasionally stopping for a coke when I could find a spot next to someone I knew. The nights always brought a sweet relief to the blistering summer days, and there was nothing better than cruising the streets of town in a car that I had spent hours washing, polishing, vacuuming and getting it in proper cruising appearance. I was proud of it even if it was nothing but a faded blue Ford Fairlane. After I pulled away from my parent's view, I would stop and remove the hubcaps from the wheels. That was the look then: stripped for speed. Nobody ever mentioned that it was your parents' piece of shit Ford. They knew I was making the same statement as everyone else. Of course the older hoods as we called them, with real sharp cars and greased hair, cigarettes hanging from the corner of their mouths, would just smirk at your pitiful efforts to make your rag-mobile look tough. But they never said much, because they knew that every sixteen year-old had to start somewhere, even if it was embarrassing. A smirk was enough of a put-down in those days.

My hometown of Maryville, a small city nestled in the foothills of the Great Smoky Mountains, had all the essentials of a small southern town. There were two main banks, one city high school and three drive-in movie theaters, which were packed on Friday and Saturday nights in any kind of weather. There were four department stores, all family owned. Most people still shopped in the downtown area because the malls were still in the blueprint stage.

Since Maryville was in the center of a vast number of farms in surrounding counties, stores were always busy on Saturday. That's when you had a combination of farmers and mountain people who could easily be identified by their washed and ironed work clothes. They also had the dour expressions of people who mistrusted "city folks."

If you wanted to take a "trip" shopping, you would drive the seventeen or so miles to the big city of Knoxville. The trip would also include a drive through, or by the campus of the University of Tennessee, the southern Mecca of college football. Almost everyone within a one hundred-mile radius of Knoxville was a rabid Volunteer fan. Three cheers for the orange and white of the Tennessee Vols. Many of the followers could recite from memory the history of the football team. Probably seventy-five percent of those orange-blooded fans had never attended a class at the university.

Small, sleepy, gossipy, sly, friendly, quietly bigoted, classy, country, growing; you had all the basic elements of the arch-typical southern town. As a matter of fact, Maryville was a microcosm of America in the sixties and had everything you could possibly need from life. It just didn't seem like it at the time.

I was looking forward to a whole summer of goofing around with my buddies and trying to get laid. If not the whole summer-just until two-a-days of football practice started in August's brutal heat. I could sweat out all the cokes then. Between the caffeine and sugar I was ingesting and a serious overload of testosterone, I was a seething mass of libidinous emotions. As I look back, I have to ask myself, "Is it really possible to occupy your mind with sex that much?" I hoped I was just a normal teenager, but I sometimes wondered if there wasn't some kind of psychological stuff that made me abnormal. Yet, when I got together with my buddies, that's about all we talked about until we got tired and shifted the conversation to sports.

I was absolutely positive that everyone but yours truly had already gotten laid the same day they got their driver's license. That's the way it was supposed to work for guys. Get your license and proceed down the hall to the door that read "Get Laid Here." The DMV probably had the office shut down for repairs or remodeling on the day I took the driver's test. Anyway, as I raised the garage door, I figured I had all summer to remedy this situation. Right now, all I wanted was a peanut butter sandwich and a glass of milk.

After my midnight snack, I washed the dishes and put them away. Not because I was such a finicky housekeeper, but because I didn't want my mother to go down into the kitchen in the morning and start yelling at the top of her lungs that "Nobody does a damn thing around here but me. I'm just a goddamn servant." Those outbursts always sent dad, my little brother and me scurrying around, looking for the cause of her irritation, each of us secretly hoping that is was one of the others. If my dad had been smart, he would have had a coffeepot, cigarettes, a lighter and an ashtray on her bedside stand so she could get a quick fix in the morning before she had any contact with another human being. Anyway, you learned. You just had to avoid ambushes whenever you could, and the rest of the time, you simply hoped for the best. That's pretty much the way the three of us worked the program.

Now, don't let me give you the wrong impression about my mother. My grandfather, as I have mentioned earlier, was a pretty hard man who rarely showed any emotion other than anger. The best person on the face of the earth was my grandmother, who I called Mama, and she tried to balance things out by being very kind and loving. But, granddaddy ruled the land with an iron fist.

My mother was the oldest of three, the other two being boys, and she was also very beautiful. Tall for a woman, she was always conscious of her figure and her blonde hair. At the age of nineteen, she had been a runner-up in a local bathing-beauty contest. I guess if there had been a talent competition, she would have arm-wrestled and beaten any man in the place. Even now, at the age of forty-three, she still looked a decade younger than her age. Growing up on a farm meant hard work all the time. Even school was better than the summer when she and her brothers labored as farm hands.

My mother loved my brother and me in her own special way. She was raising us the way she had been raised. I've often thought that if my mother were a teenager in the nineties, she would have had a tattoo on her arm that read: "Don't Fuck With Me." She had that kind of protective attitude about her boys. "Fuck with them and I'll kill you."

Dad was pretty content to stay out of Mother's way. I wish I could have known his dad. He had been a doctor who started carrying the mail because people back then paid you in chickens and corn. It wasn't exactly legal tender. My dad was overseas in the "big war," as it was called, when his dad died.

Actually my parents made a pretty good tag-team when it came to discipline. The threat of swift and sudden physical violence like a loaded gun was my mother's style. Dad, well he would just talk you to death. As I grew older, I would've opted for a whipping rather than one of dad's lectures. He was a real talkative guy. Even when we went to the grocery store as a family (this was considered a form of family entertainment), he would meet somebody he knew or who knew somebody he knew. They'd strike up a conversation and still be talking when Mother would lay her hand down on the car horn until the battery would almost go dead. Dad knew it was time to go. The endless blast of a horn had some people thinking it was a horn that got stuck. Dad knew better.

Life, as far as I knew at that age, was as good as it was ever going to get. You did what you had to do to maintain the domestic tranquillity and head for cover the rest of the time.

After making sure I'd left no traces of being in the kitchen, I went upstairs to bed. As I lay there, I started to fantasize about running for touchdowns and having everybody cheer for me. Besides sex, that was my favorite fantasy.

Chapter Three

I was awakened abruptly by my mother, standing over me, shaking me roughly by the shoulder and saying, "Wake up, Doug. Wake up. Paul's on the phone and says he's got a summer job for you. Get up and answer the damn phone." She persisted with the shaking, even though my eyes were open, as though she was attempting to not only wake me but shake away the cobwebs as well. When I looked at her and saw that excited determination in her eyes, I knew she wasn't kidding. I'd better get the hell out of bed.

Completely rattled, I sat up and pulled my pillow over my lap. Taking the hint, she wheeled out of the room saying, "Hurry up. He's on the phone." I sighed deeply and pulled on my jeans which were lying on the floor next to my bed. I got to my feet and began staggering downstairs to the kitchen to answer the phone. We were a one-phone house. The reasoning was that only one person could talk anyway. Don't need two phones. One question I had learned to never ask my mother was "why." You just did it. Now, every time I see one of those goofy commercials about some running shoe that says, "Just do it," I think of my mother. Just do it.

"What?" I asked. Sometimes you never knew what to expect from Paul. It could have been just some dumb prank to get my mother's jets fired up. Still, that wouldn't be like Paul. He knew my mother and pranks like that would've meant she would hunt him down and kill him.

"Wake up, you dumb ass. I just had a talk with the manager of this restaurant where I'm working, and she said you could have a job for the summer if you could get up here before the end of the morning shift. The shift ends at 2:30 this afternoon. Get your ass in gear." Paul was always in a constant state of excitement which was the exact opposite of me. I was always in a state of impending doom. Sort of. Maybe suspicious would be a better word.

"Slow down a minute. I just woke up a second ago. What are you talking about? What job? Where?" I spat all of this out as rapidly as I could to let Paul know that I was in no mood for one of his jokes.

"In Gatlinburg, man," he almost shouted. "I've got you a real nice place to stay with me and a bunch of other guys, and the boss says you can start the first thing in the morning. She wants to get all the paperwork done before she gets off this afternoon so she doesn't have to do it in the morning. You got any black slacks?"

A real nice place with Paul and a bunch of other guys? Got to be a reformatory. Gatlinburg? For the summer? Why do I need black slacks? My mind was working like a rock tumbler on high. I became rational enough to realize that I could get out of the house, make some money, maybe score with a girl, and be on my own. For the whole summer. With my mother's blessing. All of this was sounding like it was too good to be true. Which happened to be one of the great philosophies my dad shared with my brother and me. If it looks real good, there's a good chance it's a real bad deal.

Much later in life, I was told that you actually could be born a cynic. There was a gene for cynicism. If that were true, I was infested.

Apparently, Paul had already given my mother all of the details. I could hear her upstairs tearing through the closets to find some luggage to pack. I guess she thought this would be a real learning experience. Living on my own. Man, was she ever right.

When I asked Paul what kind of work it was, he replied, "Working in a restaurant. As a busboy. You'll make minimum wage plus two meals a day. Your bed only costs a dollar a day, so you'll be rolling in money."

Busboy, what the hell was that? My bed? Like some migrant farmer's barracks? I started having some real reservations about all of this.

"What's a busboy?" I asked.

Paul explained, "You clean up tables as soon as the people get up to go. It's real easy. The only downside is you don't get any tips. The waiters and waitresses get all those. But at least you don't have to listen to all the bitching and moaning from the jerk-off tourists. That gets old real fast. Really you don't have to talk to anybody, so I figured you'd be a natural."

It was widely known among his friends and relatives that Paul would talk to a post as long as it didn't move. Consequently, he assumed that anybody different from him was shy, stupid or a social misfit. It never occurred to him that the world was made up of introverts and extroverts. As a matter of fact, he would never have known what those words meant. I felt that there were a lot of things that Paul didn't know, but as friends go, he was true blue. What you saw was what you got. Paul's hidden agenda would never screw you because he didn't have a clue as to what a hidden agenda was. He just liked and trusted people. I sort of envied him a little for that, but then I thought it was kind of dangerous, too. Some people can turn on you in a flash.

"If you can hear my mom thrashing around to get me ready, I guess you know I'm on my way," I told him.

"Yeah," he responded. "She'll probably make the two-hour drive in an hour. I've already given her directions to the restaurant, so just get up here and I'll help you get situated. I gotta go – it's my nickel. I knew better than to call your mom collect," he said in a matter-of-fact way.

After Paul and I hung up, my mother came into the kitchen and told me to get dressed so we could go shopping to get me some new white shirts and a black bow tie. I never said anything about breakfast. Mom was in high gear. Just do it.

As I look back on the events of that morning and how it started the ball rolling that would shape my future, I guess it is fair to say that sometimes you just gotta dive in. Don't weigh in with a lot of pros and cons…just do it. Don't think-just do it. Much later in life, I found out what a dangerous way of living that can be. The "don't think" part. Somehow the word impulsive comes to mind.

Mom used to shop like a guy. Know what you're looking for, go in, get it and get out. It was almost military in the approach. As we were speeding along as fast as the old Ford Fairlane would go, she would give me a briefing on which roads we were going to take to minimize left turns. She also gave me directions as to what I should do when we got to Harman's Clothing and Dry Goods Store. Now, Harman's was not anything like the department stores you see in malls today. This old place was made of clapboard wood and had two large plate-glass windows in the front where the store's owners would paint the weekly specials and sales on a large piece of paper and tape it to the windows. They used to use white shoe polish on the windows until they got too old to clean them once a week. They only realized that after someone asked them why they had a sale on women's bathing suits in November. I once thought it would be funny to drive over to the store some night about three in the morning and paint on the windows: "All Women's Clothing Half Off."

My mother told me she would find the shirts in the size I needed, and I was to go find five pairs of black socks. When I told her that I'd be working seven days a week, she asked me if I'd ever heard of a washing machine. That pretty much settled that.

"I know you need two more pairs of black slacks, too. Lucky they've come out with that wash and wear stuff. We've got to get moving before someone else comes along and steals your job. Hurry." Steals my job. Typical thinking on her part.

Now you may wonder how my mother could have known exactly what size pants a sixteen year-old kid would need. Mom was not only conscious of her figure, she was conscious of everybody's figure. Especially mine. I had been a fat kid. Not a whale, but pretty round. I had to go to the "husky" sizes to get my clothes. I hated that. Why didn't they just say, Lard Ass Kids Clothes?

Once, my mother had discovered a doctor who had an office in a little town that you drove through when you were heading for the mountains. Early in the summer between my freshman and sophomore years in high school, my mother made an appointment to go see this doctor she'd heard about who was doing wonderful things for people who "had a weight problem." When we walked into the waiting room, it reminded me of a freak show. There was a bunch of grossly obese people-men, women and children sitting fat buttock to fat buttock anxiously waiting for their name to be called. As I studied this crowd a little more, I actually saw some skinny people wedged in between the lard. They reminded me of birds. They would nervously glance around as if the slightest noise was going to make them jump up and bay like the hounds of hell. They didn't talk to anybody; they just sat there and smoked one cigarette after another. I said to myself, "What are these people who look like the survivors of a Nazi concentration camp doing here?"

After what seemed like three hours, our name was called. I had never before seen a doctor that looked like this guy. He had a hunchback, a ratty-looking suit and a lit cigarette hanging from his lips. Man, we've come to see the hunchback of Notre Dame.

"You a big'n, aintcha?" he observed. I thought about saying that he looked like a pretzel man but just nodded my head and said nothing. "Hop up on them scales and let's see what we got here," he said while squinting through the smoke in his eyes.

"Two-hundred and twenty-five pounds," he shouted. "Damn, boy, you really must eat."

When I looked over at my mother, she just shook her head in agreement as if to say, "Say anything you want. Just make my son normal."

He then turned with what seemed to be a Herculean effort and started writing prescriptions. He told mom to make sure I took all these pills every day to see the results. Then, bring him back in a month to check his progress.

Progress was made. I was taking enough speed and God knows what else to kill the appetite of an army. Energy? I ran everywhere and talked a mile a minute. I had no interest whatsoever in food. Besides, my mother was fixing lots of vegetables and fruits and allowing no sweets in the house. Hell, everybody in my house was losing weight. My metabolism was so stoked on amphetamines, I could barely think straight. But, man, was I losing weight, and I really got caught up in it. The more I lost, the more I exercised. The more I exercised, the more I lost. Forget food. I could live on body fat and pills for the rest of my life. By the time school started in August that year, I had lost fifty pounds and would continue to lose another thirty-five or forty. Many of my friends who hadn't seen me for a few months were amazed. When I showed up for football practice, the coach took one look at me and said I'd be no good as a lineman anymore.

"As a matter of fact, if you haven't picked up a whole lotta speed, you're gonna be on the goddamn tackling dummy squad," he sneered.

"Thanks, you stupid jerk," I thought. Anyway, I wasn't too discouraged. I was still on speed and was receiving appraising looks from girls. That was the whole point of playing football, anyway. Be popular with girls. All I wanted to do was make the team and dress out for games. Fuck getting your balls knocked off. That was for idiots. Just give me a shot at the cheerleaders. The coach made me the third string fullback. Number 32. The same as Jim Brown for Cleveland. But, at third string,

I'd be lucky to score with one of the flute players in the band, much less a cheerleader.

That's just mom. After sixteen years of conditioning, I was pretty used to anything she threw my way. Even football coaches could seem loving and tender next to her; but in her mind, she was giving her son an all-out effort to see that he was gainfully employed for the summer. To her, hard work was a religious experience. Not that there was a whole lotta religion going on in our house anyway. When she wanted to make a point about someone, she would usually start with, "Any man worth his salt…." Anyway, you get the idea. Nobody needed to tell people in our house who the Higher Power was. It was her. Just not as forgiving. Later in life, I heard a joke about Irish Alzheimers. You forget everything but the grudge. That's her pretty much in a nutshell. No pun intended.

Chapter Four

Gatlinburg is a small town nestled in the Great Smoky Mountains about fifty to sixty miles from Maryville. There were actually two ways to get there. One was to take the two-lane mountain road through Townsend and Walland, negotiating a snaking path beside the Walland River or Townsend River, depending upon which town you called home. This was what you would refer to as the scenic route and the one that most everyone took on Sunday afternoons. The whole family would go on a picnic in the "Smokies.". This was our idea of a perfect day. Drive up into the mountains in a car with no air conditioning, in sweltering heat, stuck in traffic for hours just to spend two or three hours sitting on a bank by the road. There you got to eat cold fried chicken and potato salad with the ants. Now, these weren't just your regular yard ants. These babies were spawned in hell. They could take a bite out of your flesh that a shark would envy. And flies? They were called horse flies or green flies. I do think that they were the major cause of missing children instead of the deep-water "sink-holes" that everybody warned you about when you went into the water to cool off. Cool off, now there's a unique way of describing cold water shock. The water that came tumbling so beautifully down through the mountains was frigid. I always hated the cold water and the slippery rocks at the bottom. I'd get in the water gradually. So gradually in fact, that we were packing up to leave our "spot" by the time I had finally gotten totally submerged. Which suited me fine. I'd be so exhausted from trying to get into the water without having a heart attack, I'd sleep all the way home. My brother, Rob, could splash around all day and turn as blue as an undertaker's suit. He got a great deal of joy out of my misery and would snicker to himself while watching me struggle. He'd just stand in the water, up to his waist, rubbing his face, grinning at me and telling me how great the water was. He was hoping that I would lunge at him and go into a state of shock. While he grinned at me, I would just glare at him and say nothing. I was too cold to reach down into the water, retrieve a large rock and kill him with it. He knew this and so did I. This was his way of getting me back for picking on him.

Well, on this day, Mother and I didn't take the scenic route, because it wasn't fast enough. Instead, she drove over to Knoxville to pick up the four-lane highway that ran through Sevierville and Pigeon Forge. They, too, were just small towns in the foothills of the mountains-so small that if you slowed down to fifty miles an hour, you'd be through them in two minutes. Even if this route wasn't that scenic, it was still a drive that took us through some of the most beautiful farming country in the entire United States. The areas around the foothills of the Smokies were made of gently rolling hills, dotted with alternating cow pastures and various types of row crops. It reminded me of the pictures of Scotland and Ireland I had seen in National Geographic as a kid. National Geographic, of course, being the only "legal" magazine where a kid could get to look at naked women. This way you wouldn't have to steal a nudie magazine from the dark corners of your dad's closet or sock drawer. I imagine the contour of the land and the richness of the soil is what led so many of the Scotch-Irish to settle in east Tennessee. It reminded them of home. They also brought with them, as did many different peoples from across the sea, their own cultural heritage. For the Scotch-Irish, it was "work like dogs, drink like fools and make music." And it's still true today.

The farms that had the thickest vegetation were in the lower valleys of the foothills close to a river. This is what farmers called "good bottom land." The constant run-off from the mountains kept feeding this kind of land with tons of minerals to replenish the ones depleted by the years of growing use. Many years ago, farmers would use tenants as farm hands. The farm owner would allow a family to move on to the land, but not own it, and repay this privilege by working on the farm. Sound familiar? There were as many white "tenants" as there were black ones. The difference was that the black ones tended to stay longer and develop a sense of community with the other black tenants. They also attended a black church on Sunday for half a day, and spent the other half driving around visiting one another. The white folks tended to lay around and swat at the flies. Puddles of booze sweat constantly leeched through their skin from the previous Saturday night. Mother had a term for the white tenants. She called them "white trash." Anytime you were caught doing something that she considered a tasteless act (which most boys do), she accused you of being "white trash." Man, did my brother and I hate that. Not that we were so sure of what it meant, but the tone in Mother's voice when she spat out the term indicated that it was the lowest form of humanity on the earth.

Toward the blacks, she held a completely different attitude. Mother never allowed the use of the word "nigger" in her presence. She said she knew a lot more good "coloreds" than she did white people. It was her view that most black people could outwork most white people any day of the week. This went against the widely held opinion that black people were inherently lazy. Mother referred to that theory as "white trash bullshit." To Mother, it wasn't the color of your skin, but your work ethic that determined your worth in this world. In many ways, I really admired her for that outlook. To me, it seemed to make more sense.

Mother and I didn't talk too much on the way to Gatlinburg. I was sort of lost in anxious anticipation, and she was focused on not getting a speeding ticket. She was a fearless driver, and she was good, too. My father was my primary teacher for the around-the-block stuff and defensive driving skills. My mother taught me how to go on offense. With one hand resting on top of the steering wheel and the other hand flicking the ashes from her Winston out the wing window, she would pass everyone on the road. If somebody tried to speed up when she was passing, she would absolutely will that six cylinder Ford to reach down and get more horsepower and speed when you thought there was nothing left to give. As she passed the offender, she would give them a look that had "die-bastard" written all over it. I knew what road rage was well before all the sociologists, psychiatrists, law officers and others who are now analyzing what causes road rage. I can tell you exactly what causes road rage. Put a person who has all the personality traits of a mob hit man behind the wheel of anything, and they'll turn it into a lethal weapon.

Two things about riding with my mother were obvious: if you wanted to enjoy the scenery, you'd better look fast. The next thing was don't count on sleeping. I honestly believe a ride with her could keep someone with narcolepsy wide awake. The adrenaline coursed through your body like hot lead. It was similar to riding a roller coaster, except you knew the ride would end in a few minutes. With Mother, you always wondered if your body would be thrown clear enough to survive the crash. When seat belts first came out in cars, she saw it as an infringement on your personal freedom. Her brother was the same way. And he was a cop. I guess he hadn't seen too many cars crash, at least not enough to give him a clue about what the forces of gravity, steel, glass and the human body could do when they clashed. But Mother never had a wreck. I guess she always outran them, leaving behind a bloody trail of carnage in her wake. I never looked to see, and she didn't either.

Since it was a Monday, there wasn't a lot of traffic on the road up to Gatlinburg, and Mother thought that was a good sign; a sign of luck. I took it as a sign of not much traffic.

"We're making great time," she grinned. Speed always seemed to have a calming effect on my mother. It was almost as if she were out-running something. She was in a way, but that never occurred to me at the time. I just figured she had learned to drive just the way granddaddy drove-hell-bent-for-leather. My mother's uncle made his own moon-shine, and what he didn't consume himself, he sold. Nobody in the family ever talked about that openly. It was just accepted as "you know how Uncle Weston is." The family was too genteel to use the term drunken moon-shiner, so he was referred to as eccentric. Besides, he had more money than God at the time, and he kept it hidden all over the place: rolled up in his overall pockets, in a box in the barn, another box in the tool shed, in an old leather valise in his bedroom and in a coffee can in the kitchen. He knew that's where his wife, Aunt Tilda, would steal from him, so he always kept token amounts crammed into that can for her. They played strange games. I remember it being similar to the cigarette companies giving every employee a free pack of smokes every day. One, it kept them from stealing; and two, they got hooked on cigarettes. Pretty good use of human resources.

Chapter Five

Just as we were approaching the outskirts of Gatlinburg, Mother started with a litany of advice. I knew it was coming, I just didn't know when. Really she should've just published a handbook of rules and given it to my brother and me. Would've saved her a lot of breath because it was always the same old stuff.

"Now I want you to watch your ass while you're up here," she warned while giving me that sidelong look.

"What are you talking about?"

"You know damn well what I mean. Don't be up to no meanness just because you're on your own up here."

"All I'm gonna do is clean tables."

"Twenty-four hours a day you won't be. That leaves lots a time for you to get mixed up with some kind of white trash."

There she goes again.

"Come on, Mom," I said as I looked out the side window, not wanting to look into her accusing eyes. I already felt guilty, and I hadn't even had a chance to get "into anything." I wonder if she knew I was pretty well focused on using this summer job as my groundbreaking stride into manhood? Could she read my mind?

As we approached the city limits of Gatlinburg, we began to see the first indications of tourists walking along the side of the road, heading toward the sidewalks of the town. While we moved slowly through Gatlinburg, I kept swiveling my head from right to left and back trying to catch every store, motel and restaurant I could see. It was incredible. "Souvenirs," shouted one sign. "Taffy," screamed another. Vacancy. No vacancy. All rooms air-conditioned. Phones. TV. Wooden replicas of Indians stood in front of some of the shops while others had fake stuffed bears, their arms reaching out as if to be saved rather than to grab you and proceed with the horrible mauling. It still scared the little kids, though.

The realization had suddenly occurred to me that I had no clue as to how to begin the sexual conquest process. I remember reading about animals doing some sort of mating dance or ritual. Were human beings supposed to do something similar? I tried to rationalize that if a girl was wearing cut-off jeans that almost showed her panties, she was sending the message loud and clear. And that message was, "no talking, let's fuck." That was something I'd better give some thought to before I forged ahead. Maybe they expect you to talk to them. This particular aspect of getting laid had never really crossed my mind. Sports or cars don't interest girls. What the hell were you supposed to say? This was gonna need work. I guess my consternation resulted in no small amount of fidgeting.

"You gotta go or something? Or are you just nervous?"

Mom had been watching me out of the corner of her eye.

"No. I mean, I'm not nervous. And no to the other thing, too. I'm just sort of excited I guess. Where did Paul say this place was?"

I had learned that lying saved a lot of explanation. Tell them what you think they want to hear and let it go. With Mother, you learned to refine lying from a mere skill to an art form. Maybe she could tell or maybe she couldn't, but most of the time it worked. It was all in the presentation. If you came on too strong, it would be obvious. Even

Shakespeare said something about lying too loudly or something. Maybe it was in the Bible. Anyway, if you acted pretty cool about it, you could usually make people believe anything you wanted. My favorite tactic was to sort of sigh as I lied. This gave the person you were lying to a sense that nothing is amiss here. Nothing up this guy's sleeve. Also, you had to make eye contact. This is the one failure that most amateur liars make. They look off when they tell a lie. That wasn't my style. I would look right at you and tell you the worst lie in the world. But I would be so sincere about it. Actually my lying probably saved me, in my later years, from going to prison several times.

Mother spotted the restaurant before I did.

"There it is," she almost shouted. "Now if I can only find a goddamn place to park, we'll be okay."

"What about around back? Didn't Paul say something about parking behind the restaurant or in the motel parking lot next door?"

"Last thing in the world I need is to get towed in by some inbred, son-of-a-bitch, hick cop. I'll just park in the customer parking lot. It's two o'clock and I need some lunch. I bet you're hungry, too. You haven't eaten much today. Besides, I want to see what kind of place this is."

I guess that pretty much covered all the bases. She had made the assumptions, justified the rationale, voiced her opinion, commented on my lack of eating and had come to a decision. The plan was made, so the execution of said plan would be carried out immediately. That was one of the things I admired about my mother; she never second-guessed herself. She'd second-guess you in a heartbeat, but never herself.

The M&S Restaurant was right in the heart of the town, right across the street from the sky lift. The sky lift was a long steel cable that stretched over the river and way up to a lookout point on the very peak of one of the mountains. The line for that thing always went on for blocks. Parents stood sweating in the sun, while the kids alternately talked excitedly or pouted over God knows what. The heat was so bad, many of the people standing in line looked to me like they were on some kind of death march. Sort of a "we're-here-and-we're-gonna-do-this-fucking-thing-or-else." I spied one couple about my age in the line. Obviously in love and immune to the heat, they had their arms around each other as they waited their turn. When she would look up into the guy's eyes, I figured that he must have been knocking the bottom out of that. Then, why in the hell were they hanging around some cable ride when they could be in some air-conditioned room screwing their brains out? Shit. The clothesline of human figures never stopped running as people handed the guy at the gate their dollar and scrambled into a two-seat chair like the ones on a Ferris wheel. Once the safety bar was slammed down, you were on your way. Naturally, you had the environmental terrorists who would drop all kinds of crap in the river just to see it float away. Lots of shoes and sandals ended up in the water, too. They probably thought that was funny until their bare feet hit the pavement. The asphalt soaked up heat like a sponge and saved it for contact with human flesh. It was always good for sandal sales.

The restaurant didn't look too bad. It had several tables out front under a huge awning with ceiling fans. The fans, I learned later, were more to keep the flies away than to provide any relief from the heat. But at least it gave the appearance of a nice cool spot to sit and enjoy lunch or dinner. When we opened the glass doors to the main dining room, we were hit with a frigid blast of air that almost took my breath away. They must have had enough cooling equipment at work to cool off the other side of the street. I immediately wanted a cup of coffee.

The woman who greeted us was sort of attractive in a hard kind of way. She had her auburn hair pulled back and up toward the top of her head to keep her slender neck from getting sticky with the heat outside. Not in here, though. High heels that matched her sleeveless dress accentuated the soft brown of her large eyes. Her face was freckled and narrow, and her nose was a little too large. But her features all softened into a warm and pleasing combination when she smiled. Beautiful white teeth surrounded by blood red lips. Slim, but with enough curves to let you know that there were goodies underneath the clothes, she gave the impression of someone who was completely unaware of her own sexiness.

"Welcome to the M&S. Will you follow me, please?" She turned and headed for an empty table just as Paul came ambling over, pushing his hair out of his eyes, grinning a smile that said he was really glad to see me.

"Hey, Doug. Mrs. Wallace. How was your trip?" Paul and I shook hands while Lois, the hostess returned to see why we hadn't followed her.

"Lois, this is the guy I told you about. Doug Wallace. That's his mom, Mrs. Wallace." Paul explained as Lois shook our hands. She seemed to drop some of her imperial professionalism and became more natural and warm. She looked even more beautiful.

"Glad to see you, Doug. Nice to meet you, Mrs. Wallace. Paul, why don't you get us all some ice tea while I get some paperwork for Doug to fill out? Mrs. Wallace, would you prefer a booth or a table?"

My mother nodded amiably and replied that a booth would be fine. There were booths surrounding all three of the walls on the front and sides. Red Naugahyde and red Formica tabletops comprised the booths while the tables were covered with red and white check oilcloth. Small, red candles sat in the center of each table and at the far end of the booths. At the rear of the restaurant, there was a workstation where they kept clean dishes, the milk dispenser, silverware, napkins, the coffee machine and a clear glass case with all kinds of pies. One of the waiters stood back there and eyed me curiously. There was a loud clatter from a nearby table where a guy whose named I learned later was Tubby, a bored-looking busboy, was dumping dirty dishes and silver into a gray tub. Lois turned to go get whatever papers there were for me to fill out. I watched her hips move beneath the filmy dress as she walked over to Tubby and whispered something into his ear. He never even looked up from his labors or responded in any way whatsoever.

Up until this point, I had never had a job that required paperwork. The two previous summers, I had worked on a farm, baling and stacking hay for fifty cents an hour. Mr. Jackson paid us at the end of the week in a little brown envelope. This was different.

"Nice looking place," my mom whispered to me. I simply nodded and started watching the other employees as they whispered and pointed their heads in my direction. One of them was a cute looking redhead with a knockout figure. The other was a taller, slightly older blonde who looked like she was drained of energy. Her blue eyes looked sad and lifeless until the redhead whispered something in her ear that made her blossom with laughter. When she laughed, her eyes lit up and she looked ten years younger. It was almost magical. I felt myself reddening again. I was sure they were laughing about me.

Lois and Paul both returned at the same time, Lois with the employment forms and Paul with the iced tea. Mother took a pen from her purse and handed it to me just as Lois handed me the forms.

"How long have you worked here?" my mother asked, smiling.

Lois responded, "Every summer for the last five years. I worked the summers during my college years, and then I taught English at the local high school last year. It was my first year teaching, and I had a ball."

Her? An English teacher? My heart was pounding as I tried to focus my thoughts. My English teachers all looked like English teachers. She looked like a model or something. I wondered if the guys in her class ever hit on her. I wondered how they kept from it. Although, in those days, hitting on a teacher was tantamount to hitting on a nun. It just wasn't done…then. As we all know now, that social convention would fall by the wayside.

"I work at the high school that Doug attends. I'm the secretary to the principal," my mother said proudly.

"Well, Doug, I guess you don't get into much trouble at school with your mother working there," Lois said as she smiled at me.

In my most engaging manner, I replied, "Uhhhh, no." Then I put my head back down so fast I almost broke my own neck. It was a good thing, too, because my face now matched the décor of the room. I heard Paul snicker. He could probably feel the heat from my face. At that moment, I wanted to reach over and gouge out his eyeballs, but he knew he was safe in a public place. Besides, he was more afraid of my mother's reputation than he was of me. Mom, on the other hand, was behaving in a gracious and calm fashion. So far, nothing had been said that she could construe as an insult, but the conversation was still young.

After I had finished with the forms, Lois told Paul to take me back to the supply closet and get me fitted with a vest. She had already asked about a bow tie, but Mother had answered for me that I had one. When we got back, mom wanted me to put on the red vest and model it for her. Fortunately, it was still only two-thirty in the afternoon so the restaurant was doing very little business. I didn't argue with her. I just did it.

Paul glanced at his watch and said, "Quit'n time. Let's go get you settled in at the boarding house."

My mother and Lois made their gracious good-byes, and the three of us left the restaurant after Paul clocked out. Going from a meat locker environment to the oppressive heat outside gave me a real slap in the face. It made me want to turn and go back inside until October. The car was even worse. By the time the air conditioner started working, I was bathed in sweat.

I guess you're probably wondering why it was so hot in what is supposed to be the cool shady mountains. As Gatlinburg started developing as more and more of a tourist attraction over the years, more and more concrete, asphalt, buildings, parking lots and all of the other things needed to accommodate large numbers of people began to emerge. All of this stuff drew the summer sun's heat into the town and held on to it like a child holding a security blanket. The only problem was that the kid was about to suffocate. Once you got away from the heat of the town itself, the shade, the elevation and the cool streams provided a welcome relief from the heat. So much so, that the smart people stayed away from the tourist junk until the evening sun started to set. That's the time most of them began prowling the streets, looking for the perfect Gatlinburg ashtray to take back to Aunt Rose. The kids you saw were evenly divided between wearing the coonskin hats and the Indian headdresses. You sometimes wondered why some sort of ethnic or gang warfare didn't erupt, but in 1963, there was no such thing as political correctness. Too bad. I would have enjoyed watching all the parents trying to establish order amongst the flying rubber knives and rubber hatchets. Unfortunately, some of the hatchets or tomahawks as they were technically called were made of a wooden handle with a slightly flat, pointed river rock lashed together with leather. You could do some real damage with one of those babies given the right motivation and dexterity. Luckily, nothing ever happened. If it ever did, the Gatlinburg police force would have opened fire on everyone in sight. They hated tourists, too.

Paul directed us down back roads to get to the boarding house so we wouldn't have to fight the traffic on the main drag. The houses along these back streets were a big difference from all of the false faces on Main Street. These were old, old houses kept in good shape. It looked as if they were built so that not one tree had to be removed from the property. This provided a peaceful, cool relief from the heat and hustle a few blocks away. This is where real mountain people lived and tolerated the excesses of Gatlinburg. Besides, most of these people were making obscene sums of money from leases and rents on the properties they owned in town. And many of them still had their moonshine business on the side, hidden away from tourists and "revenuers." Family traditions continued. Paul kept a non-stop narrative going while on the radio, the Supremes sang in their whispery tones about somebody leaving them.

We finally came to an old clapboard, two-story house surrounded by two cars on blocks, one car that actually ran and an old dilapidated pickup truck. In the front yard, hanging from a tree, was a tire swing. The yard was mostly dirt. The grass never really got enough sunshine to grow and kids kept scuffing it away over the years.

"Here it is," Paul said proudly, "your new summer home."

Aghast is a word that you don't get to use very often, but it most accurately describes the look on my mother's face when she pulled to a stop in front of the house. There were chickens in the front yard. To go with the idly browsing chickens were a bunch of the dirtiest kids I had ever seen in my life. Even the chickens seemed to avoid the children. They, too, smelled like small barnyard animals, only worse. When they looked up at you wordlessly, you could see that their noses were running endlessly into the dirt on their upper lips, creating an effect not unlike seeing a small child with a mustache.

The front porch ran the entire length of the front of the house and was supported from the bottom with cinder blocks. Enjoying the cool beneath the porch was a couple of ugly mutts who could barely move as a result of old age or boredom. They raised their heads to look in our direction and immediately flopped down again. There was a magnitude of ticks feasting on what had to be nothing more than plasma by now. On the porch sat Mr.Cummins, who had to be around seventy-five, wearing nothing but a dirty pair of overalls. As he slowly pushed himself out of his chair, he waved with a friendly nod. He looked like a farmer who had finally given up the battle with God, the elements and the dirt. His balding head still had a few wisps of gray hair that seemed to lift and wave in the gentle breeze as he stepped toward the front edge of the porch. The wire-framed glasses he wore sat askew on his face, but he seemed not to notice. When he grinned toward my mother's direction, you could almost count the number of dark brown teeth he had left. He held on to the rail on the porch as if to steady himself, and his stooped posture gave the impression of someone who was completely used up in both body and spirit. Tobacco stains ran down his chin in rivulets, and the odor of stale whisky wafted from him like smoke from a fire started with damp wood. But that was mild compared to the musty scent of the man himself. He smelled old. I mean, he smelled like old death, nasty and rank. If anything could push your gag reflex to its limits, it was Mr. Cummins. I'm glad he didn't offer his hand to shake because I would have probably visibly shivered when I touched him. Mom? Forget it. She was still standing behind the car trying not to vomit.

"Howdy, folks," he said as he greeted us. His glassy blue eyes seemed to go in and out of focus while he stood there waiting for somebody to say something.

"Been watch'n the granchillun fer the missus awhilst she went to check on her sister," he explained as he waved his hand idly in the direction of the nearly naked kids. "She's been about to die fer a couple a years now. I jist wish she'd be done with it. End her suffer'n and my wife's suffer'n, too. Besides, I caint git no dinner till she gits back."

The compassion of this old man was overwhelming. And as far as those kids went, they could've been gone for hours before he realized he was missing something wandering around in the yard with the chickens. It wasn't until later that I learned that their daughter, Sarah Louise, had recently moved back home after her divorce from her husband of five years. She had conceived her first two children by her husband, one by his brother and the last by some guy whom she couldn't clearly recall. That's the one that caused the divorce. The husband knew about his brother knocking up his wife, but that was OK because it was family. The reason he found out about the stranger was twofold. First, he and his wife would never have any more children after Mr. Sarah Louise got shot in the testicles as he was running away from a drunken altercation in a Cocke County bar. The guy was aiming for his ass and shot a little low but dead center. The second reason was that Sarah admitted screwing another man during a drinking spree with her sister. As a matter of fact, her fifth child was this guy's too. I guess he must have been on some kind of pilgrimage to father children far and wide and still remain anonymous.

When you meet someone for the first time who disgusts you so profoundly, it is very difficult to think of anything to say. You just sort of stare, as I was doing, hoping Paul would say something in order to break the awkward silence. Here was this slovenly creature apparently doing a babysitting job for his grandchildren while as drunk as a sailor on shore leave.

"Come on. I'll show you where your bunk is," Paul said.

I looked back at Mother to see if she was going to come in, and I saw her with lines of deep thought etched in her face. She probably was trying to decide if she wanted to be exposed to this place if the outside was any indication of what the inside looked like. Paul waved to her to follow, and she quickly skirted past Mr. Cummins. Paul held the door for her and we went inside.

Surprisingly, the living room was very well kept. Everything was neat, clean and in place. Obviously, Mrs. Cummins was a little more aware of her surroundings than Mr. Cummins was. The old narrow boards that comprised the floor were shiny with age and coat after coat of varnish. The walls were decorated with various pictures of relatives and, of course, the obligatory picture of Jesus. All in all, it wasn't at all creepy but rather cozy.

As we climbed the narrow, steep stairs to the upper floor, the boards creaked but held firmly. Once at the top, the décor deteriorated rapidly. There was a large open room with one double bed and a metal cot. The cot had nothing on it but an old, threadbare mattress that I assumed was to be mine. The other bed looked as if someone just slung some sheets and blankets on them as an afterthought. On the floor were piles of dirty socks, underwear and other clothes. The double bed sat at one end of the room with the head beneath one of the two windows in this section. The other window was above the head of my cot that sat about three feet from the end of the double bed parallel to the footboard. Three separate sections of pipe were rigged to the walls to function as open closets. Against the far wall stood an antique dresser with three sets of three drawers. I supposed one column of drawers was mine. There was another bedroom slightly smaller than the "main bedroom" with one double bed and one cot. The double bed in that room belonged to a guy named Jim and the cot belonged to somebody named Dick. And a third, even smaller bedroom with two cots was for the Ledbetter brothers. Since, as I learned later, they didn't speak to each other very much, they made great roommates for the smallest room.

Mother gave everything an appraising glance and pronounced it livable although cluttered. She then tilted her head slightly back to get a good sniff of the place. Sort of like an animal checking for prey.

"Place smells like a goddamn bar. Cigarettes and stale beer. What'cha been up to, Paul?" my mother asked as she eyeballed him carefully.

"That's from the Ledbetter's room. The older one buys beer for him and his brother 'bout every other night," Paul explained. "But they ain't hell-raisers or nothin. Mrs. Cummins won't allow no loud carryin' on. She's real strict 'bout that and girls. No girls upstairs."

When my mother wasn't looking, Paul looked at me and winked. His wide-eyed explanation seemed to satisfy her for the moment.

"Well, let's get your stuff moved in. I don't want to get caught in all that Knoxville traffic going home."

We all three eased down the stairs to unload the car. When we got out to the porch, Mr. Cummins asked, "Whad'cha think, boy? Look OK?"

"Looks great," I answered. I actually meant it, because it gave me a sense of being sort of grown up and on my own. It represented a freedom that I would later discover as much a burden as a joy.

"That'll be seven dollars in advance for the cot. If'n you want to keep a box of food in the old fridgerator, it'll be an extree dollar a week."

I looked at mom while she thought this over. "That'll be fine," she said. Then she turned to me and whispered quietly, "This is a loan till you get a couple of pay days. You owe me eight dollars. Now don't forget that."

Forget it? A loan from you? Mother should have worked as a loan shark. My dad once told me that the only thing she was ever sentimental about was a dollar, and I guess he was right. She handed me the eight dollars to give to Mr. Cummins so that she didn't have to touch the mangy bastard. I got to do the honors. Then he actually licked his fingers to count the five and three singles as if to double check we weren't pulling a fast one on him. No sireee. Nobody was gonna cheat him. When he was satisfied, he nodded his head, grinned with that horrible, blackened slash of a mouth and stuffed the money into his pocket.

"You'uns be sure to let me know if you need somethin'," he said as if to reassure my mother that her son was going to be well taken care of. But of course, mom wasn't fooled for a moment. She just figured that she had taught me enough about self-reliance to take care of myself. I was pretty much on my own which was just the way I wanted it.

When my mother turned to leave, she said, "Take care and don't go get in any trouble." We stood there awkwardly for a moment, because displays of affection in public just weren't done in my family. Or in private either, for that matter. Finally, I made the first move and hugged her quickly. She looked at me with deep appreciation and turned to get into the car.

"Don't worry none, Mrs. Wallace," Paul said. "I'll take good care of him."

She looked back in our direction, rolled her eyes, and slid into the driver's seat. Then she slammed the door, cranked up the car and drove away without looking back. I guess she really wanted to beat that traffic.

I turned to Paul and he said, "Let's get you settled in and I'll show you around. You're gonna love this place."

Mr. Cummins was still sober enough to hear so he turned to us and warned, "Don't be bringin' no underage pussy in my house, lest you give me a little taste too." He cackled wildly at his own humor while we just laughed enough to let him know we were with him on the joke. I sure hoped to hell that the tourists never tried to take any back roads around town. The Yankee view of southerners was already bad enough as it was. We sure didn't need the Cummins family in the pages of Southern Living.

Paul and I dashed up the stairs and began making up my bed, putting away clothes, and getting everything situated in my new home. As I looked around, I started to feel really free rather than homesick. As a matter of fact, I never did get homesick that entire summer.

Chapter Six

Paul and I strolled toward the main drag and began to catch up on what was going on back in Maryville. Although we attended different high schools, we had gone to grammar school together and went to the same church. Our primary reason for going to church for us was to hang out in a respectable setting to discuss opportunities to raise some hell. We both figured if we did that in a church setting, no one would know what we were up to.

There were five or six of us guys that hung out together between Sunday school and the main service to review what we had accomplished or failed to accomplish by the narrowest of margins the previous evening.

When the church bell would ring for everyone to put out their cigarettes and come inside, our group would dash in and take up the entire back row. Our parents didn't mind if we didn't sit with them; they were just glad we were in church.

One Sunday, this kid named Carlos Worthington showed up to church in a full dress army uniform. He had always been kind of an outsider and was never included in our little group. Nobody really knew much about him except that he lived with an aunt and uncle and had just graduated from high school in May. He was a real quiet guy, dark skinned in a Spanish sort of way, and had real black hair. With his dark complexion, eyes and hair, he could have been a real lady-killer, but nobody knew if he dated anyone. None of us ever invited him to join our group because we thought he might have been a foreign person or something.

Well, on the Sunday he wore his uniform, he sat in the row just in front of us. This particular day, he seemed to stand a little straighter and carry himself with a degree of confidence we had never seen before. Naturally, we all viewed this as an insult. Not to allow him to get away with an attitude of superiority, we had to address this situation by vindictive means. Besides, a lot of the girls had been eyeing him before the service and whispering excitedly among themselves. As we all rose to sing some hymn, I noticed his nice, new hat sitting on the pew next to him with a bill that had a black sheen on it that you could've used for a mirror. Taking my bulletin, I rolled it up into a tube and gently slid his brand new hat over until it was directly behind him when he sat down. At the end of the hymn, we all sat and he sat on his hat. The noise was like a box being crushed, and his quick spring up from his seat was almost more than we could bear. You know how hard it is to keep from laughing when you're in a place where no laughing is allowed. There we were, Paul sitting next to me, shaking with both hands over his mouth. The rest of us were in the same boat. Carlos just pulled his hat around to his lap and sat staring at it. No emotion except a hint of sadness. As I began to watch his reaction, my mirth gradually diminished to shame. All during the service, I thought about this guy with no friends, being humiliated in what was probably one of the proudest moments in his life.

When the service ended and we all stood to leave, he simply turned around, looked at every one of us in the eyes and walked away with his head up and his shoulders thrown back. He won. We lost. Although some of my gang just kind of snickered nervously, I thought about running after him to make a public apology. But I didn't. At the time, it was supposed to be real funny, but I felt lower than whale shit. Two years later, we heard that he had been killed in Viet Nam while rescuing some of his buddies in a firefight. Won the Congressional Medal of Honor and was shipped home in a box a hero. That made me feel even worse than I had before and I still regret it to this day. What a lousy shit I had been.

As Paul and I walked along the dusty road that led to town from the house, I told him as much as I knew about who was dating who, who had gotten a cool car and what I had heard about Reverend Wilson's daughter. Now, there was one hot babe. She did more for getting guys into church than any amount of prayers and commands that could have come from Jesus himself. Paul almost went into hysterics when I told him about Sue Ann, the good reverend's daughter, getting caught bucknaked with the choir director in the choir director's office. Word was that they were going at it on top of the desk when Mrs. Wilson, who'd also been sleeping with the choir director, came in unannounced in mid-stroke. And a stroke is almost what she had. We just weren't sure if it was from jealousy or her maternal instincts kicking into gear. Whatever it was, it was a mess. The Wilsons were moving and getting a divorce, so that meant we'd be getting another preacher and a choir director pretty soon. Our church was beginning to sound positively heathen. Kinda like that Sodom and Gomorra story in the Bible and of course we all know that's where the words sodomy and gonorrhea came from. Not that I cared one way or another. Church is church and there's just one Big Guy, so what difference does it make?

"Who would'a thought?" Paul said, staring at the ground in front of him. "I wonder how long this had been going on? She always looked to be prim and proper, I thought she was a really dedicated virgin or like some kind of nun."

"Well, Paul," I explained in my wise and insightful way, "you just can't tell a book by looking at its cover. You've got to be on your toes. Watch for clues."

"What kind of clues?"

"You know…just clues."

"You don't know anything. You're just bullshitting."

"You just don't understand people, Paul. It's all in the eyes, I tell you. You just have to look hard enough. I saw it in her eyes. She was hot to trot."

"You liar. You never knew either. You've been reading so many horny books, you're starting to believe that stuff."

"Up yours," I laughed.

Since the street where the Cummins' house was was only a block off the main drag, we enjoyed the view of the back of motels, restaurants, so-called craft shops and candy shops of all kinds. It looked like a landfill had been started just behind the buildings. Behind each business was a dumpster overflowing with trash and awash in flies. There were swarms of flies diving around like tiny fighter planes in search of something really nasty. I don't know what kept them from flying into each other. There were thousands of flies that had found a place to land and were foraging around in their little spot, studiously ignoring the divebombers from above. Armies of ants marched in long, continuous lines on the ground and all over the walls of the different motels and shops apparently intent on establishing new colonies with air conditioning and an endless supply of food. At the rear doors of some of the restaurants, dishwashers and waitresses stood around shading their eyes from the sun and smoking cigarettes.

I would later learn that people in the food service industry eventually come to prefer the company of flies and ants to the company of tourists. I was still too new to the industry of tourism to fully understand this, but it wouldn't take me long to learn.

"Let's get the nickel tour out of the way, and then we'll go back to the restaurant to see if anybody sent something back," Paul said.

"What do you mean about sending something back?" I asked. "Don't the cooks just throw it away?"

"If the cook has to fix something new, they'll give it to us. We can sit on boxes back in the storeroom next to the beer cooler and eat for free. Save a lot of money that way."

I did some initial figures in my head and was starting to realize that there was a lot of money to be made this summer. I won't have to buy food for almost three months. This was great.

"But, if the food comes back with a complaint that it wasn't cooked properly, you don't get that," Paul was saying as we strolled along.

"Why's that?" I asked.

"Well…it's kinda gross, but they'll just spit on it, add a little flavoring salt, reheat it and send it out again. You don't know how many people eat food every day that has been spit on by some pissed-off, hungover cook. As nasty as some of them look, they really hate to have their cooking criticized. Let that be a lesson to you: Never send food back to the kitchen with a complaint. Just eat it the best way you can and keep your mouth shut. I always keep my eye on Roy, the morningside cook, when he fixes me something so that I don't get whatever horrible disease he's probably got. You'll get to meet him at six tomorrow morning, but don't expect a warm welcome from him. Don't let that worry you though, 'cause I don't think he likes anybody except the guy who delivers beer. He usually puts a six-pack or two in Roy's beat up old jalopy. For some reason, they're pretty good friends."

I was pretty grossed out by Paul's description of the kitchen goings-on and tried not to think about it. I figured I'd just get cereal for breakfast tomorrow and fix it myself.

As we came to the corner onto the main street, the sheer numbers of people we encountered amazed me. We went from a quiet, deserted lane to packed sidewalks of garishly dressed people, screaming children, frustrated parents and wide-eyed people of all shapes and sizes. And odors. You pack this many people in a small location and turn the heat up to about ninety-five degrees with eighty- percent humidity, and you've got the makings for a real stench. Ever been to a circus or a county fair? That sort of thing. Fortunately, the deliciously, sweet smells emanating from the candy shops would give you some relief from the human stench.

Paul pointed to his left and said, "The M&S is up that way, so let's go the other way and you can get the sight-seeing out of your system. All there is to see in the day are restaurant after restaurant, motel after motel, and on and on and on. Anyway, we can spot some sweet things and maybe talk to some of them."

I could understand Paul's optimism. Everywhere I looked were girls in pairs, girls in threes, girls with guys, girls with their parents looking bored or embarrassed. All of these nubile beauties were all wearing jeans cut off to their armpits. I was in heaven. I should have gone out with a huge fishing net, thrown it over a group of girls and scavenged for "keepers."

Paul broke my fantasy by leaning in close so no one else could hear and said, "Don't eyeball any girls who look like they are with parents or especially a boyfriend. The heat can make people do crazy things."

That was sage advice from Mr. Loopy himself. Somehow, though, Paul could really attract the women. It helped that he was about six-two, had dark hair and eyes, an athletic build and was completely unconcerned with the thought of rejection. Ever the optimist. I, on the other hand, although not as tall, figured we looked a little bit alike. I was five-ten, medium brown hair, brown eyes and about one hundred and sixty pounds. Although I was pretty athletic, I didn't look like the type. If a policeman had been tying to get a description of me, people would describe me as having no distinguishing characteristics. I really thought a mustache would do a lot for my appearance, but I was sure that if my mother saw me with it, she'd rip if off like it was a fake. I didn't need that.

"What's there to do in this town?" I asked Paul once we strolled into and out of a souvenir shop. "All I see is a lot of tourist stuff, motels and restaurants."

Paul replied, "You haven't seen the night life, yet. There's places we can go with the 'locals' and really party hearty."

"What's a local?"

"Us, you dumbass. Anybody who lives or works up here is considered a local. You always tell people in restaurants or the wax museum or the sky liftthat you're a local. Sometimes you get in free or at least get a big discount. It's a pretty good deal."

Local. I thought about that for a minute. I belonged. I was in with a special group. It sort of reminded me of people who work in a circus or something. Local. I don't think I'd ever been anything but a Methodist or a football player, so this was something really different. We had our own unwritten laws and lived by our own rules. You just said "local" and nodded your head. You were in. Just like that. It gave me a kind of adrenaline rush that I got when I first made the football team. Only this time there was no first, second or third string. Plus, you didn't get the shit knocked out of you. I had always been an outsider or loner. I had acquaintances but no real friends. Actually it never bothered me too much either. Having close friends meant nothing but heartache. They might hurt your feelings so you were a lot better off not letting yourself get too close to people. The way I saw it, being a loner was a form of protection from possible betrayal. On the other hand, this was just before all the loners got together and formed what we later called communes.

Chapter Seven

I looked up as I heard Paul calling my name, and he motioned me to come back outside.

"Isn't there anyplace to hang out around here? This gift shop and motel stuff is already boring me and I haven't been here twenty-four hours yet."

"There's this candy store I want to show you down this way," Paul said. "You're gonna love it."

We'd already been by a couple of taffy stores and that was enough to tell me that I sure as hell didn't want any taffy. It looked more like some rubber stuff than candy. But he was insistent so we started making our way through the crowds toward the next attraction. "Making our way" makes it sound sort of easy, but it was anything but easy. We were sort of like those fish that try to swim up turbulent streams to breed. Now there's some determined, horny fish. It was funny how when I looked at the other side of the street, everybody seemed to be moving in the same direction that Paul and I were going. Everyone on our side of the street was moving against us. However, I did see a positive in trying to move against the flow. You could get a better look at more girls than just watching the behind of the one in front of you. I was too shy for real eye contact, but I was great at judging bra sizes. Plus, I had absolutely no concern as to the feelings of the girls as I stared at their chests. Besides, I thought the acknowledgment and the interest would flatter them. At least I thought so.

We reached a point where the traffic seemed to have slowed and finally stopped for a minute.

"Here we are," Paul announced.

"Here's what?" I asked as I stood on the tips of my toes to get a better look.

"Kauffman's Fudge Shoppe," Paul replied. "I've got a buddy who works here in the afternoons beating fudge."

"What's so interesting about standing around watching guys stir fudge?"

"They don't just stir it, dumb ass. They beat the hell out of it. Watch them work. You've got two big brass kettles of ten to twelve pounds of fudge that needs constant stirring so it won't set up like concrete. Those four guys you see inside work in two teams."

I watched as Paul explained.

"You see that one guy with the wooden paddle in his hands and how he's working? He moves his arms and hands like pistons, working the fudge, keeping it soft. The guy that's standing next to him is there to give him a break. He's not supervising or nothing. He's waiting to make his move."

"What move?" I asked. "What keeps them from dumping the fudge all over themselves?"

"Precision, my man. This is part of the show. Old Klaus Kauffman is this big German guy you see standing in the back of the shop. He keeps his eye on things to make sure everyone is working."

I noticed that all the guys, including Mr. Kauffman, were dressed in white tennis shoes, white pants, white aprons, white tee shirts and white paper hats. I also took note that the guys going to town on those kettles had tremendous arms and shoulders. After a minute or two, the one guy standing watching the guy with the paddle would place his hands in position next to his partner as if they were working it together. Paul told me that they were getting the rhythm in sync. Soon, the first beaters stepped out of the way and the replacements took over. Then the guys taking a break leaned over with their hands on their knees looking like they were going to pass out or vomit. It also didn't take me long to figure out that a whole bunch of sweat was dripping into the fudge kettles. Maybe it kept the fudge from being too sweet. Anyway, this tag team of fudge beaters went on and on until Big Klaus waddled over and tested it with one of his sausage sized fingers. Mr. Kauffman may have been carrying an extra forty or fifty pounds on his tall frame, but you could tell there was plenty of muscle under the suet. He was also bald as a billiard ball. This gave him the appearance of Mr. Clean gone to fat. His dark, piggish eyes gave you no indication of whether or not he was pleased with the product. He simply stood back and made a rotary motion with his hand indicating for the guys to keep stirring.

"Gene, the redheaded guy, is a buddy of mine," Paul explained. "He says that this is a great job for getting in shape for football, and they make four-fifty an hour."

Four-fifty an hour? That's almost as much as my dad made as a typesetter. I filed this information away for further consideration for two reasons: one, financial and the other, football. Still, Gene looked as if getting the shit knocked out of him on the football field would be better than this. Not only that, the crowd that stood outside also included a great number of gorgeous nymphets.

"Let's go in and get a piece," suggested Paul.

"No way, man. I've yet to see a recipe that calls for a quart of sweat in it. You eat it."

At that, Paul just laughed his high pitched laugh and slapped me on the back.

"Well, then let's mosey our way up to the M&S and see if we can get something to eat."

As we headed our way back in the other direction, I noticed that the crowd had thinned noticeably and that the temperature had dropped significantly once the sun slipped down behind the mountains. Most of the tourists were heading back to their motel rooms to get ready for dinner. I'm sure they wanted to get out of sweat-soaked clothes and get a shower.

Paul said, "We can probably get a freebie tonight, because Big Bill is the night cook. He looks kinda mean, but he's really a pretty nice guy. Just don't try and piss him off. He's married to Laura, the tall blonde waitress on the morning shift. You remember her?"

I nodded my head in response as we walked to the back of the restaurant and threw open the kitchen door. Paul introduced me to Big Bill who simply glared back at me. I couldn't figure out why he was called Big Bill until I looked closer at his arms and shoulders. Paul had told me Bill had been a cook since he dropped out of school at the age of fourteen after his daddy died. He didn't get those muscles flipping burgers. He had a very unsettling stare as the result of one eye being partially covered with a cataract or "evil eye" as it used to be called.

"Whatcha boys feel like eatin' tonight? We got chicken and dumplins or cheeseburgers."

"Cheeseburger with extra fries," Paul responded quickly.

"Comin' up. Git yourself a seat in the back," Bill said with a grin.

I simply nodded my head although I would have rather had the chicken and dumplings. My grandmother always made chicken and dumplings when I came to visit her. Of course, I would have probably been disappointed if these didn't taste like home. We went to the back area of the kitchen where the cases of canned goods were stacked. Close by was a large walk-in freezer and a walk-in cooler. Paul went to the cooler and pulled out a bottle of Budweiser and asked if I wanted one.

"Just a coke," I said.

"It's okay. They don't mind as long as you don't tell anybody and don't drink too much. This is Gatlinburg, man. They got their own rules here."

I stuck with the coke and Paul just shook his head. Paul was a good guy, but I was never really too sure about his judgment. Besides, I didn't want to get fired before I had a chance to work my first day. I could imagine what my mother would do if I called her to come and get me because I got fired for drinking.

Big Bill finally called us and told us our dinner was ready. We took our loaded plates and returned to our places in the stockroom. No sooner than we had gotten settled than the owner, Sam Ronson, walked in through the back door.

Sam looked at us with watery, bleary eyes and wavered a little on his feet. He had a huge grin on his red, bloated face. His belly was large and grossly distended. His black hair was slicked back with Vitalis, and his glasses were dirty. He was wearing a wrinkled white short-sleeved shirt and what appeared to be the brown dress slacks to a suit.

"You boys gittin' treated all right? Gittin' plenty to eat?"

I just nodded nervously as Paul answered with a mouthful of food, "Yep, Sam, we sure are."

"Good, good. You work for me?" he asked as he directed his loopy grin at me.

"Yessir," I said. "Start in the morning."

"Good, good," he said nodding his head up and down.

When he offered his hand to shake, I grasped it firmly in mine. As I looked at him, a look of sharp awareness crossed his face.

He looked me squarely in the eye and said, "I can tell a man by his handshake. Yours is strong. I like that. Means I can trust you. They's not many people around you can trust anymore. You got a driver's license, boy?"

"Yes sir," I repeated.

"Manners, too. Goddamn. Now if you'll 'scuse me boys, I'm gonna squeeze by you here and get me a cold beer. Been feelin' a little parched with this heat and all."

After he left, Paul just grinned at me.

"What?" I asked.

"He liked you, dumb ass. You might get to be Martha's chauffeur this summer. She hadn't picked one yet."

"What do mean about a chauffeur?"

Paul responded, "It's easy. You just drive old Martha around to see her crony friends. It pays pretty good, too. Last I heard, it was twenty dollars a night."

I thought to myself, this town is overflowing with money. Anybody willing to work could really score big. I'd probably soon be making more money than my dad was, and that wasn't too bad.

After we finished eating, Paul and I decided to make another trek among the tourists as they began their evening ritual of patrolling the sidewalk shops for bargains. The traffic up and down Main Street had subsided somewhat from this afternoon when the street was nothing but one large parking lot. A lot of cars would get stalled in the daytime traffic because people would run their air conditioners until the engines just couldn't take it anymore and blew a hose. Picture yourself in a car with no air conditioning, a wife griping about the heat, and three kids in the back who alternately want to go swimming, get something to eat or go to the bathroom. You yourself are getting a dark brown headache from the three beers you had with lunch, and you've got heartburn. Sounds like you've got all the ingredients for a disaster. Something or somebody is gonna crack. Too much overload.

The evenings in the mountains can be very pleasant. The temperature cools rapidly and the humidity drops. People begin to slow down and start enjoying their vacation. Husbands and wives actually hold hands as they stroll along, ignoring their children's pleas for another souvenir. Peace reigns again.

Except for the rednecks. Those who hadn't had their fill of beer even after consuming almost a case of the stuff over the course of a day would prowl up and down the streets with a strange look in their eyes that said nothing good was going to come of this. The local police have more problems at night with drunks. They seem to need to stretch their legs after a long day of soaking up booze. They're easy to spot. Baseball caps that advertised a farm implement or some sort of chewing tobacco combined with tank tops and big belt buckles holding up grimy jeans are a dead giveaway. They walk along grinning at each other, winking conspiratorially and leering criminally at any woman between the ages of nine and ninety. For the most part, they were quiet, happy drunks unless they got into some moonshine. That would bring out the rebel yells, which amused the Yankee tourists to no end. Unless, of course, they were drunk, too. When Yankees get drunk, they talk even more loudly than they do when they're sober. That can be an extremely irritating sound to the ears of a Southerner. A loud, drunken Yankee in the presence of an irritable drunk redneck can start the Civil War all over again. With vigor.

Paul and I walked a few blocks toward the center of town to a motel that had a property line that ran right up to the sidewalk. There, they provided wooden lounge chairs for the hotel guests. Paul and I chose this spot to relax and people-watch. Simply watching people can be a lot of fun. For Paul and me, it was a chance to point out every little flaw or idiosyncrasy we could find. And we could find them in everybody, young or old, man or woman. Of course, we kept a sharp eye out for pairs of girls who looked like they were searching for guys. It was an especially good thing if you found girls who smoked. Girls who smoked cigarettes always "did it." All you had to do was pick the time and place and you were in. Not that I liked kissing a girl who had a mouth like an ashtray, but I would go through just about anything to lose my virginity. It always sounded so feminine to say it that way. Guys didn't lose their virginity; they got laid. Girls lost their virginity.

After that happened, then they were considered easy because then they "put out." It was the goal of every guy I knew to find a girl who would put out, but not as a steady girlfriend or anything. Just something for recreation. But if you had a steady girlfriend, you would spend untold amounts of time and money in the back seat of a car trying to get your girl to put out. Then, if she did let you do it you had to dump her because she was easy, and nobody wanted date an easy lay. This was a very clear and simple system of social standards at work here, and you had to make sure you had everything straight. I had all the rules down, but I hadn't gotten the old panties down…yet.

As the crowds started to thin out, Paul and I began to run down. He had worked all day, and I had been overloaded with new experiences. Together, we decided to make our way back to the house and hit the hay. Paul said if you wanted a warm bath, you needed to take it the night before or get up at five in the morning. If you took it at night, you could be sure to have plenty of hot water. Otherwise, if you waited until morning, you had to get up around five to beat the other guys to the bathroom. He said that the first one in would have hot water, the second one would have pretty warm water, the third would have medium and the fourth would have cold, mountain water. Those last three words were the clincher. That night, I opted for the evening bath, and by the time I crawled into bed, I was beat. I slept like a baby all night.

Chapter Eight

Paul awakened me by shaking me roughly by the shoulder. Some things never change. I swung my legs over the edge of the bed and tried to get my bearings while scratching myself from my knees to my head and most places in between. I'm in Gatlinburg, and I've got to get up and go to work, I said to myself. A tall, lanky guy began the same ritual and peered groggily at me through the darkness.

"Who're you?" he asked.

"Doug Wallace. Got in yesterday afternoon. I'm starting at the M&S today. What about you?"

"My name's Jim. I work at the Mountaineer Restaurant…as a waiter. Where are you from?"

"Maryville. You?"

"Knoxville. You know Paul?"

"Yeah. He helped get me the job."

"Good to meet you," he said as he staggered over with his hand proffered.

We shook hands firmly and nodded to each other. We ran out of anything further to say to each other at 5:30 in the morning, and I got a whiff of what smelled like booze when he shook my hand.

He stretched and groaned not so quietly, "What a party last night. **Everybody** got drunk and got laid. Maybe next time we'll get a camera."

I listened with the still, rapt attention of a small child hearing about Santa for the first time. I was also at a loss for words. He wasn't doing cartwheels or anything. Why he actually seemed a little bored by all of it. Not me. I couldn't wait to ask him about a thousand questions. Do you think they'll have a party tonight? Can I go? Can Paul go? Can I pay you anything? Please? Thank God I just thought all of this and kept my cool. Just to show Jim how cool I was, I said, "Yeah, I know what you mean."

He turned and looked at me as if seeing me for the first time and just grinned broadly.

Feeling a little awkward and embarrassed by his piercing grin, I grabbed my toilet kit and headed for the bathroom. I shaved with an old Remington electric razor my dad had given me after he got a new one for Christmas last year. It did an okay job, but not as good as a blade. I had started shaving about every three days when I was taking all of those pills during those months of dieting, and then my shaving became a daily ritual about the time I turned sixteen. I really needed to use a blade on my upper lip because no matter how hard I pushed with the electric, I always had a five-o'clock-shadow on my upper lip by noon.

I put on my new white shirt, black slacks, Sunday shoes, my bow tie and my brand new red vest. I checked myself in the mirror and decided immediately that I looked like a jerk. Some of the other guys had begun to stir and just nodded at me, acknowledging my presence, but they never commented on my outfit. I figured everybody who worked in this town had to wear some kind of clown suit. I just hoped mine didn't look dumber than anybody else's.

I stepped quietly down the creaking treads of the stairs, trying to make as little noise as possible, and I saw Paul waiting for me on the front porch. I immediately decided that I didn't want to be seen next to him. I hadn't noticed what he was wearing the day before because he had clocked out about the time my mother and I got to the restaurant. By that time, he had taken off the gold Eisenhower jacket, which had those fancy flaps on the shoulders and a black, braided cord hanging off one shoulder. But he did this morning. He also had on a black cummerbund to match his black slacks. Man, did he look good. Real professional like you would see in some fancy restaurant in Atlanta or somewhere. I, on the other hand, looked retarded. Maybe not retarded but silly. I immediately felt the class distinction between busboy and waiter. I realized that in the restaurant world, I was nothing more than a garbage man. I was starting to have serious misgivings about this whole thing.

"Mornin', Doug," Paul said as he grinned at me. "You ready to go? Lookin' pretty sharp this mornin'."

I merely shrugged.

"What's the matter? The get-up?"

"Yeah," I said, "I hate it."

"Come on, man. The other busboy wears the same thing. Besides, you guys are pretty important to the income of the waiters and waitresses. If we had to clean off our own tables, we would have to let the other customers slide. And it would slow down the traffic. The faster the tables get cleaned off, the more people come through, the better service they get and the better the tips are for us. See what I mean?"

"What does that mean for me?"

"You get to keep your job," he laughed. "Anyway, don't worry about how you look. The tourists don't pay any attention to you. They just want their food sitting in front of them about two minutes after I take their order. You'll see what a royal pain in the ass these people can be, especially the ones from up north. 'Cept for Kentucky. They're dumber than people from Tennessee."

I never really thought of people from Kentucky as being northerners, but I guess it all depends on your interpretation of geography.

The M&S was only a ten-minute walk from our house, and it was beautiful. As the red-to-pink-to-yellow dawn began breaking at the edge of the sky, you could see a gentle mist start to rise as the sun warmed the night's dampness on the mountain foliage. This mist is where the Great Smoky Mountain area got its name. Some used to say it was called the Smokies because of all the moonshine stills pumping out "white lightning," as the home-distilled product was called. There was a slight chill in the morning air that was warming in cadence with the rising sun. The only people you saw were locals on their way to face another day of catering to the number one industry in town: tourism. I was really grateful to see some outfits even more humiliating than my own. Some had to wear Indian outfits, Davy Crockett outfits, and white uniforms topped by goofy looking hats as well as many other combinations of apparel designed to be termed as "cute." Now, I didn't feel so out of place, and my original feelings of embarrassment abated.

When we got to the restaurant, the cooks were already hard at work and had cooked enough bacon and sausage for about a hundred people. The pastry lady was cutting out biscuits as several trays stacked in racks were cooling while another lady pulled a huge tray from the oven. The smell of biscuits and fresh sausage made me hungry enough to nearly drool. Paul introduced me to everyone, and I managed to forget just about everybody's name but Roy the cook and one waitress named Terry.

If someone drew a cartoon of a cook, sort of like the guy in the comic strip "Beetle Bailey," Roy could have been the model. He was a big, slope-shouldered man with huge hairy forearms. On one arm was a tattoo of an anchor and on the other one, a snake coiling around a knife. Nearly bald, he brushed the remainder of his thinning hair straight back towards the hair sticking out from the neck of his white tee shirt. Although he had what appeared to be a permanent scowl on his face, Paul said he was a real funny guy. Just not a morning person, I imagined.

When Paul introduced me to Roy, Roy look at me and asked, "What'cha want fer breakfast? Better hurry up and tell me. I ain't got all day, goddamnit."

"Uh…scrambled eggs, sausage and biscuits," I replied quickly. I didn't really want that but I had to tell him something fast or he might get pissed at me.

"Well, go grab a seat and sit your ass down. I'll bring it to ya," he said as he cracked three eggs at once onto the grill.

I thought this was pretty nice of him, so I got a glass of milk and sat at one of the tables nearest the kitchen. Almost as soon as I sat down, Roy appeared before me with a plate heaped with eggs and sausage. He slammed the plate down on the table and walked away without a word and stood sipping on a cup of coffee he had just poured from the freshly brewed pot. I felt kind of guilty that no one else sat down to join me, but I figured they had other stuff to do. I did notice that Terry and Laura stood near Roy whispering to each other and giggling. I just thought they found me to be pretty ridiculous in my vest and bow tie. I couldn't blame them for laughing. I began shoveling the eggs in pretty fast because I knew I didn't have time for a leisurely breakfast. Just as I was washing a load down with my milk, the burning started. And it grew. And it grew some more so I gulped more milk. I felt as if my face was on fire as I began to sweat. What the hell was going on? I heard full-blown laughter from the trio at the coffee machine while Paul came out of the kitchen with a big grin on his face. He strolled over to my table and looked at me, trying to muffle a laugh.

"What's so damn funny?" I wheezed.

"The newbie just got his welcome breakfast," Paul replied. "Roy dumps about a pint of hot sauce into the scrambled eggs the first time. He won't do it anymore. Just in good fun."

To demonstrate my willingness to take a joke, I grinned back at the amused threesome and nodded my head. That being accomplished, the group went back to their individual labors.

I picked up my plate with the rest of my breakfast on it, having had my appetite sated by the fires of hell, and took it back to the dishwasher.

He was laughing and didn't even see what went on. Welcome to the food service industry.

About six-thirty, the first few hardy souls drifted in carrying newspapers, guide books, maps and/or brochures about things to see and do in Gatlinburg, the Heart of the Great Smoky Mountains. They also adorned their necks with every conceivable type of camera from the most expensive 35 millimeter to the little Instamatic cameras. They wanted to capture as much of everything they could on film or slides. Great thing to invite the neighbors over when they got home and make them sit through four hundred slides of Gatlinburg's finest retail outlets. Then there were those real professionals with the movie cameras. Maybe they could film each other eating breakfast. Then old Myrtle could watch it when she got back home and show some evidence as to why she added another ten pounds to her previous weight of two-twenty.

Somewhere there must be a guidebook that tells tourists how to dress when they go on vacation. Surely to God they don't dress that way at home. Unless of course they were from Ohio, and then they probably did. Even at weddings. It appears that people on vacation either do not pack enough clothes or don't like the ones they brought. When they started coming in, you could tell by the fold wrinkles in the tee shirt that read something like "I Saw A Bear Eating Garbage In Gatlinburg And Lived To Tell About It," or something just as snappy and humorous. Then there were the hats and caps. Why would anyone with an IQ slightly above that of a houseplant ever want to own a baseball cap with a feather sticking out of it? The kids looked kind of cute in the Indian headdresses and coon skin hats, but the adults were absolutely astonishing in their poor taste, not to mention their ignorance of financial value. There were some hats that had "Scalp Protector" emblazoned on the front. I later learned that was the most popular cap among guys from Ohio.

My thoughts were interrupted when Lois came up to me and told me that it was time to get me trained. Trained? To clean up tables? But I simply agreed enthusiastically to show her that I was a real go-getter. An elderly couple who appeared to be in their late fifties had opted for a quick breakfast so they could take advantage of the absence of traffic at the early hour. After Lois had rung up their ticket, she came back and grabbed a large, gray plastic bus tray. It was about twenty by twenty inches square and about eight inches deep. It also had a permanent film of grease covering every square inch of its surface so you had to handle it carefully unless you wanted to create a huge mess in the dining room. Lois and I went to the booth where the couple had been sitting and she began teaching me how to clean a table.

"First," she said, "scrape the leftovers onto one plate. Then, stack all the plates with the garbage plate on top. Grab the silver and put it in the bottom of your tray, and then load the rest of the cups, saucers and glasses. Put the salt and pepper shakers back in place, wipe the table down with this wash cloth that has a little ammonia in it. Kills germs. Place the tip in the center of the table for the waiter or waitress, and then wipe down the seats. This last part is the one that most restaurants fail to do, and people judge your restaurant by the cleanliness they observe as they are being seated."

As we worked side by side, our arms and hips occasionally brushed together. I could feel the cool softness of her slender arms and smell the light, fragrant perfume she was wearing. When she looked directly into my eyes to make sure I was learning the procedure, I felt an enormous urge to kiss her full on the mouth as a way of saying "thank you for training me so well." However, common sense prevailed this time, and I resisted. I took the dish tray back to the kitchen and began unloading it in the dishwashing prep area, after I dumped the garbage from the top plate. The dishwasher would then give the dishes a spray rinse and stack them into the dishwashing machine. I guess he had the most boring job in the whole place, but he seemed to enjoy his work because he sang along with a radio sitting nearby. His name was Donnie, and he looked like he was about fifteen years old. His lank blonde hair was held in place with a paper skullcap that everyone in the kitchen was supposed to wear. Well, everyone but Roy. But, what the hell, he was only the cook. He said it made his brain hot. Donnie had some tattoos as well. On one hand, he had the letters l-o-v-e on each finger. On his left hand, he had h-a-t-e. When I asked him about this, he said it was just like his dad's tattoos that he got in prison. I suppose he was carrying on a family tradition. When I asked him why his dad was in prison, he grinned proudly, revealing three missing teeth and replied, "Grand theft auto and armed robbery." I gathered this was something that he found rather dashing about his father. I was also surprised to hear him use the legal terminology so well, figuring he must have been exposed to the legal system early on in his brief life.

Donnie had a small transistor radio sitting on a shelf about ear level to which he had tuned to a Knoxville rock and roll station. "Louie, Louie," by the Kingsmen was wailing away on the radio, and, as was my habit, I stopped to listen for a minute to concentrate on the so-called "dirty lyrics." I still couldn't tell what the uproar was over. I guess you just had to pretend to hear dirty lyrics, so that way you were sure to hear them. I once asked a guy about the lyrics as we were riding along in his car, and all he would do was look at me and say in an unbelieving tone of voice that he couldn't believe I couldn't understand the lyrics. So he told me what they were, but his explanation differed from what Paul heard, which was different from some of my buddies back home. But it had a good beat and I like to dance to it. That ruling was courtesy of some greaser from downtown Philadelphia being asked to judge the merits of the song on American Bandstand. It always amazed me how a guy like Dick Clark could pretend to be sooooo interested in what some of those losers had to say. He should've gotten an Oscar.

I was jarred from my musical reverie by the shouting match between Roy and Terry over an order of pancakes that got sent back. Terry was telling Roy that the customer said that they tasted like pie crust and that she tasted them and had to agree.

"Whatta ya mean pie crust?" Roy screamed in defiant outrage. "Thems pancakes, goddamn it!"

Terry, whose face had turned a fiery red because she hated Roy, strode over to a large stainless steel bowl with what was apparently pancake mix. She jabbed a finger into it and put it in her mouth.

"Taste for yourself, you dumb sumbitch!" she howled just as both doors to the kitchen were open to the dining room.

When he tasted the mixture, he yelled, "Who put goddamn pie crust in the goddamn pancake bowl? I'll kill the bastard."

Terry, not the least bit interested in a hunt for the culprit, lashed out at Roy saying, "Just make some pancakes, you asshole, and make 'em fast."

In order to calm things down, Lois came dashing through the "in" kitchen door to stop all of the screaming and yelling. I figured it was time for me to get the hell out of the kitchen. I grabbed my tray and went to look for a dirty table. When I got out into the dining room, a few people were laughing hysterically at what they thought was a show, while others just stared at each other in stunned disbelief. The lady who sent the order back was demanding that her husband should do something, and he was. He was laughing his ass off. This just pissed his wife off that much more.

Lois got the whole issue resolved in a pretty quick fashion. She asked the pastry ladies to mix up some more pancake mix and throw out the pie crust mix that had now had had an untold number of fingers in it. She then went out to the customer whose life had been ruined by this unfortunate mistake and told both the wife and the husband that there would be no charge for their breakfast and that a new order of pancakes was on its way. This seemed to satisfy all of the parties in this modern-day Greek tragedy or comedy, depending upon your point of view. It then occurred to me how deftly Lois had remedied the whole situation. As a teacher, she probably missed her calling and should have been a union negotiator.

Not being used to seeing adults who weren't married fight, I was slightly unnerved by the entire event. I wondered if somebody would be fired or something. Instead, when I went back into the kitchen through the "out" door, Terry hissed at me to go through the right door and get the hell out of her way. Roy observed this little confrontation with his permanently arched eyebrows that gave him a look of perpetual surprise and asked, "The hell's wrong with you, boy? 'Cain't you read?"

I shrugged and asked what he was talking about.

"Them damn doors. One says 'in' and the other says 'out.' The reason fer that is we don't want the garbage haulers, bumping into the waiters and waitresses. I'll, by God, make you cook an order iffin' you knock one down. Whatta ya think of that?"

"I'll watch it, Roy," I replied sheepishly.

I stayed pretty busy, but without any incidents until the breakfast rush subsided around 10:30. By then, most of the tourists had eaten and headed out for another day of whatever attractions spiked their interest.

Terry caught my eye and waved me over to the area where the service people could sit down for a break and a smoke. As I headed her way, I tried to remember any other blunders I had made that morning that could've pissed her off. She had a temper to match her reddish-blonde hair. She also had the most beautiful green eyes and the fairest skin I had ever seen. About five feet two and a hundred pounds, she was hot. I was sure her boyfriend looked like Frankie Avalon.

When I reached her, she guided me by the shoulder to one of the break booths and told me to sit down.

"Sorry 'bout that."

"What?" I asked.

"Gittin' on your ass 'bout the door and all."

"Oh, that was my fault. Can I call you Terry?"

"What the hell else would you call me?" she asked grinning.

"Uh...." I was such a dumb ass trying to talk to her and not let her catch me looking at her bust. Look at her eyes I told myself. Then, I got lost in those as well.

I've always kept it a secret from my buddies, but I have always found the eyes to be the sexist feature of a woman. Somehow, I thought women liked eye contact when you talked to them. That way they would think you weren't thinking about them naked.

Guys would classify themselves according to a woman's body parts. You were a leg-man or a tit-man or whatever. Could you admit to being an eye-man? No. You'd get labeled as a weirdo for sure. I already had enough problems fitting in without making things worse.

"Here...have one," she said as she slid a pack a Marlboros my way.

"Thanks." All I had ever smoked until then was a puff or two shared with some buddies when we camped out or something. I had never really smoked in public, but I figured it would make me look older and more sophisticated. I took her lighter and lit up. I immediately had the urge to cough but smothered it as Terry stared out the window at the passing horde of people. The next puff went down okay, and I began to get a little light headed, a sensation that was not unwelcome.

"Does your boyfriend smoke Marlboros?"

"Don't have one since I caught him doing it with my older sister. They deserve each other so far as I care. Both of 'em drink too much anyway. You drink? You look too young to."

"Aahh...I have a beer once in a while," I lied.

"Ever get drunk?" she asked, eyeing me carefully.

"Nope."

"Good. I don't mind a beer myself now and again, either."

"Maybe we could have one together sometime," I said hopefully.

"Maybe so," she replied while she looked at me as though she were evaluating me.

"Great," I said.

We both rose and went back to work. I went about washing down all the tables and booths in preparation for the lunch rush which started around 11:30. I kept glancing over at Terry, but she appeared oblivious to my observation. I was already feeling a rush of infatuation and eager anticipation. I was in heat, and I bet she could tell it. That was even better. She wasn't a bit threatened by my intentions, and I bet she could look right into my thoughts with those green eyes. God, what a woman. After I cleaned a few tables, I went out back to have another smoke and commune with the flies.

When I went back inside, the lunch rush was in full swing. The other busboy and I were moving like pickpockets at a county fair, cleaning our way around the dining room in order to make room for more diners. Our work was not unnoticed by Lois and the other waiters and waitresses. They really appreciated our efforts. Plates, silver, cups and glasses flew with a blur into the tub. Double time back to Donnie, the dishwasher and back out again. Tubby, my counterpart, asked me if we were racing. He had the stone face of someone who is not particularly bright, which in Tubby's case was a real understatement. Tubby was the retarded cousin of some relative or something and giving him this job was going to be the top of his career for the remainder of his life. I felt sorry for him. At least this was just a summer job for me, but for him, this was going to be his life.

The lunch rush flew by without incident. About 1:30, the last of the customers were finishing and none were coming in to replace them. I thought it was time to sit down, until I was told we had to get everything ready for the evening shift. Salt and pepper shakers, catsup bottles, sugar dispensers and napkin dispensers all had to be refilled. The area in the back of the dining room was being replenished with clean utensils, coffee cups, salad bowls and glasses. The salad ladies were preparing huge mountains of tossed salad in large stainless steel bowls. I asked Laura why the night shift didn't do its own work. She told me that in the restaurant business, one shift always prepared for the other. The night side would get everything ready for the morning shift and so on.

When I finally sat down about two twenty, I suddenly realized how tired I was. My feet and back were killing me. Even my hands were sore from carrying tub after tub of dirty dishes. I don't think I'd ever been this tired after football practice. When Terry noticed me slumped in a booth, she came over to me, smiling.

"You beat, Doug?'

"Yeah. You, you look like you could still go a few rounds."

"You'll get used to it. Don't worry about it. This was just your first day. Maybe tomorrow we can have a beer when we get off work. What you think 'bout that?"

"That'd be great Terry, but I don't have a fake ID. I can't get served."

"Don't worry 'bout that. You pay for it, and I'll buy it from a guy I know who owns a beer store. We'll go back to my place."

I had a sudden adrenaline rush that could've allowed me to work another ten hours. Instead, I jumped to my feet and asked, "That's a date then?"

"Yeah," she grinned, "that's a date."

Chapter Nine

Paul was still waiting on a late lunch couple and told me he'd be home later. He didn't want to miss his tip. One of the other waiters walked up to me and told me his name was Larry.

"I'm sorry I didn't introduce myself earlier," he said, "I was so tired from last night, I could hardly stand up."

"It's okay," I said. "You go to the same party as Jim did last night?" I was hoping for a really graphic account of the previous evening's activities.

"Naw, man. I was working."

"You work two jobs?"

"Well…sort of. I chauffeur Sam around to his drinking buddies every night. He had his driver's license pulled about five years ago for drunk driving. Pays twenty a night for easier work than this."

I thought the hours were a killer, but that the work itself was pretty easy. I asked him, "When do you sleep?"

"In the afternoons until about seven then in the morning from about four until five thirty or so. Only problem is that it really cuts into my drinking time," he laughed.

I did a quick mental calculation and arrived at one hundred and forty dollars a week, tax-free. Hell, tuition at the University of Tennessee was only ninety dollars a quarter. If I could score a job like that, I could pay for lots of college and have money to burn. Larry interrupted my financial wool gathering with a statement that almost knocked me out of my socks.

"Sam was talking about you last night before he got out of it. He said he was thinking 'bout making you Martha's driver for the summer since you were so well mannered and everything.

"What's she like, anyway?"

"Sam's wife? She's an alky, too. Always needs somebody to drive her around to see her drinking buddies. They both have a different circle of friends so they go their separate ways. Besides, Sam's a quiet, cheerful drunk, and old Martha's just the opposite. She's loud as hell and would whip a bear if she decided to fight one. Want me to tell Sam you're interested?"

"Hell, yes," I said. I wasn't concerned about Martha. I was raised by a tough woman, and she was stone, cold sober. A drunk like Martha would be no more trouble than baby-sitting.

As Larry and I walked out the back, he put his finger to his lips to tell me to be quiet. He then eased open the beer cooler and pulled out a six-pack of Budweiser. Picking up some newspaper from the top of a stack of boxes, he wrapped up the beer securely and tucked it under his left arm.

"Employee compensation," Larry explained with a wink.

Bullshit. That was stealing, I thought. But I kept my mouth shut anyway.

When we stepped out into the glare of the hot, midday sun, we were both temporarily blinded. Larry pulled off his waiter's jacket, took out a pair of mirror sunglasses, slipped them on and looked at me for approval. He then pulled a pack of Marlboros out, flipped open the lid and shook one out for me.

"Thanks. I need a light, too."

"Shit, man. I feed you, dress you, take you to school, and you eat the teacher." He laughed heartily at that overused phrase.

"I'll buy my own on the way back," I said while grinning at his stupid comment.

There was a motel next to the restaurant that the Ronsons also owned. We ambled over to the pool to see if any good looking chicks were laying around basting in suntan oil. All we saw was one big fat woman, shielding her eyes from the sun, while two small boys screamed and argued over a float. She should've drowned both of them. Those two little monsters were loud enough to get a ticket for disturbing the peace.

Larry and I made our way across the paved road, past an auto repair shop that had what appeared to be both living and dead autos parked in no particular fashion around the building. The fading yellow paint on the cinder block shop had grease and oil in places you would think were impossible to reach. Different auto parts lay in disuse on the ground, and a very old dog wandered aimlessly amid the trash as if he were looking for a tool he just dropped.

"If you ever need a car fixed, old man Duggan is the best around when he's sober enough to work. All the Ronsons take their cars to him. He's cheap, too. Only needs enough money for booze and what little food he eats. He lives in this old dump with a cot, a TV, an old fridge and not much else."

As Larry was telling me all of this, I began to wonder if drunks populated the entire city of Gatlinburg. Must be all that bourbon in the water.

We finally got to the dirt road that led to Mr. Cummins boarding house. When we arrived, he was sitting on the front porch with a glazed grin on his face.

"Get a lot of work done today, Mr. Cummins?" Larry asked. He turned to me and winked.

We got no response. Mrs. Cummins came out on the front porch, glanced at her husband and slowly shook her head. "Sometimes I wisht he wouldn't drink so much. But at least he don't git out an git in no trouble. Jus drinks hisself to sleep ever night. Could be worse, I reckon."

I really felt sort of sorry for her. She had that look in her eyes that revealed compassion, disappointment and defeat all at once. Dressed in a pale blue gingham dress partially hidden by a faded apron that she constantly twisted in her hands, she made me want to reach out and smooth a loose strand of gray hair that hung over her glasses. She was the picture of everyone's grandmother, only sadder. Finally, she looked up at us and smiled.

"You boys git outta them monkey suits an git comfortable. I jes made a whole batch a sugar cookies," she said proudly, breaking the severity of the moment.

Larry and I bounded up the stairs to change into shorts, sneakers and tee shirts. I hung up my slacks, figuring I could get two or three days out of them before they needed washing. My shirt was another matter. I'm glad it was this new "wash and wear" stuff. I thought that maybe I could wash my clothes in the tub the same time that I took my bath. Kill two birds with one stone. I'd have to think about that one. None of the other guys was back from work yet, and that pleased Larry to no end. He wouldn't have to share the beer with anybody but me.

Larry left the beer wrapped in the newspaper while we went downstairs to grab a couple of cookies. The smell coming from the kitchen reminded me of my grandmother's house. She was always making a "homemade" something or other and it was good reason to overeat. As Larry and I sat down to a heaping plate of still-warm sugar cookies, Mrs. Cummins poured us both large glasses of cold milk. Great, I thought. This'll be dinner, and beer for dessert.

Watching Larry eat could test a pig farmer's gag reflex. He talked with his mouth open as he ate so that you had a very clear view of the initial digestion process. With a hard swallow, he would grab the glass and slosh down some milk, spilling some on his chin in the process. Bits of food would wash back from his mouth to float in the milk until the next big draining started. If you sat too close to him, you would get covered with the spray of wet, chewed food as he talked and gorged simultaneously. It was pretty gross.

After inhaling about a dozen homemade cookies, most of which Larry ate because I lost my appetite, we thanked Mrs. Cummins, who seemed to take a lot of pride in watching us stuff ourselves. I guess where she was from bad table manners were a compliment to the cook. We thanked her profusely and bounded up the stairs to unwrap the package smuggled from the M&S.

Larry acted like a kid on Christmas morning as he tore into the newspapers holding the six-pack. From a drawer containing socks and underwear, he pulled out a bottle opener, or church key as we called them, and pried the lid off the first bottle.

As I watched him make swift work of the bottle top, I asked him, "If you hadn't had that church key, how would you have gotten the beer open? With your teeth?"

He laughed and said, "Watch this."

He then took the next bottle and placed the lip of the bottle top against the latch plate of the door. Holding it steady, he then slammed his hand down firmly on the bottle, sending the bottle top spinning into the air. As the beer foamed quickly to the lip of the bottle, he jerked his head down and placed his mouth over the opening, preventing any of the froth from hitting the floor. The whole five-second scene appeared to be a mime of the word desperation. He pulled the bottle from his mouth only to laugh. He immediately put the bottle back to his mouth, tilted his head back as far as he could and began draining the bottle. When the gurgling stopped and he came up for air, only half of the beer remained. Wiping his mouth with the back of his hand, he looked at me quizzically and asked, "If you don't want that, I'll drink it."

"No thanks. I'll take it from here," I said. I took a big swallow of the cold and slightly bitter beer and grinned back at him.

We sat across from each other in the small bedroom that Larry shared with his brother Lonnie. I asked if he and Lonnie were twins, and he said that Lonnie was a couple of years older than he was but was still a senior in high school. He'd failed a couple of grades and was the oldest kid in his class at nineteen. He kept plugging away at school so he could get his diploma before he enlisted in the Navy.

"When's Lonnie get back?" I asked.

"'Bout a quarter after four. That gives us about thirty minutes to finish these beers before that lazy bastard gets back and wants some of my hard-earned compensation," he said with a cocky grin.

Halfway through his second beer, I asked him if he had the night off from his chauffeur's job.

"Night off? Shit, man, are you crazy? Drunks don't take a night off. I don't usually pick up Sam until around seven so that gives me time to get some sleep before I go to my second job. I usually have a couple of beers to help me relax and go to sleep for a few hours. After that, I'm ready to go. I suggest you do the same thing."

"Why?" I asked.

"Cause you made an impression on old Sam, and he told me to bring you over tonight for Martha to get a look at you. See if you're what she wants."

"You mean an interview?" I was beginning to get nervous.

"Yeah. She wants to make sure you've got arms and legs and ain't blind." Larry found his own joke hilariously funny.

"Don't worry. You've already been picked by Sam. You're coming along in case Martha wants to ride around tonight," he explained.

I finished my beer, and Larry immediately handed me another. I was already beginning to feel a little lightheaded from the first one and wasn't sure I ought to have another one. But I took a long swallow and watched Larry start in on his third. No way was I going to keep up with him.

I got up, stretched and told him I'd better get a nap.

"You want your other beer?" he asked.

"No thanks. You can have it or give it to your brother."

"Fuck that bastard. I'll drink it," he responded.

"What if Sam smells beer on you? Won't you be in trouble?"

"Him? Smell beer on me? You've gotta be kidding. He and his old lady both smell like an entire bar. Anyway, they push enough booze stink around for both of them to be declared lethal weapons."

I walked into my bedroom and sat down on the edge of the bed, sipped on the beer and reflected over some of the day's events. I made it through my first full day on a real job, met some neat people, drank some beer and was later going to possibly drive a drunken woman somewhere. Then I began to realize: "I don't know my way except from here to the restaurant. What if I get lost? Can a drunk woman give me directions?" All of this ran through my mind until the beer started ordering me to lie down. I wasn't too sure that I was getting off on the right foot or not, but it was great to be on my own and not have somebody trying to tell me everything to do. I decided I could do just fine without the guilt trip. Before I could get a clear thought going, the beer lulled me to sleep.

After what seemed like only fifteen minutes, Larry was kicking the foot of my bed and telling me it was time to go. Being a little disoriented, I asked myself:

"Go where? Where was I? Who is this guy?"

After a moment, it all came back in a rush and I remembered I was supposed to go with Larry to meet Martha. I noticed that Larry was wearing the same shorts and tee shirt he had on when I conked out, so I figured I could go dressed the same way. As I looked around, my roommates were either reading or sleeping. It sort of reminded me of an army barracks; the army of locals against the army of tourists. Larry was in a rush so instead of introducing myself to some of the others, I bounded down the stairs behind him out to the front porch.

Mr. Cummins had a Mason jar tilted to his lips when he saw us come out of the house. "Don't you two bastards go gittin' in no trouble tonight. Yuh hear?"

"Aaaww, come on, Mr. Cummins, we're on our way to church," Larry told him.

"Bullshit. You two bastards is goin' on a pussy prowl. I know you, so don't try to fool me," he said, nodding his head.

Larry immediately confessed and complimented the old man on his sharp skills of observation. His ugly grin widened as he nodded his balding head even faster.

I noticed that I had been called a bastard for the second or third time today. I wondered if people around here used it as a term of endearment or a formal greeting. I then concluded it was also a very valuable adjective used to describe just about anything. Bastard heat. Bastard tourists. Bastard traffic. Bastard this and bastard that. The word eventually lost any meaning at all other than a major component of the vocabulary of mountain people.

As Larry and I walked along the road to the Ronson's house, I asked him how he could be so sure that I'd get the job? He just told me not to be so bummed out and let him do most of the talking, as if I had an alternative.

When we walked into the Ronson's house, I was surprised to see a very neat and clean place. I expected to see liquor bottles and cigarette butts piled all over the place. Sam welcomed us in as if we were long, lost relatives and asked us to have a seat. The room was very large with one wall that was entirely composed of a river-rock constructed fireplace. Gray paneling covered the walls, and a thick, plush dark gray carpet lay underfoot. The furniture was all crushed red velour in sizes I imagined were for extra large people. When I sat on the couch, I felt as if a whale had swallowed me. There were only two lamps lighting the room, giving it the effect of a funeral parlor. Nice house, but no home sweet home.

"You fellas want a Coke or somethin'?" he asked, ever the gracious host.

Larry said yes for both of us, and I nodded in agreement.

Sitting in a huge, overstuffed velour chair, Martha looked like a little lost girl. She was staring at me without blinking. I was beginning to squirm nervously until she finally decided to speak to me.

"How old are you, boy?" she asked while squinting through the smoke from the cigarette stuck between her lips. She was wearing so much make-up, she looked like a wax person. Must have been a pound of dark red lipstick alone.

"Sixteen," I replied, looking directly back at her coal black eyes.

"Old enough for me," she said, grinning lasciviously.

Sam saw all of this and laughed a loud rumbling fat man's laugh. He wheezed out, "She's a pistol, that Martha. Ain't you sweetie?"

She never took her eyes off me and replied to Sam, "I am at that and this boy's my new chauffeur if he'll keep his goddamn hands offa my little girl."

What little girl, I wondered? My question was soon answered when a dark-skinned, long legged, black-haired beauty twisted her way through the living room on the way to the kitchen. At around five-four and one hundred and ten pounds, this was one walking work of art. She said nothing and never acknowledged anyone's presence. She must mean **that** daughter. In her tight cut-offs and sweaty white blouse, she looked like the model for all the covers on those cheap porno books that occasionally made the rounds at school. But she also looked as friendly as a pit bull. The words spoiled and rude came to my mind, and I took an immediate dislike to her. Damn the hormones, a man has to draw the line on principle. Of course, it was more like a dotted line. A pale dotted line.

Larry came to my defense saying, "He's already got a girlfriend, Mrs. Ronson."

"Yeah. And I know a lot of guys with wedding rings on too."

All I could do was sit there and turn about the same shade as Martha's lipstick.

She finally stood up somewhat shakily and said, "Let's go, sweetheart. Got to see some people."

You could tell that she was once a real good-looking woman just like her daughter. At about the same height but probably ten pounds lighter. I found out later that people who drink a lot don't eat very much. Sometimes, they get real skinny. Martha could use a few cheeseburgers from the restaurant to bring her back up to fighting weight. She was wearing black slacks and a yellow sleeveless blouse. She probably knew that the yellow in her blouse highlighted her natural olive complexion. All in all, she wasn't bad looking.

She then walked over to Sam and said, "Gimme a kiss, Daddy, so's I can go."

Sam and Martha kissed each other for what probably passed as a goodnight kiss, and she turned to me and tossed me a set of keys.

"The red one. Let's go."

As we walked out of the house, she took my left arm for support.

"Hurt my knee playing tennis with Kat this afternoon."

"Who's Kat?"

"My daughter. Kat's short for Kathleen. And you mark my words, that's all you're gonna know about her. I won't allow her messin' with the hired help."

I held the passenger rear door for her as she climbed into the seat. I shut the door and walked around the rear of the car and got in. It was the first time I had ever sat in a brand new car. Much less a '63 Pontiac Bonneville. The red leather seats and all of the other bells and whistles gave no indication that there were about four hundred horses under the hood. Larry told me that every car Sam buys, he specs it out with a police pursuit engine.

From the rear Martha said, "Can you handle it? This car's a sonovabitch."

"Yes ma'am."

"What do I call you besides boy?"

"My name is Doug," I answered.

"Okay, Doug, let's get this show on the road. I got some people to see."

With that, I cranked up the powerful motor and asked. "Which way?"

Chapter Ten

After Martha directed me to take a right on Dogwood Lane, she told me to just head down toward Main Street. When she got into the car I got a look at some of the things that I supposed were her traveling supplies for the evening. On the floor next to her feet were a small ice bucket and two bottles of what I figured was gin. On the seat next to her were what appeared to be a big beanbag and a carton of Winstons. I could hear her in the back, dropping a cube of ice into her glass then pouring herself a refill from one of the bottles. I wanted to ask her about the beanbag, but I was too nervous to talk. She looked to me like she was someone who had a real short fuse.

"Don't you ever say anything?" she asked. "Cat got your tongue or something?"

"I…uh…well…I wasn't sure I was supposed to do anything but drive," I answered stupidly.

I looked in the review mirror and saw her looking me right in the eyes. She had a smirk on her face that even further intimidated me. The different neon lights from the gaudy places we drove by cast a rainbow of garish colors across her face like a clown constantly changing his make-up. I looked back at the street and waited for her to respond.

"You're supposed to be a driver, companion, bodyguard, delivery boy and any other damn thing I want you to be," she snarled.

"Can we be friends, too?" I asked.

When I looked into the mirror, I saw a startled and quizzical look on her face. She seemed almost shocked by my question. Then her face began to soften perceptibly enough to give her a near girlish, innocent look. The change was incredible.

"Wanna start over, Doug?" she asked softly, with an almost pleading look on her face.

"Start over what?"

"Us," she stated simply

"Sure. My name's Doug. Nice to meet you," I said as I watched her in the mirror.

She leaned forward from the back seat and lightly grazed my right shoulder with her long, red nails, and said, "Hi, Doug. I'm Martha. Glad we could get together tonight." With that she slumped back into her seat and awaited my comment.

The chill in the car that wasn't coming from the air conditioner began to warm.

"My pleasure, ma'am."

"Call me Martha. Ma'am makes me feel too old even if I am old enough to be your mother."

I decided to be daring and grinned at her saying, "You sure don't look that old."

A wide grin came across her face as she gave me a sidelong glance. "You're some kind of bullshitter, aren't you? Doesn't matter. I love it."

Obviously once beautiful, her looks were beginning to succumb to the ravages of booze and tobacco, and she and her husband probably hadn't 'done it' in a long time. He was probably too busy drinking with his cronies. Actually I felt sorry for her.

We drove along in silence for a few minutes, watching herds of tourists grazing up and down both sides of Main Street in search of I'm not sure what. Maybe they were just enjoying a view that was different from their own boring homes. Anything would be better than that.

Finally, from the back, Martha said, "take a right up there at that Hilltop Hotel. Can't remember the name of the road. But I do know you have to go past two more roads on your right and take the next left that goes up a long hill. Turn in the third driveway on your right."

I nodded and listened while she fixed herself another drink. That woman could drink like a horse. I don't know where she put it, but she still didn't appear to be drunk at all.

I pulled into a long driveway that led to a huge house on the side of the mountain. Lights shown brightly in the darkness surrounding the house, giving it an inviting warm look. When I stopped the car, I got out to open the door for Martha. She had already opened it and was a little surprised to see me standing there offering my hand to help her out.

"Goddamn, Sam was right. You are real polite. You're a real southern gentleman, ain't cha? I like that," she said as she stood facing me. Now I could see her eyes better, and they appeared to have a thick coating of clear glass over them. For a moment I thought she was about to cry. I learned later that I was staring into the glass-coated eyes of a drunk. When she took her first lurching step toward the house, I caught her arm to steady her and she looked at me thankfully.

"Why, thank you sir. These damn shoes, you know."

I simply nodded my head in agreement.

The front steps leading up to the house were built from river rock curving gently up the slope of the hillside. Little recessed lights had been installed along the way to help prevent someone from stumbling, which I found very helpful as I negotiated my way up the steps with Martha now leaning heavily on my arm. A huge brass doorknocker was on the front of the heavy oak door. As I reached for a lighted doorbell, Martha grasped the knocker and began pounding away, generating a noise that reminded me of a battering ram. I held off on the bell, anticipating someone quickly opening the front door to see who was trying to break it down. I glanced over at Martha, still clinging to my arm, and she had her head down as if she were trying to memorize what her shoes looked like. After a minute or so had passed with no response, Martha raised her head to say, "The old bitch ain't home, I reckon. She's prolly out screwing somebody's husband. You know she screwed her first two husbands to death. Doctors said heart attack, but I damn well know better. Married these old coots, screwed them dead and inherited all their money. Her ass is a lethal weapon. They outta throw the old murdering whore under the damn jail."

"If you hate her so much, why did you come to visit her?" I asked.

"Hate her? Hell, she's my bes' friend. Whatta you mean hate her?"

She was laughing so hard; she started a horrible coughing fit. She bent over at the waist both laughing and coughing at the same time. When she finally straightened up to look at me, she had a strand of long, dark hair hanging over her face. I thought about brushing it back for her, but when I raised my hand in the direction of her head, she jerked away quickly. Neither of us commented on that brief moment.

"Well…uh…. I don't know. You just called her a bitch and a whore and all. I thought you were mad at her about something and came here to settle it."

"Figger of speech. Don't mean nothin'."

"Ah," I thought. Sort of like that "bastard" thing. I guess I needed to learn to cuss in a flattering manner if there was such a thing. "Good morning, you murdering bastard. How's things with your lying ass today?" That would really help me break the ice with people.

"Come on, Dougie. Let's us go over and see Mrs. Lucy Anne Compton. You know the way to her fine house?"

Dougie.

"No ma'am. I'm still new to the area. You'll have to give me directions."

"Hell fire, boy, do I have to tell you ever which way to go?"

"If you want to get anywhere, you do," I said, immediately regretting the way it came out.

She burst out cackling again and said, "I'll say one thing: You got a smart mouth on you. And you got balls. I like that in a man, Dougie. You 'n me are gonna make a fine fuckin' pair we are. Can't wait to show you off to my gal friends. Let's git movin."

As we made our way down the stone steps, she continued to giggle girlishly. I finally had to ask her what was so funny.

"You. You ain't a bit like them other boys Sam gits for me. You ain't scared of me; I can tell," she said winking at me.

I was glad she couldn't see me blush. I thought my face would burst into flame at any second. I just mumbled something about respecting my elders as I helped her into the back seat and closed the door. The thing she didn't know was that my own mother was as scary as they come, and she didn't even drink.

As I made my way around the car, I could see her fixing herself another large glass of gin and ice. I wondered if she was going to be able to talk enough to give me directions. She was so disoriented, we could have ended up in another state.

"Okay. Let's go back the way we came and git back on the main drag. Lucy Anne lives on the other side of town."

When we got to Main Street, the tourist traffic was out in full force both on foot and in cars. Martha looked up and down the street, tilting her glass often and smoking one cigarette after another. I had to roll down my window slightly for fear of getting poisoned from booze odor and smoke. When I did, the cool fresh air caressed my face, making me feel a little better.

"Lookit all them bastards. Spend that money, folks. Don't dare take none home with you. We know what to do with it," she howled drunkenly at the crowd.

Fortunately, her window was shut tight and no one heard her. I was beginning to think this chauffeur job wasn't all it was cracked up to be.

I followed Martha's directions to her next visit. This house looked almost small next to Martha's and the last house. It was a cozy split-level sporting a huge porch on the front of the house. I parked the car right in front of the steps leading to the entrance and helped Martha out of the car. With all the trouble she was having trying to hit each step, I probably should have carried her up the front door. I rang the doorbell and waited, while Martha wavered slightly and held on to my right arm. After some minutes of doorbell ringing, Martha realized it was a lost cause.

"Goddamn. Where is everbody? Ain't nobody here."

I really didn't know what to say. There was a plaintive quality to her voice that could almost inspire pity. Pity for a child who'd come running into the house crying that there was nobody outside to play with. I stayed silent.

She jerked upright suddenly and snapped, "Take me home. Now."

"Yes ma'am," I said, leaving off the salute.

Driving back, she was very quiet. Then, I heard her snoring softly. She was out like a light. Once home, I carried her into the house. Luckily, the front door was unlocked, so I went right on in. Kat was sitting on the couch watching TV and drinking a coke.

"Don't tell me. She's drunk."

"She's had a few," I replied.

"Well, don't put her to bed yet. We gotta get her to pee first. She wets the bed when she gets that way, and that's most nights. Take her over to the bathroom down the hall on your left. I'll give you a hand."

Kat seemed to know the drill pretty well. When we got to the bathroom, I sat her mother on the toilet.

"Raise the lid, you dumb ass. Don't they have indoor plumbing where you're from?" she snarled.

Embarrassed, I lifted Martha off the seat and lifted the lid.

Kat continued her instructions with, "Undo her slacks and slide them down off her. Panties, too."

I was almost too shocked to say anything. I thought I'd just deposit the body and let Kat do the rest.

"What are you gaping at? You've got to know how to do this because I won't always be here when you bring her home. I got a life, too, you know. Besides, think of it as changing a baby or something. That's all she is anyway. A helpless, thirty-seven year-old infant," Kat said as she stared at her mother.

I did as I was told and removed the clothing.

Kat then leaned down to her mother's ear and yelled, "Take a leak. Time to piss. Do it so you can go to bed."

Although Martha never once acknowledged another presence, I heard the stream hit the water in the bowl. Amazing. Kat appeared to be yelling at a dead person, and the corpse was responding. She should go to medical school.

"Wipe her off with some toilet paper and put her to bed."

I was beyond humiliation. My movements were mechanical, as if what I was doing was not me, but rather a robot following instructions.

"You know you're not just her driver, but her nurse as well. You might as well get used to it. This is about a full time job in itself. She pay you?"

"Naw, that's okay," I said.

"Wait a minute. I'll get you your money. You earned every damn dime of it."

With that, she spun around to go get the money. As she was walking away, she yelled, "Put her in bed and throw a blanket over her. Her evening is over."

I lifted her from the toilet and carried to the large bedroom just off the bathroom. There was enough light from the hall to find the bed and throw a quilt over her. When I got back to the living room, Kat was holding out a twenty. I took it and thanked her.

"Just take good care of her," she said sadly and turned away.

Without saying anything else, I walked out the door and back to my house.

When I finally climbed into bed around one, I tried to review the events of the day, but they seemed to envelop me like an old blanket. There was so much stuff going on in my head, I didn't know what to think. All I could think of was that line from that Wizard of Oz movie that pointed out to the little girl that she wasn't in Kansas anymore.

Chapter Eleven

The small alarm clock that I brought with me sat on the floor next to my bed sounding a head-splitting blast at five in the morning. I had set it a half an hour earlier to beat the rush to the bathroom. As I fumbled in the dark for it, I heard someone bark out for me to shut off the damn alarm. I sat up and put my bare feet on the wooden floor, pulling my tee shirt over my head. I stopped about half way and sniffed. Smoke. All the smoke from the night before had clung to the fabric of my shirt making it smell like an overfilled ashtray. I threw the tobacco-stinking shirt under the bed with the intention of washing a load of laundry in the afternoon. Then it occurred to me that I really didn't have enough for a whole load, so I retrieved the shirt from under my bed and carried it downstairs with my shaving kit and clean underwear. I figured I could just wash it in the tub with me as I took my bath. What a stroke of genius.

    I padded quietly down the stairs and went into the bathroom, turned on the light and closed the door. The main thing I did not like about the bathroom was the lack of a shower. One of the guys had bought some kind of rubber hose sprayer deal that sort of worked like a shower except you were sitting on your ass in the tub. I turned on the water to the tub, regulated it to the right temperature, and threw in my dirty shirt as the tub was filling. The water pressure was very low, so I had time to shave as the water slowly flowed into the tub.

After I finished shaving, I stepped into the bathtub and sat down. The water was perfect. I grabbed my tee shirt, soaped it up and left it in the water to soak. After washing off, including my hair, I pulled the stopper out of the drain. I then slipped the hose over the mouth of the faucet and again adjusted the water so I could rinse my shirt, the tub and myself. The plan worked to a tee. When I finished, I dried off and began twisting the tee shirt as hard as I could to squeeze out all of the water. It was still coming out a little soapy, but it smelled a lot better.

After I gathered all my belongings, I went back upstairs to finish dressing. At the top of the stairs, Jungle Jim was waiting. We called him Jungle Jim behind his back because he was hairy as an ape. He looked like a gorilla. My private name for him was the "Missing Link." You only had to see Jungle Jim once in his underwear to realize that Darwin was right. This guy was living proof.

"I'd better have some hot water or you're in trouble," he warned.

I smiled, nodded my head and told him to fuck off. I don't think he even heard me because he just looked at me with a glassy stare and went down to the bathroom.

By now, Larry was up and getting dressed. I hung my wet shirt on a hanger and hung it up to dry on a nail that had been driven into the wall for just such an occasion. As I was finally putting on my clip-on bow tie, Larry walked up with a big grin on his face.

"How'd it go last night with Martha?"

"What do you mean?"

"You know…any problems?"

"Nope. She was fine. We went to visit some friends of hers who weren't home and then we just drove around for a while. She got really drunk and I had to take her to the bathroom and then put her in bed."

"Did you get any on you while she was passed out?" He had a huge leer on his face

I was a little stunned, and I told him so. "You are one sick son-of-a-bitch. First of all, she's old enough to be my mother. Second, she was dead drunk. I'm not into screwing dead people like you obviously are. And finally, her daughter, Kat, was right there in the living room. She's the one who paid me."

Larry just laughed and told me I'd get the hang of it pretty soon.

Hang of it? What the hell was that supposed to mean? To me, this was nothing more that a well-paying baby-sitting job. No more or no less. I finished dressing without further conversation and we headed out the door and down the road towards the restaurant.

"You pissed at me?" Larry asked.

I sighed and said, "No, I just think you were being a little crass back there."

"Let me tell you something," he began. "You may call it crass or whatever you want. But this is my second year up here, and you've got to grow up some. We're living in an adult world now. No more cruising drive-ins, mom doing your laundry, cheerleaders or any of that other shit. You're on your own with nobody to answer to but yourself. What I'm tryin' to tell you is that you got to take advantage of the freedom you've got right now. When the summer ends and you go back home, you're gonna feel stir crazy. On time for dinner, curfews, homework, football practice-all of that stuff doesn't exist right now."

I stopped walking and looked at him. "So that means I can become a criminal, now?"

"No. It's just that you have the opportunity of a lifetime to experience a lot of things the other guys back home will have to wait years to do. Right now, we're bullet-proof."

I thought about what he had said as we continued walking. That stuff about being on your own made sense to me. Besides, life **is** short. Who knows? A truck could hit me tomorrow. I decided right then what my new outlook would be. Carpe Diem! My Latin teacher from last year was always using that phrase and telling us to learn as much as we could every day. I figured that phrase should apply to my summer up here as well.

I turned to Larry and asked to bum a smoke.

"Carpe Diem." I shouted as he handed it to me.

"What the hell does that mean? Thank you in Slobovian?"

"No. It's Latin for 'seize the day'," I replied.

"I still don't know what you're talkin' about, man. What's it mean?"

"Means I'm gonna do just what you said."

"I didn't say anything about carp or seizing the day."

"Yeah you did. You just used a lot more words to say it."

Larry took that as a compliment on his vocabulary and began rattling on mindlessly about a tourist yesterday who stiffed him on a tip. He was talking about seizing that guy by his silly-looking shirt and beating a decent tip out of him.

We got to the restaurant a little early and had time for another cigarette and a cup of coffee. One of the pastry ladies brought us some biscuits and jelly that we devoured instantly.

While we were sitting there, a blonde woman in a low-cut sundress unlocked the front door and came inside. Let me rephrase that. She made an entrance. Her blonde hair was cut short. She walked with very proper posture and was sporting the largest set of boobs this side of Hollywood. I mean, we're talkin' Mamie Van Doren at least. She looked neither right nor left, but strode directly back to the prep area to get a cup of coffee. I suddenly realized that I had not chewed my food from the time I saw her come in.

"Who's that?" I mumbled around a mouthful of biscuit.

Larry looked up and said, "Oh, that's Julie. She's the hostess on the night shift but a lotta times she and Lois switch off. Lois is taking some kind of class at night school. Besides, Julie would rather work days so she can go out and play at night."

"Go out and play?"

"Yeah," he said as he stared at her.

"She married?"

"Yep, but she ain't braggin' about it. Her old man's a truck driver and is gone most of the time. He gets in about every two weeks for three or four days. I think he goes back on the road to keep from getting screwed to death. What a way to go."

Julie spotted us and walked over to the booth where we were sitting and squeezed in next to Larry.

"Mornin', boys. Been gittin' any on ya lately?"

Larry laughed and said, "I been gittin' so much, I can barely walk."

"Liar. Who's he? You gonna be polite and introduce me?"

When she turned from Larry to look at me, I was nailed by two of the clearest blue eyes I had ever seen. Her complexion was as smooth as silk and her cupid's bow mouth was covered with hot pink lipstick. It's a good thing that her face was so mesmerizing because I was trying desperately not to stare at her breasts. Those two melons could've been the eighth and ninth wonders of the world, and the low cut of her sundress showed plenty of deep cleavage. She had a small smirk on her mouth like she was reading my mind or something.

"That's Doug, a friend of mine from home. He started to work here yesterday," Larry replied.

She sized me up for a moment and stated, "You look awful young. How old are you?"

"Sixteen," I managed to croak.

"Good age. I member when I was sixteen. How old do you think I am?"

Crap. Guessing a woman's age can get you in big trouble. My mother always said to guess way low if ever I was put in that position. I thought about saying twenty-five because it would probably take a woman that many years to grow melons that size. But twenty-five was a little old so I guessed twenty-one.

"Give the man a cigar," she said laughing. "What else can you guess about me since your eyes are sizing up my bra size?"

I wanted to ask what that was, but thought better of it.

"Well, Doug, it's nice to meet you. You and me, we'll have some fun together before the summer's over. How's that sound?"

I was so far in heaven, all I could do was nod my head like a real jerk.

She winked at me and got up to leave.

"Times a-wastin', boys. Let's get these hungry tourists fed and watered."

As she rose to leave, she seemed to lean over towards me a little to give a closer view of the goodies tethered precariously in her dress. I disregarded all pretenses and gaped openly. From the grin on her face, I had done exactly what she wanted me to do. She was having a ball at my expense, and I didn't mind in the least.

As the first few customers came wandering in the restaurant, I made sure there was plenty of orange juice in the cooler. Then I went over to the milk can and gave it a little tilt to see if it needed changing. It felt about half full, so I figured it would last until the lunch crowd started coming in. I liked being busy so I would make coffee, fold napkins, wipe down the prep area and just about anything else I could do between bussing tables. My extra efforts didn't go unnoticed by the waiters and waitresses either. They appreciated seeing someone who wasn't getting any tips pitching in and helping out. I started getting a lot faster at clearing tables and setting out clean utensils, but the learning curve on this job was a pretty short one. Besides, the work was kind of relaxing in a mindless sort of way. Kinda like mowing the yard, except you didn't get rocks slammed into your legs. Plus, the busier we were, the faster the time passed. As far as I knew, I couldn't tell one day from another. With no days off and driving Martha around at night, I seemed to be on an endless merry-go-round of work, nap, drive, nap, work, nap and so on.

One day, I noticed that there seemed to be no let-up with the lunch crowd. Even more than that, they seemed a little better dressed than usual. As the night side started coming on their shift, the day-side was still waiting on people who were seated before their shift was up. They didn't trust the second shift to fork over the tips that they earned. So, as new people came in, the new crew would start waiting on them. One of the second shift busboys called and said he would be in a little late, but he would be in. I decided to stay and help out because I didn't want Tim, the only busboy remaining on the night shift to get overrun. When word got out that I was staying over to help out the crew, waiters and waitresses came up to me and thanked me for pitching in. They even told Julie that they wanted me transferred to the night side.

I was feeling pretty good about all that, but I had never seen us as swamped as we were. I asked one of the waiters if we had advertised free deserts or something, and he looked at me and laughed.

"Don't you know what day it is?"

"No. I don't, but what difference does that make?"

"It's Sunday, man. The locals take their Saturday night bath, go to church and go out to a restaurant for lunch. I guess mama says no cooking on Sunday. If God gets the day off, so does she. Then we get a lot of people who come in from Sevierville and even as far away as Knoxville that'll come up here for Sunday dinner. Best night of the week for tips. I'll probably clear sixty or seventy five dollars tonight. Easy."

It didn't take a brain surgeon to figure out I was in the wrong uniform. Although I was getting an extra twenty a night to roll Martha around, it still wasn't sixty a night. But then again, I also had it pretty easy, too. Just ride around in a big car and do whatever Martha wanted. I decided to take things the way they were and not concern myself with trying to change shifts. Maybe I could ask Martha for a raise. Maybe I could move her to twenty-five a night. That would add up to one hundred and seventy-five a week with no taxes. Hell, all things considered, I was making almost as much money as my dad and having a hellava lot more fun. I thought that I should make sure my situation stayed just as it was because I had a real good deal going.

The days tumbled onward. There seemed to be no end to the number of tourists that flooded into town. Naturally, all the locals were making a killing. Tips for the waiters and waitresses were great and Sam gave me a twenty-five cents-an-hour raise. Martha had bumped me up to twenty-five a night, so I was pretty flush.

On a Monday or Tuesday morning, I'm not sure which, I was sitting in the back booth with a cigarette and a cup of coffee. Martha had run me ragged last night visiting almost everybody in town. It was like she was desperate for attention. It was pretty sad. Julie came bouncing in, got a cup of coffee and slid into the booth next me so close that you couldn't have gotten some dental floss between us. And I sure wasn't struggling to get away, either.

"Mornin, sugar. You look like something the cat drug in this mornin. What've you been up to?" she purred into my ear.

"Been working a lot, driving Martha around."

The lunch crowd was a bit slow today because there had been a break in the heat. Many people opted for picnics in the mountains rather than going to a restaurant. We even advertised picnic lunches with all the fixins'.

Around 1:30, I sat down with one of Roy's extra thick, extra greasy hamburgers and a large ice tea. I didn't realize how tired I was until I sat down. I guess a lack of sleep was beginning to take its toll.

I was sitting with my back to the front of the restaurant and was slightly startled when Terry quietly slid into the seat across from me and lit a cigarette.

"What's that? One of Roy's giant gut grenades?" she asked.

"Yeah, tastes good, too. Makin' any money today?"

"Not bad. I had a group of four old ladies who didn't understand the concept of tipping so they left me a quarter. Should've followed them out of the place and thrown it at them. Bitches."

"Yeah, that's tough," I said.

"I saw you this morning," she said as she stared at the tip of her cigarette.

"Saw me what?"

"Flirting with Julie."

"I wasn't flirting with her," I said, blushing.

"Look at you. You're getting red as fire. That means you're tellin' a lie when you get all red like that." She looked at me with a funny grin on her face.

"I'm just teasin' you. But you better be careful with her. She never met a man she didn't want to fuck. I'd swear that's why she married that truck driver so she could cat around on him when he was gone on a trip. And be extra careful of him, too. I hear tell he beat a man to death down in Alabama fer pullin' a knife on him. The judge declared it were self-defense."

As I sat and listened to her story, I asked her, "How do you know so much?"

"You just pick up on things here and there."

I felt a stirring in my groin as I watched her smile and stretch her arms in a way that made her breasts jut forward. My mind raced. Sweaty sheets, feverish skin, urgent clutching, deep kissing, pausing for air only to dive back in again. The sounds of passion: moans, whispers, pleading, and sounds of the bed almost walking across the room. These images sped through my mind's eye in a flash, and the sexual tension began to reach the boiling point as I tried to put all of this in some kind of order. I pictured her....

"Hey, anybody home?" she asked as she tapped me on my forehead.

I jumped a little and laughed sheepishly. I wondered if she could tell by the look on my face what I had been daydreaming about because I didn't want to get slapped right here in front of everybody in the whole place.

I smiled back at her and realized I've got to be the luckiest guy in the world. Got a great day job, a fantastic night job and an eighteen year-old beauty that obviously wants to screw my brains out. I'd found heaven.

Chapter Twelve

The days began to turn into weeks. Each day had its own ritual, and I took comfort in that I was the one who decided what and when I did anything In those days, I thought I was experiencing freedom when I had actually become no more than a slave to others and myself. I just didn't know it at the time.

When we got back to the house, a couple of the guys were already home. I could hear the distinctive sounds of the Tokens as they sang a song that I really didn't understand but liked a lot anyway.

In the jungle, the mighty jungle, the lion sleeps tonight,

In the jungle, the mighty jungle, the lion sleeps tonight.

Then the background singers would come in with some kind of stuff that was probably African in origin or something. I used to change the chorus to "I wing my whip, I wing my whip" thinking it was about some lion tamer getting some lions whipped into subservience so they wouldn't eat him in front of small children during a circus performance. That would be one hellava news story. "Lions Eat Trainer in Front of Vomiting, Screaming Crowd. Film at eleven."

We started up the steps to the house, nodding in Mr. Cummins direction.

"Whatcha got in them pokes? Groceries, I bet," the old man cackled loudly at his own humor. He knew damn well what we were carrying upstairs and thought highly of us for doing so. He never said anything to Mrs. Cummins and wasn't about to. It'd spoil our fun.

Larry grinned and winked at Mr. Cummins, "Yeah, we got some groceries. We got to eat 'em before they get warm…I mean spoil."

This brought on another unusually loud burst of howling from the old man, which was followed by a nasty coughing and spitting fit that was still going on when we walked into the house. None of us asked if he was all right or anything. The poor old bastard was about dead anyway, so we declined to be observers to his hacking up some kind of major organ. Let the old woman clean up the mess.

When I got to the top of the stairs, I saw Paul propped up in bed reading the latest issue of Playboy. While he was reading, he seemed to take little notice of Jungle Jim standing next to his bed, pleading with him to just let him see the foldout.

"Come on, you asshole, quit hogging the damn thing. Just let me see the Playmate of the month," he whined desperately.

Because Jim was so hairy and had a five o'clock shadow by noon, watching him aggravate Paul reminded me of a child arguing for a new toy. It also reminded me of my younger brother when I got something that he wanted to see. Rob could get on a dead person's nerves and that reminded me of Martha.

"Larry," I called out, "are we driving tonight or what? Did you see Sam or Martha either one today?"

"We drive every night unless we're told otherwise," he replied.

Yesterday, I'd had two beers and a nap and felt pretty good all night. Based on that logic, I could have four beers, go to sleep and feel twice as good with my three and one-half hour's sleep. I was the sort of person who would look at a bottle of aspirin, and if it said take two every four hours, I'd take four every two hours. Anyway, four from six was two, so I offered a beer to both Paul and jungle boy. They accepted my offer with a look of surprise and thanked me. I sat on the edge of my bed, lit a cigarette and opened my first beer of the day. I tilted it to my mouth and swallowed half of it before coming up for air, just as I had seen Larry do several times before. After a couple of drags on my smoke and a wall-rattling belch, I finished the bottle with a second hit. Somebody applauded my belch and gave it a nine on decibels and an eight point five on duration. To us, belching loudly was an acquired skill that, performed well, could give you a real high standing among your peers for manly behavior. I thanked them for the recognition and told them I was saving my best ones for later when I had more suds under my belt. With that, I quickly opened the next beer with my bottle opener that I had bought at a little gift shop the other day. Its handle was a piece of bark-covered wood and coated heavily with shellac. I thought it was pretty neat. The second beer went down almost as quickly as the first, and when I dropped the bottle into the metal trash can, Jim looked over at me.

"You in a race?" he asked.

"Nope. Just thirsty. Got a problem with that?"

"Hey, man. Don't get pissed. I was just kidding," he replied.

"Its cool, man," I said.

Jim turned back to Paul and was trying to read over his shoulder. I sat there thinking I give the guy a free beer and all of a sudden, he's my den mother. Sonovabitch could get his own beer next time. I opened my third and went into Larry's room but he was reading some car magazine. With nobody to talk to, I went back to my bed to smoke, drink, relax and think about home for some reason. The thing that sort of surprised me was that I didn't miss it at all. As a matter of fact, I dreaded going home at the end of the summer. I was in a different world here. Different people, different morals, different outlooks on life, and it all seemed perfectly normal to me. I was in real life while home was like some twisted Ozzie and Harriet nightmare. How could I ever go back to that?

I had developed the ability to stay awake after a few beers and thought that I'd better do something about the huge pile of dirty laundry in my duffel bag. I don't think my bathtub laundry was working out as well as I planned, because my shirts and my underwear were beginning to look a bit dingy. What the hell, with all the money I was making I could throw them away and buy new ones. Sure I could, I thought sarcastically.

"I'll see you later, man. I've gotta go do my laundry."

"Later," Larry responded.

I slipped on a pair of cut-offs, a tee shirt and my tennis shoes over bare feet. That way, I figured, I could get just about everything I owned washed.

Doing my laundry was something I definitely knew how to do. Because my mother worked, she often got up at five on Sunday mornings to do a whole week's worth of washing in one big marathon. I had to go with her to help with the folding as well as keeping her company. We always went at five on Sunday mornings so we wouldn't have to mix with any "white trash" that didn't even own a washer and dryer. We had both, but mother always insisted on doing it all at once rather than a little bit every night. I never questioned her logic. She would view that as a challenge worth fighting over.

It was still fairly early for the tourists to be up, but most of the businesses were open so the locals could get all of their errands and shopping done. Warrren's Pharmacy was one of those so I stopped in to see if I could find a small box of detergent. Jeff was working behind the counter and waved at me as I came in.

"Where you goin', Santa? Little early for Christmas isn't it?" he asked, laughing at his own joke.

I laughed back at him to let him know I could appreciate his humor. If some people asked me the same question, I would have walked over and tagged them on the nose. When it came from Jeff, you just knew he wasn't insulting you. He was just trying to make you feel a little better about the lousy task you had facing you. I asked him if they stocked small boxes of washing detergent, and he pointed me to the aisle and shelf it was on. When I took it up to the register, he looked at the price and then looked around to see if anyone was near by.

"You get the local's price rather than the tourist's price," he said as he rang up the purchase at half the regular price. "Even at that, we still make good money," he winked.

I thanked him and left for the laundry, which was located on a back street not far from the M&S restaurant. As I entered the dirty, low-ceilinged cinder block structure, I saw only one other patron in the place. A vision in pink she was. A pink sleeveless top, checked pink shorts, well-worn pink flip-flops on dirt encrusted feet, all set off by large pink curlers in her hair. It also appeared that she had purposely fitted a hundred and seventy pounds on her five-foot frame into an outfit designed to fit someone in the range of a hundred and twenty-five pounds. The black bra she sported underneath the straining blouse added a dash of contrast to her ensemble. At her feet sat an absolutely feral-looking child of undetermined gender clothed only in a diaper that looked as if it had been worn without benefit of change for at least three weeks. The odor emitted by these two individuals was stronger than the soap powders and bleach clinging to the walls. I caught myself staring as one would at freaks in a side show. I willed myself to walk to the far end of the washing machines and start loading my clothes. I couldn't cram my load into one washer, so I pulled everything out and started over, this time separating the light colored clothes and whites from my dark stuff. I turned around to retrieve my detergent from my chair, and I dumped some soap on the clothes after closely studying the directions on the washer. These machines could be very different from the ones back home. Placing quarters into the sliding slots above the machines, I shoved them in, listened to the washers start up and went over to sit down with a paperback book.

After what seemed like a long time, I went over to check the progress of the washers, hoping that by lifting the lid I could hurry up the process some. The first washer was still thrashing away, and I closed the lid. When I opened the lid on the machine next to it, my heart skipped a beat. Someone had stolen my clothes literally from beneath my nose. Nothing but water was sloshing in the machine. While I resisted the urge to yell, I slowly surveyed the rest of the place, only to see the pink lady and her kid who was now playing with the cigarette butts that were accumulating at its mother's feet. Casually, I looked into the machine on the opposite side of the washer that had my clothes in it. When I lifted the lid, I saw dry dirty clothes covered in dry clean soap powders. With a sense of frustration and relief, I shoved more quarters into the silent washer and started it up.

All I could think was that I was going to be stuck in this filthy place all morning on my only day off. That was infuriating. I went outside to smoke a cigarette and get away from the causes of my frustration and anger. I hated coin wash places. Give 'em to the Russians. They deserved places like this. Better yet, make convicts work in laundromats, checking to see when clothes were dry and folding the dry ones. A few years of that and the crime rate would really go down.

After a few moments, I turned to go back just as Mrs. Pink and her little pig were coming out. She had a load of laundry under one sweaty arm and a cigarette dangling from the corner of her mouth, and she kept jerking the arm of her offspring so that its toes only touched the ground every few feet. Man. Mother of the Year.

As soon as I got to the top of the stairs, Larry was waiting for me.

"Time to go, man," Larry grinned. "God waits for no man and neither do Sam or Martha."

"Gotta brush my teeth. I'll be ready in a minute."

"Hurry up, man. You're gonna make us late."

I dressed in six quick movements into sneakers, clean shorts and tee shirt, the uniform of the evening. Instead of taking my toothbrush and stuff downstairs, I just squeezed some toothpaste onto my finger and rubbed it all around my teeth and gums. Then I worked up some spit and swallowed.

By the time we got over to Sam and Martha's, I felt pretty good. This time Kat answered the door and stepped aside to let us in. She didn't acknowledge us at all with any kind of "come in" or "nice to see you again." Deep down, I figured she hated us for some unknown reason. Damned if I could think of anything I had done to make her so cold toward us. It was probably Larry she didn't like because he always had this I-know-something-you-don't-know grin on his face. It really irritated the shit out of most people.

Sam, smiling broadly while rubbing his huge belly, asked, "We make any money today, boys?"

Larry answered, "Made so much money, I'm not comin' to work tomorrow. Matter of fact, you could close the restaurant for the night right now and still take a truck to haul all your money to the bank."

Sam laughed uproariously at Larry's comments. I thought they were kind of stupid, but it sure made an impression on Sam.

"You smart as hell ain't cha, Larry?"

"No sir. I'm just lucky. I'd much rather be lucky than smart."

Again, Sam laughed loudly. I just reckoned he would laugh at a soup label if you put it in front of him. Apparently, he had started drinking earlier in the day without the benefit of a nap. I glanced over to Martha and nodded to her as if to say hello. Tonight she was wearing white slacks, a red blouse and red shoes, and somehow, she got all the reds to match her lipstick. She really looked good. She looked a little younger than I'd ever seen her look, too. I guess the booze was acting as an anti-aging medicine because she nearly looked better than Kat, who sat cross-legged on the couch, her hair in tangles and her clothes all wrinkled. She looked like she had slept all day and had just gotten up.

Larry and Sam continued to carry on while Martha rattled the remaining ice cubes in her glass and asked me to fix her one for the road. I took her glass over to the large bar on the other side of the room. There was a big mirror behind the bar that looked like it was composed of a bunch of one foot by one foot mirror squares with random gold lines running over them. I took a look at myself in the mirror as I picked up the bottle of gin that resembled the one I had seen in the car last night. The label read Beefeater's. I put two cubes of ice in her glass that I had gotten from the small icemaker under the bar. I watched myself fix Martha's drink and thought I was pretty cool fixing drinks as I poured the glass full of gin. I strode back to Martha and handed her the drink. When she took the glass from me, she gently brushed her fingers against mine and locked her eyes on mine for a beat or two. I broke the contact and turned to see if anyone was watching us. Luckily, everyone else was absorbed in anything other than Martha. She could have been another piece of furniture for all they cared.

"Thanks, Doug. You're a real sweetie."

"Yes ma'am," I said.

"Just one favor, Doug, before we go out tonight. Call me Martha. Not Mrs. Ronson, just Martha. I'm gonna introduce you to some friends tonight, and I don't want you callin' me Mrs. Ronson in front of them. One, it makes me sound too old. And two, we're friends now. You're just not my driver, you're my escort."

I felt a little awkward, but I said, "Okay…Martha."

She smiled at me and asked, "Ready?"

"Let's go," I said and held out my hand to help her up from the chair.

When I pulled her up, she accidentally bumped up against me causing her drink to slosh onto my shirt.

"Whoops. Didn't mean to get any on you," she said, giggling.

Kat had been watching this whole exchange and left the room in a huff. Nobody else seemed to pay any attention to her as if it was something she did all the time. I, on the other hand, felt as if I had been caught doing something wrong. Actually, I was a willing subject to what was apparently a come-on from Martha. It was kind of weird but not all that uncomfortable. I guess my view of what was attractive in a woman was broadening since I had gotten away from home and my immature buddies. They were probably wearing the tires out on their parent's cars between the Little Big Boy and the A&W Root Beer place just looking for high school chicks. Kid stuff.

When we walked out to Martha's car, she hesitated for a moment and looked at her car.

"I want you to bring the Bonneville down to the motel tomorrow when you get off work and give it a good washing. We need to look good when we're out and about."

I remember seeing Kat washing her car in an area right next to the motel pool, so I supposed that was where she meant.

"Bring your swimsuit. You can cool off in the pool with a beer if you want."

"Sure, Martha. Anything you want," I said with a smile.

When I backed out of the driveway, I asked her where we were going tonight, she said to drive over to her cousin's house.

"Lucy Ann. You remember, don't you?"

I replied, "Yes, I do." But I thought, "Do you?"

"Bunch of us old hags are havin' a card party tonight. Might even have a cocktail or two."

I glanced at her in the rearview mirror and said, "If it's for old hags, then I better take you someplace else. You don't qualify."

Her large smile dissolved into a sardonic grin.

"You puttin' some kind of snow job on me? You tryin' to get lucky with an old woman?"

I had the feeling she was fishing for compliments so I was adamant in my denial when I caught her eye in the mirror and said, "Snow job? Tryin' to get lucky? Absolutely not, Martha. I'd never lie to you; you been too good to me. I respect you, and I think you're an attractive woman. I mean, you look a lot better and younger than your friends. I mean that."

Her grin faded into a somber look as she whispered, "That's the sweetest thing I've ever heard, Doug."

Probably the only thing she remembers hearing today, I thought.

"Why are you so good to me? I bet you've got some kind of interior motive," she said.

Ulterior, Martha, and yes I do.

"No I don't Martha. I believe you just don't trust a soul."

"Why the hell should I trust you, then?"

"Have I ever lied to you? I'll answer that. The answer is not in the slightest. All I've ever tried to be was your friend. You okay with that?"

"Yes," she replied in a pouty sort of way.

We drove on in silence, she in her thoughts and I in mine. I had no clue as to what was going on in her pickled head, but I was aiming to try to squeeze some more money out of her. In retrospect, I really did feel sorry for her. She deserved better treatment than she got.

When we got to Lucy Ann's house, I quickly ran around to the other side of the car to get the door for her. She looked up at me with a girlish grin on her face and smiled at me.

"I hope some of them old bitches are lookin' out the window. If I knew one of 'em wouldn't tell, I'd kiss you full on the mouth," she said with a leer.

With that, I raised her hand to my mouth and kissed it a tad longer than plain hospitality allowed while looking into her eyes. She glowed beautifully. I believe, at that moment in time, I had given her more simple happiness than she had experienced in years. And, scumbag that I was I knew I was only putting on a performance. I had definitely become a whore, and I was okay with that.

At the front door, we didn't have time to ring the bell. Lucy Ann opened the door as soon as we hit the top step. Martha was right; somebody had been watching.

"MARTHA, hooonnneeeyyy," she screamed. "So good to see you lookin' so fine. And who's your young friend here? Don't kid old Lucy Ann Compton and tell me he's just your driver."

"He's my friend first and my driver second," she replied nonchalantly.

"Well, I'd say he was a friend with the way you two was givin' each other them goo goo eyes and all," Lucy said as she sized me up like someone looking at a car they were going to purchase. "Martha, I do declare, you are a real pistol. Come here and give your cousin Lucy a big old hug."

When they broke apart, she looked at me and asked, "Do I get a hug, too, sugar? How old are you anyway?"

"Old enough," I said with a cocky grin.

Lucy Ann took me by the hand and led me into the den where a card table was set up. She then introduced me to the others. There was a chorus of hugs and kisses and "oh my's" and good cheer for everyone. It was like they were seeing long lost relatives, when in fact they got together like this at least once a week. I'd seen some of my relatives carry on like this so I figured it must be some kind of fake adult ritual dance or something. I was bored out of my mind.

"Sugar," Lucy asked, "would you be a sweetheart and find out what everyone is drinking and fix us a little one?"

"Sure, Lucy Ann, I'd be happy to."

Martha had been watching this and offered, "Fix me the usual, honey. The same way you always do. Girls, tell my Doug what you want to drink."

A woman named Alice told me to fix her one with a lotta bourbon and a little branch water. The other two said they'd have what Martha was having, just like I fixed hers.

I went to the well-stocked bar and poured the rounds. When I was serving them, the one named Pat winked at me and grabbed my arm with a jewelry-covered hand and said, "Don't wander off now. You heah?"

I just winked at her and walked over to the bar.

"Help yourself to a beer, honey," offered Lucy Ann.

I glanced at Martha who winked back at me and discreetly held up one finger indicating that I was on a limited quantity for the evening. I pulled a Heineken out of the fridge, opened it and sat down to nurse it through the night. No sooner had I plopped on the couch than Alice shook the remaining ice in her glass at me for a refill. I felt a surge of anger and blushed to show it. She could've at least asked rather than treating me like some kind of trained animal. Old bitch. But I said nothing and performed my duties. When I handed Alice her drink, I surveyed the levels of the other three and asked if anyone needed a "refresh" as Martha called them. With the "no thank you's" all around, I went back to my beer and a magazine.

"Damn, that young man can fix a drink," said Lucy Ann as she sipped it then held it up to the others for appraisal.

Pat, who had been more restrained than the others all evening, suddenly asked, "Can I borrow him for my next party, Miss Martha, or can I just borrow him whether I have a party or not?"

This question generated a gale of whooping laughter from all of them as well as another chorus of questions aimed at Martha as to whether my services just stopped at being her driver. Martha simply smiled and refused to answer by shaking her head. Not too convincingly, I might add.

I couldn't believe the constitution of these women. If I hadn't watched it for myself, I could have sworn they were pouring their drinks into a potted plant or out the window.

Just about the time that I was ready to tell Martha it was time for her to go home, their gleefulness and laughter began to die as quickly as a summer afternoon shower. The room had turned from a slumber party to a funeral wake in a matter of seconds.

Lucy Ann finally broke their silence with, "Time to close up, girls. I've damn near drunk mysef sober."

"Me too," said Alice. "Dontcha just hate that when it happens?"

I thought they were crazy. Drink yourself sober?

When Martha rose from her chair, she stumbled slightly, but caught herself on the edge of the table. I quickly went to her side to keep her from falling down.

"My, these new shoes are giving me a fit," she explained.

Where had I heard that before?

"I know exactly what you mean, Martha. Those damn people in Japan or one of those countries over there just can't make shoes like people in America can," agreed Alice.

"I been havin' the same problem with my shoes for some time now even though I go all the way to Rich's Department Store in Knoxville to buy mine," Lucy-Ann said with a nod to the others.

Funny how they all seemed to agree on the idea that the quality of their shoes was the culprit in their failing equilibrium rather than the consumption of enough booze to fill a bathtub. I guess they all reinforced the same excuses for each other.

As I walked Martha to the door, Pat said, "You two go straight home now. Don't be drivin' up to River Falls overlook." River Falls was a beautiful spot overlooking a sparkling mountain river and the town of Gatlinburg. It was also a notorious parking spot for anyone who enjoys sex in a car. Paul once said he went up there during the day and found enough latex on the ground to sew him an inner tube to float down the river on. Pretty gross idea.

Martha simply turned and waved in a lazy way, and we went to her car. I helped her get in, and shut the door. When I got in the car, Martha said, "Thanks for being such a good sport tonight. I know putting up with a bunch of old sots like us musta been humiliating."

"Nope. I really had a good time, Martha. Your friends have a real sense for fun," I lied.

"Liar," she said as she slumped over against the door to fall asleep.

When I pulled into the Ronson's driveway and turned off the engine, Martha awoke with a start. She rubbed her face and eyes with her hands, thoroughly smearing her make up.

"Home already?" she asked.

"You bet. Safe and sound."

As I took her inside, she seemed to have regained a great deal of sobriety. She called out for Sam or Kat only to meet with the silence of the house and the ticking of an ancient grandfather clock that sat in the corner of the den. She turned towards me and said goodnight. I nodded slightly and patted her on the shoulder and told her to get some sleep. Without warning, she grabbed both sides of my head and pulled my mouth down on hers. Her kiss was passionate, wet and warmed by the stale odor of booze and cigarettes. Rather than jerk away from her, I allowed the kiss to go on until she decided to break it up. When I looked her in the eyes, they had filled to the point of near overflow with tears.

"Thanks for playing along tonight, Doug."

I started to ask what she meant by "playing along," but I knew she figured that I was smarter than that. I just hung my head, blushed and muttered "no problem."

With that, she turned and walked to her bedroom, and I walked out the door.

After I had bathed to wash off the evening's party, I lay on my bed with my hands behind my head and thought about the world in which Martha lived. The only time she seemed truly happy was when she was drunk, and even then she sometimes broke down in tears for no apparent reason. I often wondered if she was hiding from something or someone so she wouldn't be scared or feel pain. Feeling no pain. I had heard that used many times when people were talking about Sam or Martha. At first I thought maybe they had some kind of back trouble or arthritis or some other kind of physical pain. After spending so much time with Martha, I began to get the feeling that the pain was in her soul. To me, pain was always related to some kind of sports injury, but I had never seen someone suffer so much pain with nothing to show for it like a bone sticking out of their skin. Maybe she should try to talk to a preacher or someone like that. At least she should try to find a preacher who didn't fool around on his wife. Whatever she needed, she didn't seem to be finding it in liquor. It didn't affect me that way, then. When I had a few beers under my belt, I felt relaxed and confident. I also think it made my mind focus more clearly on things that I was confused about. Where alcohol made me smarter, it was making Martha miserable. If I was her, I believe I'd slow down on the booze until it brought you right to the level you wanted and stop there. It sure worked for me, so there is no reason why it couldn't work for her. The next time I got a chance to talk to Martha alone, I was going to tell her about my theory. Then maybe she could drink just enough to have a good time instead of going overboard. As I learned later in life, so much for good theories.

I fell asleep thinking how practical my idea was and how much help it could be. I was also confident that if my idea was good, I might even write a book about it. I could call it "The Secret to Drinking for Effect" or maybe "Drinking Made Easy." That last one probably wasn't too good because just about everyone I knew had an easy time drinking, including me. However, I was going to make sure I didn't end up like Sam or Martha. They were crazy.

I had a bad nightmare that night. I dreamt that I was being carried down a rushing mountain river without the benefit of a paddle or a life jacket. I was trying to steer the canoe by holding onto the sides and rocking the boat away from large jagged rocks. It was dark and there were no people around me to help me stop, so I kept dipping, leaning and sweating my way down hoping to reach some calm waters in order to save myself. When I finally awakened, I felt as tired as if I had not slept at all and my sheets were soaked with sweat.

Chapter Thirteen

When I got to work, one of the pastry ladies was at the grill frying bacon and sausage.

"Where's Roy?" I asked to no one in particular.

"Runnin' late this mornin'. Said he got drunk with some young gal last night, and he thinks she broke his back," answered Donnie from his dishwashing area. He was chuckling to himself as I walked over to ask if Roy had been in an accident or something.

Donnie looked up at me and grinned, "Hell, man, don't you know nothin'?"

I just stood and waited for him to further my education.

"Some gal he was with last night 'bout fucked him to death. She musta been mighty drunk, or she's one a them women that like hairy old ex-convicts. Some women like to git it on with some guy they figure is dangerous," he explained.

"Anybody know how she was?" I asked.

Donnie whooped, "Whatta you wanna know fer? You jist a boy like me."

Not exactly, I hoped.

I grabbed my cleaning rag and went out to give all the tables a morning wipe-down. Terry, Laura, Lois and Larry were all sitting together having a cup of coffee, and they waved me over to join them. I looked around for Paul and saw him sweeping the front patio area. I shrugged and went over to grab a cup. Paul walked up beside me to get a cup as well.

"Why were you sweeping? That's my job."

"I'm tryin' to impress Lois with my hard work so she'll maybe put me in for the night side."

It was well known that the night side crew made better tips even though they only worked the one meal. Breakfast tippers were usually pretty good, but the lunch tippers were cheap. The people who came in for dinner were the best tippers. I guess it was because they got cleaned up a little and had a chance to have a beer or two in their rooms before heading out to dinner.

"Good luck," I said.

"Yeah, thanks."

Since their booth was full, Paul and I sat down in the one behind them. Paul sat facing the front of the restaurant, and I sat facing the booth with the women whispering to each other. Terry, who looked rather sad, seemed to take the least interest in the conversation. I thought about asking her to join Paul and me, but then I decided to keep my mouth shut. Paul leaned his head down and lifted his cup toward his mouth to blow on the coffee to cool it down a bit before taking a noisy slurp.

"How's that night job of yours goin', sport?"

"Oh, its okay. The money's good, but I don't know, man. Martha seems kinda sad and lonely all the time and it's getting to be a real bum deal. I mean, they could pay me top dollar to shovel shit, and I'd still be shoveling shit. You know what I mean?"

"Hell, dumb ass, shoveling shit is almost what you do here cleaning up these crappy tables. At least with the night job you get to drive around in that big monster B'ville. 'Sides, you're not doing this for the rest of your life. It's just a damn summer job with a whole lotta perks. Think about our buddies back home driving around, wearing out the old man's car, tryin' to get laid, living at home and probably making a lot less money than we are."

"I know, but…"

"But hell. You need to get away from old Martha for a while and join the living. She's so fucked up, no wonder you're down in the dumps. You don't wanna end up like her do you?"

"No. I guess you're right. But how am I gonna get any time off?"

"Switch with Larry and drive Sam around for a while," he replied

"Now, there's a brilliant suggestion. Trade one messed up drunk for another. You don't even make any sense," I told him.

"Well, at least he's a man and won't get all weepy and snotty and stuff all the time. Men drunks have fun. Women drunks just get all sloppy and cry a lot. There should be some rules about how much a woman should be allowed to drink."

As usual, Paul had figured he had come up with one of the solutions for a major world problem: put a two-drink minimum on women and a five-drink maximum, I guess.

"Why don't you run for President of the United States, Paul? You're so damn smart and all. Hell, President Kennedy's only thirty-something, I think. And he's got a hot looking wife."

Paul just grinned hugely and said, "I might just do that."

I liked Paul, but sometimes I think he was so optimistic, he was delusional. Got on my nerves.

Lois got up from her booth behind us and said, "Doug, you can take tomorrow off. Paul you get Monday off. Larry, Tuesday. Sam told me to start letting everyone have a day off every two weeks. Except for the weeks before and after the Fourth. Okay?"

"Great," I exclaimed. My mood had instantly taken a definite turn for the better.

A little before lunch, my day took another small leap forward. Sam and Martha came into the restaurant together, wearing sunglasses naturally, and they were actually holding hands. I was so surprised that I had to catch myself to keep from staring.

Lois went up to them, suggested they grab a booth and have a cup of coffee. They both said they'd like that and slid into one of the booths as Lois went for the coffee. Very shortly, one of the pastry ladies came out with two plates of chicken and dumplings, green beans and a little side bowl of canned peaches. Martha just shook her head no and held out her hand as if she were defending herself. Sam laughed and said, "Nettie, you somethin' else. I don't want nothin' to eat. I just had my breakfast. Besides, I need to lose a little weight anyway."

"Vodka and tomato juice don't count as no breakfast. You need to eat some real food to keep your health. You and the missus, both," Nettie replied in a commanding way.

Nettie worked in the kitchen as a pastry lady and had been with the Ronson's longer than anybody could remember. She was really more like family than an employee.

"Now, eat. Both of you."

Sam shook his head and began attacking the food hungrily. Martha gently picked her fork up and started moving food around on the plate the way a small child does when it doesn't want to eat. Nettie simply stood there and glared at them with her hands on her hips. Finally, Martha started putting some food into her mouth until Nettie wheeled and stormed away. Martha put her fork down on her plate and picked up her coffee cup with both hands, which seemed to tremble at the weight of the cup. As soon as Nettie came out of the kitchen again, Martha resumed her efforts to get something into her stomach.

I took a load of dirty dishes back into the kitchen and heard her saying, "They's gonna starve to death on that damn booze. Booze ain't food; it's just poison. I know, cause my Luther died of it. God rest his sorry soul. If them two don't eat, they's gonna end up dead and buried."

Being an experienced dieter myself, I asked Nettie why Sam was so fat if he didn't eat much.

"Just likker fat. Beer and shine. Kills your appetite so's you don't want nothin' to eat. Just a damn shame." She said shaking her head.

I asked her, "Why isn't Martha fat like Sam?"

"She started out kinda small anyway. As a young girl, she had a great figger like her daughter Kat. Sam, believe it or not, started out bigger'n he is now. Now he's all beer-belly."

I thought about all I had been through to lose weight and about all the beer I had been drinking lately. Shit, I thought. I better switch to bourbon or wine or something. I sure didn't want to pork up again. I decided that beer was okay if you were working it off while you were drinking it. Like car washing or yard work. The other stuff was for relaxing with friends or at a party. I suppose some people just don't know how to drink, and it gets them all messed up.

When I went back out to the dining room, I heard Lois talking to Sam and Martha about how great getting away for a while would be for them. A few minutes later, Lois came over to me and said I was getting a vacation myself.

"Martha and Sam are going down to Knoxville for a few days to visit some relatives. Martha wanted me to give you this and said for you to keep the car washed. She said you could drive it all you wanted. But it better be in the same condition as she left it."

Having said that, Lois slipped some folded bills into my shirt pocket and placed her finger up to her lips to indicate to keep it to myself. I then went out to the back for a smoke and pulled the bills out of my shirt pocket. Five twenties. My stomach jumped to my throat. I had never held so much cash in my hand at one time before. I was already making almost two dollars an hour on my regular job. This was like getting over two week's pay for doing nothing. I quickly shoved the bills into my pants pocket where they seemed to rest hotly against my thigh for the rest of my shift.

I spent the rest of my day waiting for the second shift to start so I could go home. I didn't know what I was going to do tonight, but I knew I wouldn't be driving for Martha. For a moment I considered hopping into that Pontiac and heading for Maryville. I wasn't going to stop by my parents house; I just wanted to show off that car to some of my friends that the boss's wife and I were pretty tight so she lets me use her car anytime I wanted. I didn't care if it was a lie, she still told me I could drive while she was out of town. I could see the looks on peoples' faces as I cruised around the drive-ins in that brand new car. On the other hand, somebody was liable to see me and tell my parents. Shit. What would I tell them if that happened? Case of mistaken identity? Not much chance there. To be safe, I just thought I'd ride around town a little and turn in early. I hadn't had a good night's sleep since Sam had hired me to be Martha's driver. Besides, I remembered that I was wearing the same socks I had worn yesterday, so I guess it was time to find a coin wash place. Sometimes, living on your own could be very time consuming.

When I got off work and went home, I was a bit lost for anything to do. Usually the pattern had been to have a few beers, catch a nap and go over to Martha's. Tonight I had the night off, so the nap wasn't a necessity, but I decided to have a couple of beers anyway. I didn't get any from the restaurant this afternoon, but I still had a few left over from last night. I went down to the refrigerator and got a large glass and filled it with ice cubes. If it worked for cokes, it'd work for beer. I went back up to my room, opened a beer and poured it slowly over the ice. The cubes popped and crackled like tiny icebergs, and the beer almost foamed out of the glass. After I got the foam under control, I sat on my bed, leaned back against the wall and lit a cigarette. Nothing was better than a beer and a smoke after a fun day of cleaning up after people. Actually, you did appreciate your time off more than if you were just hanging around a bunch of losers all day. As I sat there, I realized that I didn't know what to do with myself tonight. I figured I would wait until

Larry and Paul got in and see if they wanted to go out and prowl around town for a while. We could even use Martha's car.

I stubbed out my smoke and picked up a paperback novel I had gotten interested in a few days back. After I had read just a few pages, I fell asleep for about fifteen minutes. Paul came in, waved a greeting and said he was not going to his other job.

"What other job?" I asked. "When did you start working two jobs?"

"Just got hired a few minutes ago by old man Kauffman at his candy shop. I stopped on the way back here and asked him if he needed anybody part-time. He told me part-timers were all he used, so I could start this afternoon at four and work until seven. Pays pretty well, too."

"What do you do?"

"Beat fudge," Paul replied.

"Beat fudge?"

"Yep."

"For three hours?"

"I can do anything for three hours," he said, staring at me in his tough guy way.

"Good for you, big guy," I replied without looking at him. "Lemme know how it goes."

That was one of the main reasons for spending a whole summer up here anyway, I thought. Most of us were putting away money for college so our parents wouldn't be so strapped. We figured we could have a social life when we got back to school, but for now, all that mattered was how much work you could do. All but one of the guys in the house had an extra job besides their full-time job. Richard Wells was a slim, quiet blonde guy who seemed to keep to himself a lot. Although he insisted we call him Richard, we all called him "Dick." One guy called him "Money Dick" and it stuck, because he obviously wasn't working to pay for school. As a matter of fact, his parents came driving up in a big, blue Mercedes every other weekend to take him out to eat. His mother also did his laundry for him when she was here. His father was some kind of big shot surgeon in Knoxville and was making about a million dollars a year. I think old "Money Dick" would have rather been home loafing around with his country club buddies at the pool. Besides, he didn't drink, and we were a little suspicious of someone who thought he was too good to drink with us. We just let him go his own way.

Larry and Paul came in with their usual six-packs and started working them over pretty well. The conversation led up to what to do for the night. Larry had the night off, too.

We sat around and lost track of time until Paul jumped up and said he had to go meet somebody. It was a little before five, so Larry and I said we would walk with him down to the drugstore.

When we got there, Paul introduced us to this guy our age who was leaning against a red sports car convertible. This guy apparently didn't need any money either. A plain tee shirt wouldn't do for this guy. He had on the kind of shirt golfers wore with some little alligator on the shirt where a pocket should have been. He was also wearing seersucker shorts and leather loafers with no socks. Handsome, tanned and friendly, Jeff Warren shook my hand like a politician. You couldn't help but like the guy, even if you were a little jealous of him. He seemed like a genuine person and not some stuck-up, snobbish country-club type. As we talked, I learned that his grandfather owned the drugstore as well as a few other stores on the main drag. Jeff sort of helped out wherever he could. I asked him what kind of car he had, and he said it was a Karmen Ghia. I'd never heard of one but I didn't let on. Obviously, a lot of girls must have known what kind of car it was because several of them slowed their pace as they passed us by. It finally dawned on me what he was doing, slouched against his car. He was deciding on a female companion for the evening. Like a kid in a candy store. I really admired his style and thought that hanging around him would be good for picking up leftovers, but Larry started talking about getting something to eat. I told Jeff I enjoyed meeting him and he shook my hand again and said the same thing. For some reason, I felt this guy was going to do okay in life. He just had that confident attitude that everything was going to go his way. He wasn't cocky, just confident.

Larry and I started going back and forth about where we wanted to eat, even though it was only about five thirty. After naming a few places and weighing the pros and cons of each restaurant, we made our decision on the singularly most important feature the restaurant had to offer. A free meal. That left only one place so we headed up the street to see what Big Bill was cooking up for the night-side crew.

Instead of going in through the front, we opted to go through the kitchen and see if Bill was in a generous mood or a stingy mood. It kind of varied with Bill. It wasn't that he was so big that made him intimidating; it was the fact that you never knew where he was coming from. One day he was like Santa Claus, all jolly and friendly, and the next day, he could be like a wounded bear. Kept you off guard. We ambled into the kitchen slow and easy, nodding to different members of the crew, trying to gauge the "temperature" of the kitchen. If everyone was talking and laughing, then Big Bill was probably happy. If people were tiptoeing around, Bill was wounded. Luckily, Bill spotted us and yelled, "What are you two bastards doin' here when youins is supposed to be off work? Ain't they any women out there to be chasin'? Couple a peckerheads."

Larry and I cut our eyes at each other. Bill was in a good mood.

"Ain't got the energy to chase women, Bill. We're starvin'," replied Larry.

Big Bill looked over at us and grinned as he said, "You two bastards ate yesterday, didn't ya? You got some hogs at home that need feedin'?"

"Naw, Bill, we just wanted to get some food cooked by the master chef himself," Larry said as he looked down and kicked at a small piece of bread lying on the floor. "How about a couple of cheeseburger plates?"

"How about a big old steak and some vegetables?" Bill asked.

We couldn't believe our luck. Maybe Bill had taken a snort or two of bourbon before he came in to work. Whatever the reason, we were ecstatic. Bill told us to grab a seat and tell him how we wanted our steaks fixed.

"If you'll find you a place in the back room, you might find a cold beer or two in there somewhere," he said with a wink.

About that time, Julie walked in, saw us and gave us both a big hug. Man, what an appetizer she would make. She had on one of those "cigar" dresses and I still didn't know why they were called that.

"Julie, why do they call those dresses you wear 'cigar dresses'?" I asked.

"Watch this," she said.

With that, she brought her elbows tightly against her sides and leaned waaaayyy over at the waist. For a moment, I thought she was going to spill out of the top of her dress. She stood up and winked at me.

"Close your mouth, boy. Flies will be runnin' in there," she laughed.

She glanced out the door to the dining room and saw a man at the register waiting to pay his check.

"Watch what this guy does when I ask him if he would like a cigar."

With that she left the kitchen and headed for the front. The man at the register was about forty or fifty years old; it's hard for me to judge the age of old people. But, he had the tourist outfit on which consisted of sandals with floppy black socks, plaid shorts, and a tee shirt with something about moonshine on it. I could see Julie as she smiled at this guy, flirting with him while ringing up his bill. When she handed him his change, she had obviously popped the question because he took a step back, looked down at the case, looked back at Julie and nodded his head. Just as Julie started her slow bend downward, the guy froze. Then, he seemed to bend over too, catching up with Julie so as to maximize the view behind the glass case. I can tell from where I was standing, it was awesome. The only reason a normal man would not do the same thing would be if he were in a back brace or lacked a pulse.

After what seemed to be an inordinate amount of time selecting a cigar, the guy's wife came over to see if his back had gone out on him or something. I could see her eyes darting back and forth between Julie and her husband, analyzing the situation at hand faster than a hawk on the alert for prey. She quickly poked him in the ribs, and he straightened up suddenly and pointed to a box of cigars in the case. Julie bent over just a little bit farther to reach in and snatch a cigar from the display, stood up, brushed her hair away from her face and handed the man his selection. Actually, she handed him two of them because he was going to pay for whatever she came up with. Very profitable little case the restaurant had going there. He handed Julie some bills and waved away the change. Julie smiled and thanked him as his angry wife was leading him out of the restaurant. When she came back into the kitchen, she was laughing and shaking her head.

"That man gave me a two dollar tip for two fifty cent cigars. But he sure got his money's worth. I could feel these puppies starting to shift some."

Big Bill glanced at her and said, "Julie, you let them things get loose and there'll be a riot started. Maybe heart attacks. Them's about lethal."

She grinned and winked at me as she ran her fingernails lightly across my back. I was speechless, but my bloodstream was working okay. My dick was harder than Chinese arithmetic. Larry started applauding her and asking when the next show would be. Julie just turned and bounced back into the dining room.

"Food's up," Bill yelled.

We grabbed our plates and headed for the back room. Once we sat down, Larry looked at me and smirked.

"Why don't you set that plate on your tent pole there and spin it like that guy on the Ed Sullivan show does every other week?"

I blushed. "Just shut up, will you?"

We wolfed down those steaks in record time, only pausing to flush our mouths with mouthfuls of beer. Once we had finished eating, Larry opened fresh beers for both of us, and we lit up cigarettes.

"Man, that was good," I said to Larry.

"Yeah," he replied as he blew smoke toward the ceiling. "It was priced right, too."

"What do you want to do tonight?" I asked him.

"I don't know. What about you?"

"Let's do something that doesn't involve driving a car. I never thought I would ever say that in my life, but I'm really sick of driving all around this place. We ought to walk around and just act like tourists," I suggested.

"No. We'd have to buy stupid-looking clothes. Besides, if we looked like tourists, we wouldn't get any 'locals' perks."

"How about that fake-looking wax museum? If we get in free, we aren't out anything."

Larry responded, "I've been there, and it's not even a deal for free. I've seen more realistic mannequins in a store window display. It amazes me that more people don't ask for their money back when they come out of that place; it's so fake."

We sat in silence for a while and smoked. I was really too tired to do much of anything, and I bet Larry was, too. We were just unwilling to admit it to each other. Sometimes having fun can be a real chore. I'd be happy just to sit here, smoke and drink beers, but our location lacked a certain atmosphere. Cases of canned food and a garbage dump nearby did nothing to elevate our moods. Finally, I came up with an idea, but I didn't want to suggest it with too much enthusiasm for fear of being labeled an old fogey.

"Why don't we go down to the Greystone River Motel and sit on those lounge chairs near the sidewalk? We can watch people walk by and rate them on their stupidity level."

Larry surprised me by showing real enthusiasm for my idea.

"Hey, that sounds good. Why don't we finish these beers, knock down two more real fast and go do that?"

"Hell, why don't we wrap up a six-pack to go? Get some big paper cups so we don't get caught drinking beer in public." I suggested.

"A restaurant is a public place, and people there don't get arrested for drinking in there. Why should we worry?" Larry asked as he gaped at me with a lopsided grin.

I could tell he was already getting a little loopy.

"We're only sixteen you, dumb bastard. Had you forgotten that?"

"Funny you asked that because, yeah, I had forgotten that I was too young to drink. Since I've been drivin' Sam around, I've felt older. How bout you?"

I didn't answer him immediately because I was taken somewhat off guard by his question. It was real hard to explain, but I just felt older than sixteen by at least ten years. I glanced up at Larry, and locked on his eyes.

"Yeah. I know exactly what you mean," I finally answered.

In an attempt to get us both fired up, Larry clapped his hands together and jumped up.

"Let's get that six-pack and go," he said hurriedly.

"While you get the beer, I'll go in and see if I can get a couple of those large 'to-go' cups for ice tea and stuff."

I walked a little unsteadily through the kitchen to the paper goods bin and got out two paper cups.

Big Bill spied me and asked, "Been into the dessert, have you? Brown bottle dessert?"

I just winked at him and told him what a great chef he was.

"Lyin bastard," he laughed as I walked out the back.

About a week ago, Paul had suggested we go to a grocery store and ask for some regular size grocery bags, so when we carried the beer home it would look like food instead of stolen property. We had stopped at one of the main grocery stores and asked a bag boy for some sacks. He pulled a big stack out of one of the bins at the checkout stand

and gave them to us. He could tell we were locals. From then on, we put our beer in those bags and fooled everybody.

After we packed our provisions for the evening, we started strolling down the sidewalk at a leisurely pace, enjoying the sights and sounds of the crowd. The air was cool and comfortable, lending further to the relaxation we were both feeling. Once we reached the motel, there were several lounge chairs left, and we picked two and moved them close enough together to set our grocery bag between them. I reached into the bag and pulled out the cups. When Larry started to pull out one of the bottles, he stopped and looked at me in a funny way.

"Shit."

"What's the matter?"

"No church key"

"I thought you had one?"

"I thought you'd get one when you went to get the cups."

We were both pissed at our own stupidity.

"Well," I said, "one of us better go to that tourist trap across the street and buy one."

"You do it. I got the beer," Larry whined.

"Let's flip for it. Tails goes across the street and heads stays and guards the beer. Call it in the air," I said as I flipped the quarter from my fingers.

"Heads," I shouted immediately.

It came up tails.

"You lose. Go get the church key."

Larry had observed this whole brief process without uttering a sound.

"Hey. That's not fair," he finally said.

"I said tails goes and heads stay. Wanna do it again?"

He just shook his head no and got up to attempt to make it across the street without getting run over. I watched Larry as he made his way through the traffic like a broken field runner, picking his spots as he ran. Although traffic was creeping along at about ten miles an hour, there was always the danger that occurs when tourists and/or teenagers decide to troll up and down the main drag. The first concern deals with their attention to driving. Most of them are rarely looking at the vehicle ahead of them, but at the brightly lit stores and the people strolling up and down the sidewalks to avoid going back to a cramped hotel room. Up and down they went in a never-ending parade.

I shifted my attention to the people strolling just in front of me on the sidewalk. There was more variety of ages, sexes, sizes, shapes and methods of dress than you could classify. There were the old tourists inching their way along, talking very little, but seeming to enjoy the crowd and air of a resort area. There were the parents with small children, usually happily licking ice cream cones or pouting about something they just had to have in the last gift shop they passed. The parent seemed to either take no notice of their whining, or they would shake them roughly and tell them to shut up. Which, of course, made the poor kids even more miserable. I think the kids who got the cold shoulder treatment fared better than the complainers. When they finally learned that their parents were ignoring them completely, they seemed to give up and turn their attention towards a sibling to see if they could get some kind of response out of them. This action usually ended up in some sort of argument of one kind or another.

Larry seemed to be taking a long time to pick out a simple can opener. Maybe he was going to try to shoplift one when no one was watching. That would be like him; steal something and find a reason to make it warranted.

A family had stopped right in front of me to discipline their three small children. The mother was about ninety pounds dripping wet and had that worn, haggard look of someone who was getting old before her time. The father was a classic. Goofy baseball cap tipped back on his head, tank top tee shirt, baggy shorts that couldn't reach his waist due to the massive beer belly he was sporting. He had the country look of a mechanic and the glassy eyes of a drunk. With a cigarette dangling from the corner of his mouth, he was threatening to wear the kids out if they didn't shut the hell up about souvenirs. Mom just stood by nervously smoking a cigarette with her arms crossed in front of her. She was constantly glancing around to see if anyone was paying any attention to Daddy's angry lecture.

"If you goddamn little pecker woods don't shut the hell up, we're gonna go back to the room, and I'm gonna wear your asses out," he complained bitterly to the three children who stood staring at their feet.

The wife leaned near him and said, "Now, Randy..."

He wheeled on her and said venomously for her to "shut her fuckin' mouth if she knew what was good for her."

She simply bowed her head and drew shakily on her cigarette.

In the mean time, big Randy took a break to take a huge gulping swallow of beer from the can in his hand, belching loudly when he finished. After he wiped his mouth with the back of his meaty paw, he told his family to get moving. And they did.

I thought to myself what a lousy shit that guy was. Threatening his family and all. There was really no cause for him to go off on those kids and his skinny wife like that. My mood began to sour. If I'd had a gun, I would have shot the bastard dead right on the street. I hated people like that.

Larry came trotting up nearly out of breath with a church key in his hand.

"Got it," he said, grinning.

"What'd you have to do? Get one special made?"

"No, man. It was the girl at the register. When she started to ring up this one dollar opener, she asked if I was a local. When I told her I was, she just looked around real cool-like and rang that sucker up for fifteen cents. Man, I think she wants me real bad."

I wanted to ask him how that brief retail exchange would lead him to the conclusion that she wanted to jump into bed with him, but decided to be charitable and listen to his outrageous fantasy as it unfolded.

"So I asked her what time she got off work. Then she asked me what I wanted to know for and I said so I could walk her home. She ain't real good lookin', but she might put out. Anyway, she said okay and for me to be back at nine."

I just stared at him for a minute and finally said, "Way to go, slick. Now, gimme the damned opener."

He handed over a genuine, hand crafted, birch handle bottle opener that was made in China. I just shook my head and reached down to pull a beer out of the sack. I did so slowly and set it behind that bag to hide it from the prying eyes of the people on the sidewalk. I told Larry to hold on to the bottle while I opened it. I pried the top off and began pouring the beer into the large paper cup. We repeated the process for Larry. I sat back in the lounge chair and lit a cigarette. I was still in a funk over that greasy guy and his family, but I decided to pass on telling Larry about it. He wouldn't have understood anyway.

"Look at those two blondes giving us the eye. We ought to go talk to them," Larry said excitedly.

"Yeah. Let's go ask them what they want for their fourteenth birthday next summer. That'd really be nice. Why don't you pick out some girls who are at least in high school?" I said disgustedly.

He just looked back at me grinning and glassy-eyed and replied, "Good enough to bleed, good enough to breed."

"You are one sick bastard, you know that Larry?" I asked. With that, I turned my cup up and drained it, grabbed another beer from the sack, placed it between my knees and opened it. I didn't try to hide it as I poured it into the cup. If anybody said anything, I'd just tell him or her to mind their own damn business. For some reason, I was beginning to get a little tired of the way the evening was turning out.

"Why don't we rate people on how stupid they look," I said to Larry. "We'll go on a scale of one to ten, ten being the best."

Larry immediately perked up and pointed to a rather obese lady and said loudly, "You're number one," while holding up his index finger.

I happened to have a mouthful of beer at the time he said this and I instantly spewed it everywhere while choking with laughter. The woman just glared at us and picked up her pace.

"You dumb sonavabitch," I laughed at Larry.

We continued to play this game until we came down to the last two beers. After opening these, I took the cigarette out of my mouth with the intention of flipping it out into the grass across from Larry's chair. I misfired and the fiery butt landed in his lap.

"Goddamn you, you cocksucker," he yelled as he leapt from his chair.

This reaction led to a complete halt of traffic on the sidewalk in front of us.

"You tryin' to set me on fire?"

I just shot him a bird and told him to go fuck himself.

Somebody from the crowd on the sidewalk told us to shut our filthy mouths. Another one said that they were going to call the sheriff because we were disturbing the peace.

I turned to the crowd, placed my beer on the ground at my feet and raised high the middle fingers of both hands and shook them at the crowd. Larry couldn't contain himself, and he began roaring with laughter. One large man made a step toward the low wall separating the sidewalk from the grounds of the motel. As soon as I saw that, I snatched my beer from the ground and told Larry to get out of here. We both ran full tilt to the back of the motel near the river and stopped to see if anyone was in pursuit. When we saw the coast was clear, we both broke out into spasms of laughter again. We finished the beers in a single long gulp, and proceeded to urinate in the river. A voice came out of the darkness behind us, scaring both of us silly.

"What the hell you two think you're doin'?"

Some old guy was leaning over the first balcony, looking down at us. I couldn't make out his features in the dark, but I could tell from the tone of his voice that he wasn't amused by our antics. Larry and I started running again. This time we went along the bank of the river toward another street that was about a quarter of a mile from where we were. Once we got back to a street crowded with tourists, we tried to blend in with them. I noticed that I was taking steps in a very deliberate manner because the sidewalk seemed to want to move a little. I turned to look at Larry and saw that he was walking in such an upright posture, he was beginning to lean backward and list a bit to his right. That was enough for me. I quickened my pace to put as much distance between us as I could. I didn't know if there was a law in this town against being drunk in public, but I sure knew that sixteen-year-old guys were in trouble if they got caught. After I had walked briskly for a couple of blocks, I turned to see if Larry was anywhere to be seen. He wasn't. Good. I crossed the street against a green light and was looking at a short busty brunette, when my foot hit the curb, sending me sprawling on my hands and knees on the sidewalk. Some guy in his forties wearing a stupid looking tee shirt helped me get back on my feet. When I got up and started to thank him, he apparently got a strong whiff of my beer breath and looked at me disgustedly.

"You better go home, kid."

I was so embarrassed by then I didn't even bother to brush the sidewalk grit off of my knees. I just headed for home.

Once I got back to the house, I could see the glow of a cigarette coming from the front porch, but I couldn't see who was smoking.

"What cha been up to, you little turd?"

Mr. Cummins.

"Nothing much. Just sightseeing a little."

"Why dontcha' sit a spell with me? I'll give you a taste of my corn likker," he offered hopefully.

In a way, I felt a little sorry for the old bastard because everyone tried to avoid him.

"I'll go get a glass," I said as I started to open the front screen.

"Shit, boy. This stuff is strong enough to kill polio germs. We'll jist share outta my jug here. Hit won't kill ya."

I took the offered jug and raised it to my lips. I had no idea as to the volume contained in his jug, but when I titled it, a flood of the homemade whiskey washed into my mouth and down my throat. After swallowing, I thought the top of my head was going to explode and I gasped for breath.

"Holy Jesus. That stuff tastes like airplane fuel or something."

Mr. Cummins was chortling and saying, "You'll git used to hit. It'll getcha there real quick like. Don't be pukin' on my porch, now. Ya hear?"

A warm glow spread from my stomach to my cheeks to my brain. I lit a cigarette and immediately felt lightheaded from the strength of his whiskey. Soon, I began to feel a sense of well being.

"That stuff's not too bad."

"I figgered you'd like it. I seen you as a young fella that likes a snort or two."

I began to relax and actually enjoy Mr. Cummins' company. "Where did you get that limp of yours? Fall off a horse?"

"No. I got shot in the leg in the first war. Got me a medal fer hit too. Saved the lives of a bunch a young fellers that was about to get overrun by some of them German bastards. I got a holt of their machine gun and mowed a whole bunch of them down. Then reinforcements came an' took me to a field hospital where they patched me up. They ended up sendin' me home cause I couldn't walk so good no more. They's real nice to me onct I got home. Treated me like a real hero and ever thing. Old man Ledbetter gave me a job down at his hardware store, and me and Missus Cummins got hitched. Worked for the old bastard from 1920 to 1961 when I retired. The missus and I raised three boys and two girls and buried two chillun that died not long after they's birthed. Thass my story."

I was fascinated. This dried up old piece of shit was a real live war hero and raised five kids to boot. He went on to tell me that every one of his kids got a college diploma from the University of Tennessee.

"I's real proud of all of 'em," he said staring out into the night.

I just sat there quietly, listening to the sounds of the wind rustling the leaves and the squeak of Mr. Cummins' rocker as he rocked back and forth between hits from his jug. This wasn't some old drunken bastard; he was a success in a lot of ways. If he wanted to spend some time relaxing with his moonshine, more power to him. He wasn't hurting a damn soul. "Stay drunk all the time," I thought to myself. "You've earned it."

I slowly pushed myself up out of my chair and told Mr. Cummins good night. As I climbed the stairs somewhat unsteadily, I sort of regretted making fun of the old man. He wasn't all that bad a character. He was probably just kind of worn out. And so was I. I fell into bed and slept a dreamless sleep.

Chapter Fourteen

As it got closer to the Fourth of July, there was no let-up in the tourist traffic. The streets were crawling with people who seemed to be determined to have a good time regardless of the noise, heat, crowds and general misery generated by crowding too many people in such close proximity to each other.

I had finally gotten a much-deserved day off after I had been there for almost four weeks. With nothing really to do, I walked by the M&S and saw that things were starting to pick up steam in there as well. Terry spotted me as she was serving some ice tea to a family who had chosen to sit out under the canopy under the large ceiling fans.

"Hey, Terry. How's things?"

"Pretty good. There's going to be a big party tonight at Julie's place. Some of the day-side crew will be there around eight and the night side will have to play catch up when they get off. You're gonna be there, aren't you?" she asked while shading her eyes against the glare of the sun.

"You inviting me to be your date?"

She thought for a minute and said, "Yeah. You'll be my date. See you later."

I watched her twist her way among the tables as she walked away from me. She was as much fun going as she was coming. Then I noticed a huge lump in my throat about the size of a grapefruit. My heart was beating so fast, I thought it was going to pound right out of my chest. At that very moment, I found myself profoundly in love. This gorgeous redhead with a body right out of Playboy was going to be my date. As I reflect on the way I felt, it was a feeling as strong as any chemical I had ever ingested since. I was having a rush of hormones that put me into some sort of lustful nirvana that I didn't want to leave. The faster the fantasies of the evening flashed through my head, the quicker the lump in my throat moved to my groin.

Suddenly I realized I was standing there and staring into space. As I became conscious of my present time and space, I looked around to see if anyone was watching me. I decided to leave before someone called some guys with a net and a straightjacket. I was walking on air as I headed back to my room.

When I got home, Mr. Cummins was sitting on the front porch in his rocking chair, stopping every once in a while to lean over and spit a brown stream of tobacco juice at one of his dogs. They seemed to sense when it was coming, because they would jump away from the direction of the porch as soon as they heard a stop in the creaking of the rocking chair. This game seemed to amuse the old man to no end.

"Howdy, sport. How you a-doin' this mornin'?"

"Fine, Mr. Cummins. How about you?"

"Fair to middlin'. Can't complain."

Not with a jug of airplane fuel close at hand, I thought. When I got upstairs, Larry was hard at work, sweeping, dusting and straightening up everyone's bed. I asked him what brought on this burst of domestic activity.

"Hell if I know, man. I just thought I'd do it for the hell of it. Place was beginning to smell," he explained.

I did notice that he had emptied all of the ashtrays and there was a strong scent of ammonia in the air. He was right. Once you smelled the upstairs with less sweat, smoke, stale beer and dirty clothes, it was almost pleasant. With the windows wide open, a cool breeze caused the flimsy curtains to flutter gently.

"Good job, man. Come on, I'll buy your lunch at the M&S," I told him, both of us knowing we'd still get a free lunch even if we were off that day.

On the way to the restaurant, I told him about the party that was planned at Julie's house. He seemed to perk up at the mention of a party.

"Great. At Julie's place? You know how to get there?"

"No, but we can find out at lunch. She's working the day shift for Lois."

"You gonna drive Martha's car?" Larry asked.

"Hell yeah. It needs to be run every day to keep it sharp," I replied.

"What about the cops? I mean if you drink at the party and all?"

"Screw them. I'm sure Sam will fix things. He hired just about all of them anyway. Besides, they're so used to seeing me behind the wheel, they'll probably think I'm driving old Martha around as usual. No sweat, man," I assured Larry.

He just gave me a sidelong glance and said nothing in reply.

When we got to the restaurant, we went in the back way to ask Roy what the special of the day was.

"Chicken 'n dumplins. Better'n snuff and ain't half as dusty," he answered. "Whatta you wanna know that fer? You two bastards, all you ever eat is goddamn cheeseburgers."

"We'll have the special, Roy," I answered.

He fixed two large heaping plates with chicken and dumplings, green beans, slaw and a roll. Just before he sat them under the counter under the warming light, he cleared his throat noisily and acted as if he was going to spit a huge hawker in my plate. Instead, he spit on the floor and just laughed.

"Keep you on your toes, you cocky shit," he said grinning at me.

We took our plates out to the dining room, stopping to pick up utensils and iced tea. When we got seated in the back booth, Julie came over to us with a sly look on her face. "You two hot shots ready to git down and git tore up tonight?"

"Yeah," we piped up in unison.

"Good. I'm gonna have some fun with you two tonight," she laughed as she twirled away to seat some new diners.

Larry and I just looked at each other and let our imaginations take us on our own mental pleasure cruises. We talked very little during lunch; we just wolfed down the food like we had a car double-parked outside. When we were through, we took our plates and glasses back and sat them down on the dishwasher's bin.

When we got outside, I saw Kat sunbathing by the pool. She looked over at us from behind her large sunglasses and waved us over to join her. The pool for the motel was only about ten feet by twenty-five feet. It was just big enough for the Ronson's to advertise that there was a pool on the premises. Apparently, Kat had dumped a bunch of chemicals into the water because today you could see the bottom. Most of the time, the water was sort of murky. Kat wasn't a bit murky. She had a bikini on that covered just enough to keep her from getting arrested. Both Larry and I tried not to stare openly at her, but we caved and gaped at her like two guys who'd spent far too much time in the company of other males. She knew the effect she was having on us, and she liked it. She had oiled her tawny, muscular body until it glistened brightly in the sun. Being unencumbered with large breasts, her slim body and long legs made you think of a ballerina or an athlete. Definitely built for speed.

"Hey, guys. Get your swimsuits on and join me. No little kids around today."

"Do you have a swimsuit?" I asked Larry

"No. You?"

"No, but I saw some at Warren's the other day when I was in there. Let's go over there and see if we can get the local's discount," I suggested.

Larry hollered at Kat, "We'll be right back."

She waved to us in acknowledgement, and we took off.

When we got into Warren's, Larry was suddenly struck by a really great idea, as great ideas go for Larry.

"Let's dye our hair," he said excitedly. "We can get Kat to help us. I bet she'd love to do that."

Since we both had dark brown hair, I asked him, "What color?"

"Blonde as hell, man. It'll be real cool."

Our tab came to eight dollars even for two bathing suits and two bottles of a platinum hair color. We were sure the plain blonde wouldn't work as well as the platinum, so we decided to go for the strong look.

When we got back to the pool, Kat told us to go change in unit number twenty. They never rented that one out because it was kept for family use only. When we told Kat we wanted her help in dying our hair, she was extremely enthusiastic about being a part of helping us to look as foolish as we possibly could.

"That's a great idea. I just wish I had thought of that," she said looking back and forth at us as though she was seeing us for the first time. "Go into twenty and get changed. I'll go get some towels from the maids."

With that, we charged into the motel room and got into our suits as quickly as we could. Pure excitement coursed through me over something as simple as changing the color of my hair. I decided I needed to get out more often.

When Kat got back, we were both studying the instructions that came with the color kit.

"You can throw them damn instructions away. I've done this a bunch of times with my girl friends. Never a guy, but, hell, hair is hair," she said when she returned.

Larry and I just looked at each other and grinned. We ditched the instructions.

Kat pointed to me and said, "Let's start with you first, Doug. Your hair is darker than Larry's, so it'll have to stay on longer."

I can remember having my mother wash my hair over the kitchen sink as a small boy, but this experience was altogether different. First, Kat pulled one of the pool chairs into room twenty and placed it in the shower stall. Then after regulating the water to the proper temperature, she told me to get in and sit down. She began by thoroughly washing my hair with a baby shampoo. I sat with my eyes tightly closed as she massaged my hair and scalp with her long fingernails. Being in a shower stall with a beautiful girl washing my hair, occasionally bumping up against me, was one of the most erotic experiences I had ever had. And it showed. I heard Kat snicker so I quickly placed my hands over my lap, hoping that I could force things under control by using the Boy Scout method of applying pressure to the area. Boy, was that a mistake. It only made things worse. I could hear Kat trying to muffle her chortles until the tide broke and she burst out laughing so loudly, she stepped out of the shower to walk around holding her stomach. At first, I was humiliated, but I began to realize how funny the situation was, so I started to laugh as well. The swelling started subsiding, and Kat was getting control of herself. When she finally started applying the dye, the nasty odor burned my eyes and nostrils and my brain moved from my lap back to its rightful place in my cranium.

"Holy Jesus, Kat," I cried. "You're going to burn my skin off. Are you sure you've done this before?"

"Quit being a big baby. And, yes, I have done this before."

"Are there any survivors?"

The only answer that question got was a brisk slap on the back of my head.

After she had massaged, twisted, rubbed and patted my head, she handed me a towel to wipe off my face. She then put a clear plastic disposable shower cap on my head and told me to get a beer out of the fridge and sit quietly on the bed.

I did as I was told, stopping only to check myself out in the mirror as I carried the beer back to sit down. Amazing. Larry came in and caught me in front of the mirror and whooped with glee.

"Goddamn. Ain't you a sight. Wish I had a camera because I could blackmail you for big bucks."

I merely raised my middle finger to him and gulped down half of my beer. I sat on the edge of the bed, turned the bottle up and emptied it. I sat there for a moment and listened to Kat give Larry the same instructions she had given me. The burning sensation in my eyes and nose was still a problem, so I walked over to get another beer. Within twenty minutes, I was in the middle of the third beer when Kat told me to join her in the shower. By now, I had that slightly drunken grin plastered on my face.

"Sure, baby doll. Whatever you say," I responded as gallantly as I could.

As I padded across the shag carpeting, I looked closely at Larry then caught my reflection in the mirror. We looked like we belonged in a ward somewhere. It was all pretty bizarre, but Kat seemed to be having a great time, clapping her hands close to her face as she looked from one creation to the next. By this time, I had pretty much lost my sense of smell, whereas Larry was now complaining about his eyes and nose.

"Stop your damn whining and drink some beer. Make you feel better," I told him as one orders a child to shut up and eat.

Kat took me by the hand and guided me over to the shower.

"Sit down in the chair and tilt your head way back. We don't want this to get into your eyes," Kat said as she directed me to the chair.

I grinned my loopy grin at her and said, "Okay."

Sitting there with my head back, I ogled Kat openly as she rinsed my hair. She didn't seem to notice, paying more attention to my hair than my intentions. Just as well.

"Damn, boy, you look like you just flew in from California. You look like one of those Beach Boys."

She then started towel drying my hair, told me to stand in front of the bathroom mirror and be still while she dried it with the hair dryer.

"Good God," I gasped. There was a stranger staring back at me with hair the color of spun gold with tinges of red.

Larry stuck his head into the bathroom and whooped loudly, "Your hair. Man, it looks great. You'll be getting some pussy, now, I bet."

This, of course, coming from an individual whose perception, judgment and taste were all suspect. Besides, he had a belly full of beer, too. Kat did not seem the least bit bothered by his reference to female genitalia, but even found his comment to be rather amusing. She, too, had been into the beer cooler.

After working her magic fingers on Larry's noggin, he was equally impressed with his new appearance. We both decided that this was one of the greatest ideas in the world, and we had done something of major importance regarding further defining who we were. Much later, Jungle Jim summed it up very distinctly when he looked at us and said, "You two got drunk, didn't you?"

Larry and I stood side by side in front of the mirror with Kat in the background, and we all gaped at the reflection with broad smiles. With toasts all around, we finished our current beers and opened new ones to go out and sit by the pool.

I shielded my eyes with my hands because the sun seemed unusually bright. I guess there was extra reflection from the glare of our new hair. I sat with my feet dangling in the water and waited for hoards of beautiful girls to come leaping into the pool and commenting on how masculine I looked with my blonde hair and brown eyebrows. I personally felt that the contrast was what would really turn them on. I looked over at Larry, and he was beginning to drool slightly from staring into the pool so long without blinking an eye.

"Hey, retard. What's wrong with you?" I asked.

"My mom's gonna kill me," he replied.

"Your mom ain't here."

"I mean when I go home at the end of summer."

I thought he was maybe a little too drunk to appreciate the steps he had taken in defining himself. I figured he needed my analysis of the situation to make him feel better.

"Screw it. It'll be all grown out by that time," I told him.

Kat responded, "Not by a long shot. You're good until Christmas anyway."

With that comment, I, too, began staring into the pool. My mother is going to beat the living shit out of me. Probably out in the yard in front of the neighbors, too. As a warning to my brother Rob not to mess with what she and Dad had created.

"Could be worse," Kat said, "Could've been a tattoo."

"What beautiful logic," I thought, "a tattoo. I'd just tell my mother that I'd opted for a little dye job instead of a tattoo. That would have to make her calm down. My mood jumped from the bottom of the pool to the trees above us. I had my bases covered. No problem here, folks."

"You're great, Kat. That's exactly what I'll tell her, " I said as I saluted her.

"But there's no place in Gatlinburg to get a tattoo," Larry complained.

"Shit. You can get anything you want in Cocke County. Bet your ass on it. Everybody knows that," Kat said, nodding her head as someone who had wisdom in such matters beyond our pathetic scope.

"Will this wash off if I get into the pool?" I asked.

"Jump right in, big boy. The chlorine in the water and sun will help set the color," Kat advised.

Into the water I went. When I came up for air, I splashed Larry and urged him to get into the water. He finally pushed himself into the water and began coming back to life. After frolicking in the water for a while, I decided to catch some sun, open another beer and join Kat as she listened to a rock station on her little transistor radio. This was the life.

When I settled in next to Kat, she shielded her eyes as she rolled over to inspect her work.

"You do look kinda cute," she said. "At least your hair isn't doing what Larry's is doing."

I looked over into the pool at Larry. His hair had started to turn green. The chlorine.

"Get outta the water, Larry," I shouted. "Your hair's turning green."

Startled, Larry quickly got out of the water and ran into the room to look at himself.

"SON OF A BITCH," he screamed. "I'm dead for sure."

Kat was almost doubled up with laughter. I had run into the room myself to see if my hair was doing the same thing. It wasn't. Poor Larry stood stock still with both hands clutching wildly at his hair. In a moment, Kat came in and told Larry that it was way too early to slit his wrists. She'd just get a different brand of hair color and redo his.

"Let's do it now," he begged.

"Can't. Burn your hair off if we try it now. Got to wait twenty-four hours," Kat explained.

"What about the party tonight? I can't go looking like I'm made up for Halloween. You've got to do something, now."

Kat answered Larry by handing him a freshly opened beer.

"That's all I can do for now, sport."

Larry sat on the side of the bed and groaned, holding his face in his hands. Kat shook her head and retrieved another towel from the closet.

"I hear you got a date with Terry. That right?" she asked.

"Yeah."

"Well, good luck. I don't think you know what you're getting into," Kat cautioned me.

I didn't think too much about her comment at the moment, but much later in the evening, I found out the hard way.

Chapter Fifteen

I was trying to figure out what Kat meant by "what you're getting into" when I fell asleep in the lounge chair by the pool. When I awoke, the only people I saw were a mother in a bright blue bathing suit and her two little screaming kids. They'd dip one toe into the water, let out a nerve-shattering shriek and run back to where the mother was sitting listlessly, staring at the water. Since I wasn't wearing a watch, I had no idea of the time, but I could tell I had been asleep for a while. I looked down at my chest, and it was a bright pink. So was my stomach and the fronts of my legs down to my ankles. Fortunately, someone, maybe it was Kat, had carelessly thrown a towel across the tops of my feet. They were still white.

As I started to push myself out of the lounge chair, I felt a sharp jolt of pain run through my eyes, to the back of my skull and back out my ears. My mouth felt as if a circus had traveled through it as I slept. I lay back for a moment and tried to remember what I needed to do. **Vinegar**. I've got to get some vinegar from the kitchen to put out the fire of my sunburn. There was some kind of acid in vinegar that stopped the cooking process once you got in out of the sun.

I finally managed to get upright on my feet and staggered over to the number twenty unit to get into my shorts, shoes and tee-shirt. I stripped off my bathing suit and surveyed the damage in the mirror. I was cooked to the bone. I needed some first aid before the nerve endings in my skin awakened and started screaming. When I pulled my tee shirt over my head, it lay on my chest like sandpaper. Great, I thought. This was going to be **my night** with Terry and I looked like a huge lobster. I ran into the back to the kitchen and asked Big Bill if there was any vinegar around I could take back to my room.

"Mix some butter with that vinegar, boy, and you'll turn brown as a berry," offered Bill. "I've seen sunburn like that before, and I'm here to tell you, you better mix you up some butter and vinegar or you're gonna be sick as hell."

With his expert medical opinion in mind, I gathered up the supplies I needed, picked up two six-packs and shoved everything into a large brown grocery bag.

When I got to the front porch, I hurriedly spoke to Mr. Cummins and started to go inside.

"It's hell, ain't it?" he asked.

"What are you talking about? What's hell?"

"Getting the spins so early in the day. Wears your ass out," he replied, nodding his balding head.

"What do you mean the 'spins'? I don't understand."

"Drunk, you peckerhead. What the hell'd you think I meant? I could smell it on you afore you got to the porch and yore damn eyes are redder than a damn Georgia roadmap. That's what I'm a talkin' about. Anyway, what'd you do to yore damn hair? Dye it?"

I didn't respond other than giving him a sheepish grin.

"Whatcha got in yore bag there? Sunburn ointment or hair rollers?" he asked, cackling like mad.

He was really enjoying himself.

"Anybody tell you 'bout vinegar and butter? It'll work real good, but you got to take yoreself a good cold bath first. Then you put the ointment on. You'll be okay."

Well, I was reassured by a second medical opinion. I thanked Mr. Cummins and told him I'd get right to it.

"Whatever else you got in that there poke will do you good, too. Good pain killer," he volunteered as he winked at me.

I thought, that old bastard is smarter than he acts. Nobody fools him.

I ran up the stairs, sat my bag down and opened a beer. After drinking deeply, I held the cold bottle against my burning skin, and I felt instant relief. I then stripped down to my shorts, grabbed my towel and headed for the bathroom. I ran the tub full of cold water and started easing myself into it by sticking a toe in the water first. No sense falling in and getting a heart attack. This water had to come from one of the coldest streams in the Smokies. I was more worried about frostbite than sunburn. When I finally got settled in, the burning on my skin started to disappear. I just lay in the tub, sipping on a beer and thought about the evening's upcoming activities. Terry hadn't said anything about picking her up or anything. I figured we'd just link up at the party.

A loud pounding on the bathroom door jarred my from my reverie.

"Hey, Doug. You in there?"

Larry.

"Yeah. What do you want? I just got in the tub."

"Just checking old buddy. Kat and I couldn't wake you so we left and went back to her house," Larry answered.

"Get any on you?" I asked

"She tried bleach on my hair and it got the green out of it. Damn stuff liked to have blinded me though. Thought I'd never recover."

"There's beer upstairs if you're up to it," I yelled at him.

"Thanks. I'm gonna down a quick one and take a nap. You've had your nap today. I need to rest up to have some more fun. See you later."

Rest up to have more fun. We must all be crazy, I thought.

After a few more minutes, I got out of the tub and began to dry myself off. Actually I had to gently pat myself dry because my skin was so tender. When I got back upstairs, I put some butter and vinegar in a soup bowl that I had gotten from Mrs. Cummins' kitchen. I hated the smell of vinegar, but I knew I had to go through with this. Smearing the mixture all over the front of my body made me shiver in disgust. I walked over to my bed and carefully lay down so as not to get my sheets dirty. In about thirty minutes, there was no burning. It was a miracle. The pain of the sunburn was completely gone. I decided to leave the mixture in the bowl just in case I needed some more when I got back that night.

I went downstairs to the bathroom, washed the medicine from my front, and shaved. The anticipation of tonight's party was pumping more adrenaline into my system. I felt energized by my fantasies.

I climbed back up the stairs and saw Paul peeking at my bowl. He turned and looked at me quizzically. "What the hell's this stinking shit?"

"Sunburn medicine. And it works great," I said proudly. I demonstrated by vigorously rubbing my red chest.

"Hmm," he said with some interest. "Hey, I need a favor. My alarm clock quit working, and I don't want to buy another one. Can you reset your alarm to go off at six thirty since you get up at five thirty? I'd really appreciate it."

"Sure. I can do that," I replied.

"Thanks."

With that, he fell onto his bed for his nap before he went to the fudge shop. Poor bastard. He works harder and more hours than any of the guys in this place. Gotta admire his work ethic. My mother would have definitely rated this guy as a real worker.

About that time, Jungle Jim and Money Dick came bounding up the stairs and headed for the room they shared with a mere nod to me.

I stuck my head around the door and asked, "Where's the fire? You guys got something hot lined up?"

They glanced at each other briefly before answering. Finally, Money Dick said, "We're going to see a play. We met a couple of the actors, got to be friends with them, and they gave us these tickets for free. They also invited us to the party afterward. They're really neat people, being from New York and all."

"New York? What the hell are they doing in the mountains of Tennessee?" I asked.

Jim replied, "They're actors. They got this off-Broadway play that they take on the road. They'll spend a month here or two weeks there, traveling around the country. They have some really great stories."

The ape-man surprised me. I always thought he considered raunchy sex novels to be literature. That's all you ever saw lying around his bed. Although I never actually saw him reading one, I figured he was a habitual jerk-off artist or something else just as bent.

"Maybe I'll catch you two high society types later. We've got a big party tonight, and it's gonna be great."

Money Dick then asked shyly, "Is that why you dyed your hair blonde? It looks really good on you, with your dark eyes and all."

"Uh, no. I mean thanks…I guess. Yeah, thanks." I wasn't used to getting flattering compliments from another guy and it made me a little uncomfortable. Then I noticed Jungle Jim looking like he was getting steamed about something. He was a real weird guy what with his mood changes and his secrecy. As a matter of fact, I didn't know much about how Dickie-boy spent his time either. I guess they were just two odd ducks in the same pond.

I stepped out of their room and grabbed a beer. It was starting to get a little tepid, but it went down pretty easy. I thought I'd better take it slow if I wanted to show up tonight. My headache had cleared up somewhat, and I was beginning to get another rush about this evening. I wondered if I'd be able to make it with Terry. I must be crazy; we hadn't even had a date yet. I'd be lucky to get a kiss. But then again, she did lay a huge lip-lock on me the other day right in front of everybody.

It felt great, but it really embarrassed the shit out of me. She didn't seem to mind at all. I guess she was what my grandmother would call a "brazen hussy." If that was what one was, bring' em on. I finally reached the conclusion that she was hotter than a firecracker, and in a few hours, I'd reach home plate. Better get ready for the big game.

Sleep was pretty much out of the question because Larry was in the other room snoring like a chain saw. I was surprised he didn't awaken himself. It sure didn't bother Paul either, but that poor guy was practically dead on his feet most of the time. He could've slept through a car wreck.

Since the stink of the vinegar had started to fade, or my sense of smell was screwed up, I decided to grease myself up one more time before I took another bath. I sure didn't want to meet Terry smelling like a jar of pickles. I slathered the "medicine" on again and lay down on my bed with a cigarette and a beer. Man, this was the life. Nobody to tell me what to do, where to go, when to go or when to come home. This was almost more freedom that I could stand, I thought smiling. I dropped the cigarette butt into the empty bottle and went to sleep.

"Hey, asshole. Wake up. Time to go, man," Larry hollered as he shook me awake.

"What time is it?" I asked groggily.

"It's almost eight, but we've got to stop by the restaurant and bring some beer to the party. I talked to Julie a little while ago."

"I've got Martha's car. What's the big hurry?" I asked.

"You gonna drive it to the party? We'll all probably get drunk."

"I said I'd drive it **to** the party. I didn't say anything about driving it home. We can walk if it comes to that. I sure as hell don't want anything to happen to her car." I responded.

As I was getting dressed, Larry went to his room and came out with two bottles of Schlitz.

As he handed me the beer, I asked, "What'd you do? Change brands? Is this any good?"

"Anything in life that's free is good. Don't you know that?"

I thought for a minute before answering. For some reason, I felt that the real answer was not a yes. The statement briefly startled me into a few seconds of introspection that seemed to last for an hour before I responded. Is anything in life that is free a good thing? Starvation is free. Is that good? The stuff we never paid for was free. Or was it? Do you pay a penalty for that kind of logic? I certainly had been enjoying plenty of freedom as opposed to my life at home. That was definitely good. Or was it? I had to force my mind to turn down another avenue because I didn't like to argue with myself over something that made me uncomfortable.

"You're right," I responded, "a free beer has got to be a good beer."

With that, I hastily gulped down half the contents of the bottle and erupted with a roof-rattling belch. Larry immediately responded to this macho challenge with a belch so violent, I thought he was going to dislodge an organ in his upper torso. I mean, it had to have **hurt**.

"Jesus. You okay?" I asked.

Larry began to laugh so hard, I thought he would surely wet himself. This primitive form of entertainment and competition probably started with the cavemen as they sat around the evening fires grunting and grinning at each other. Maybe Darwin was right after all. My friends and I often displayed all of the social graces of cavemen in spite of what our parents had tried to teach us. I supposed getting older would take care of that. But, hell, if it was funny, why would the aging process take away from the humor? That was the big problem with parents of this day and age: they had no sense of humor. They needed to quit being so straight-laced and stiff. If every meal was followed by a big belching contest, I bet more families would sit down to the dinner table together instead of the kids eating in front of the television while the parents argued at the table. At the dinner table in my house, dinner was usually held in a silence that resembled a momentary truce to fuel up for the next battle. I guess that's why my little brother didn't like to eat. He was always too nervous, waiting for some sort of skirmish to break out right at the table. Me, I just ate as fast as I could then asked to be excused. I could then beat a hasty retreat to anywhere I could find that was not within sight of my house. Rob usually wasn't far behind, hollering for me to wait up. And I did.

I finished getting dressed and downed the rest of my beer. Considering how much I had had to drink today, I was in great shape. I guess the key to controlling over-consumption was to take little catnaps. That way, you had some downtime to rest up and let your brain catch a breather from the massive assault on the cells in your brain that enabled you to put one foot in front of the other without falling down. Besides, there was no way anybody in their right mind would drink as much as Sam or Martha. They were insane.

I went downstairs and out to the front porch where I found old Mr. Cummins sitting in his rocking chair. He looked at me with his rheumy, blue eyes and mumbled something I couldn't quite understand.

"Say again, chief?" I asked him.

"Becairfulouddere, " he repeated.

"Be careful? Is that what you're saying?" I really felt sorry for the old bastard. He was totally shit-faced.

With that, he simply nodded and waved a gnarled hand as if pointing in the general direction away from where he sat. He didn't have a clue as to where he was or whom he was talking to, I'm positive. He was also sweating like crazy, so I wondered if he was sick or something. I just shook my head and walked toward the big red Pontiac where Larry was leaning on the front fender smoking a cigarette.

"What were you and the old coot talking about?"

"Nothing much. He's drunker than hell and makes no sense. He's also sweating a lot, too. Do you think he's got a fever or something?"

"Shit, no," Larry snorted. "He's just got the drunk sweats like my old man gets from time to time."

"What's the drunk sweats?" I asked.

"I don't really know. Mom told me it was all that booze trying to find a way out of your body before you died from it. It was like a natural protective reaction sort of like puking when you drink too much. My old man's done it lots."

I didn't really know what to say to Larry, but I hoped his dad didn't drink as much as Mr. Cummins. I believed he might consume more booze than Sam and Martha put together. The undertakers would never have to embalm him; he was already pickled in moonshine.

Larry and I just stood there for a minute and stared at the old guy as I lit a cigarette. I guess we had sort of lost our sense of humor for the time being and were lost in our own thoughts. I was thinking that I was glad my parents didn't drink like that, and, at the same time, felt sorry for Larry who seemed to be a little embarrassed by the things he had just said about his father. I could tell he felt both love and shame because of the way his dad drank, but I didn't know if I could say anything to cheer him up.

"Let's go, man," I said, finally breaking the silence.

We got into the car, and I started the engine with a roar. As I backed the car around in the yard, I could see Mr. Cummins still staring straight-ahead as if watching a movie only he could see and only he could hear.

I headed the car down the short dusty road in the direction of the restaurant. I had planned on putting as much beer in the trunk as this big car would hold. Larry was still very quiet, and I began to feel a little uncomfortable.

"Come on, Slick. Tonight we're gonna get loaded and get laid. Cheer up, will ya?"

Larry seemed to come back to life and nodded his head. "That's right. Loaded and laid. It's even in the Constitution of the United States of America."

"No shit?"

"Yeah, man. We're in the pursuit of happiness, aren't we? You know, 'life, liberty and the pursuit of happiness'?"

"Hey," I responded, "you're right. I'd never thought of that. If we get into trouble, I want you as my lawyer."

Larry looked at me and said with a grin, "My dad says lawyers are assholes."

By the time I steered the car to the back door of the restaurant, we had managed to shake off the blues and were getting into the mood of the evening.

We noticed Big Bill standing out the back door, smoking a cigarette.

"Hey, Bill. Goin' to the party tonight?" Larry yelled.

"Damn right. Gonna make sure none a you peckerheads tries to put a move on my wife," he said, eyeballing us.

"Shit, man. We're cool. We wouldn't do anything like that," I said earnestly.

"You might not, but the whiskey would," he replied with a grin. "How'd you two think I got these here scars on my arms? Cut myself shaving? Hell, I got cut up by another man's wife so I shot the bastard. Damn judge give me three years in the pen. Didn't matter none that it was self-defense. He tole me I shouldn't have been porkin' another man's old lady. He didn't say 'porkin', but that don't matter. I got a nice place to stay for a while and got me some jail-house tattoos to boot," he said showing us his hands and arms.

I could tell they weren't the same quality that I had seen on my Uncle Dave's arms. He'd been in the navy during World War II and got them overseas. Looked like a real artist did my uncle's arms, but Bill's looked cheap and messy. I, however, declined to point out this difference. That was to be one of my only wise decisions of the evening. I didn't know at the time, but it was going to take a real turn for the worse in a few short hours.

Chapter Sixteen

After we had loaded several cases of beer into the trunk, we put a six-pack in the front seat between us for the trip to Julie's place. I started the engine on the powerful Bonneville and revved the engine a couple of times to let the car know who was in charge. After the engine slowed down to a comfortable idle, I slowly pulled out of the parking lot into the crawling Main Street traffic. Larry turned the radio on and slipped in an eight-track of a new group from England called the Beatles. They had some real catchy stuff.

"Turn it up loud," I told Larry. "Let's let everybody know this is a party wagon that's headed for a good time."

Larry complied, immediately attracting the attention of the people on the sidewalks and in the cars of the oncoming traffic.

I thought Larry seemed to be lost in thought as we made our way to Julie's. As I took a swallow of beer, I asked, "what's bugging you?"

He waited a minute before answering. "I don't know, man. For some reason, I just feel like something is going to go wrong tonight."

"Go wrong? What do you mean?"

"Well I can't really explain it, but I get this feeling of impending doom or somethin'."

"Impending doom? Man, have you been reading a dictionary or the Bible or what?" I asked. "That sounds pretty deep to me."

"Naw, I've heard my old man talk about the times when he had the feeling of impending doom. He used to talk about it a lot before he quit drinking," he responded, staring out the window.

I didn't want to push him any further. He seemed like he was going somewhere that I wasn't welcome. In a way, I was a bit disappointed in his attitude. He had barely touched his beer, and he gave the impression of someone going to see the dentist. So I left him to dwell in his own world, hoping that he would come out of it pretty soon.

As for myself, I was almost nervous. Terry had been acting like we were going together for a while lately. Sometimes, she would stop me in the kitchen, straighten my tie, pat me on the cheek and then wink at me. It made me feel great 'til once I saw Roy staring a hole in me. I just shrugged it off as another bad hangover day. He couldn't be jealous of us because Terry was way too young for him. Besides, he looked more like an ape than a man. He had huge, hairy hands and arms that almost hung to his knees. He even had only one eyebrow that ran all the way across his forehead, there was so much hair between what should have been a break in the hair. He was brutally muscular, though. If I showed up at fall football practice looking like him, I'd get the starting linebacker job for sure. Even our tackles didn't look as strong as he did. They were big and lifted enormous amounts of weights, but Roy had this natural build of a man who had worked at hard labor all of his life. He looked tough. He was going to be at the party tonight, so I hoped he was a gentle drunk instead of a mean one like Martha. God forbid he'd get like her.

Rather than think about that ugly bastard, I wondered how I would be able to get Terry alone tonight. I'm sure she was probably thinking the same thing at this very moment. Maybe she had a plan already worked out. That would definitely take the pressure off me.

It had been enough pressure to go into Warren's drug store to buy some rubbers. Now **there** was a bit of utter humiliation in my life that I would spend a long time trying to forget. I went into the store hoping that it wouldn't be busy and that Jeff would be working behind the counter. When I got there, the store was packed and some **girl** was behind the counter. Damn. I spent a good hour reading and staring at the magazine rack in hopes that things would clear out a little so I could make the dreaded purchase. I tried to think of ways to approach the counter by maybe saying I needed to buy some for a shy friend. Hell. I knew that wouldn't work. Every idea I came up with had a flaw in it as big as a mountain.

I was about to throw in the towel when I heard her tell the pharmacist that she was going on a break. Now what, I thought. No sooner had she left than the pharmacist came down to the register to take over for a few minutes. At least he was a guy and would probably be sympathetic to my situation. I glanced around like a thief about to make his move and noticed that there were very few people in the store. They were mostly in the back and were staring at souvenir crap. I marched confidently up to the counter and told the pharmacist, in my loudest whisper, that I wanted a package of condoms. I thought using the medical term for rubbers might make me sound more mature. When he looked at me, he started to grin slowly. The bigger his grin got, the more I had to disguise the shaking in my legs. I even tried to affect a bored look on my face as if to say, "Yeah, need about a dozen; gonna be a fun weekend."

He finally asked me a question that I hadn't anticipated.

"Sheik or Trojan?" He shouted. I can't remember if he shouted or not but it sure seemed that way.

Shit, I thought. I forgot those things came in brands. I thought there should be a plain box with the word condoms printed on it. Just condoms. Like you go to the store and ask for salt. You go to the aisle and get a box that says salt.

"Well, sir?" he asked looking at me straight in the eye as a few people got in line behind me. The huge hole in the floor I was hoping would open up and swallow me never happened. But there was no turning back now. I was in the game.

I didn't know what shake meant so I went for the manly sounding ones. "Trojans," I gasped.

"Excellent choice, young man. Use them myself. Got a real natural feel to them," he said as he leaned over the counter and placed the box in front of me, winking at the same time.

"If you know what I mean," he whispered conspiratorially.

"YYYeahIknowwhatyoumean," I mumbled as I struggled to get the cash out of my jeans.

"One dollar and seventy-eight cents for a package of three," he announced.

I shoved the money at him, all the while feeling the stares of people behind me. I was sure I was headed for hell and damnation in their eyes. My neck felt as if you could fry an egg on it, and I was beginning to shake visibly.

I got my change, and he handed me the small Warren's bag saying, "You hurry back now. You hear?"

I responded by dashing out of the store and following any direction my feet would take me away from there. I was positive that he was now relating my story to all of the customers that remained in the store. I'll bet he even knew where I worked and was telling them to go eat at the restaurant and ask me if I got any. Shit.

I took another swig of beer and asked Larry which turn we were supposed to take after we passed the city limits. He took a rumpled piece of paper out of this pocket and studied it for a minute.

"Take a right at Smooth Rock Lane," he said. "Then you follow Smooth Rock for four tenths of a mile till you come to Logger's Road. Turn left on to Logger's, and Julie's house is the second one on the right."

"Got it," I answered. We were on our way.

There were three cars parked in the front yard with one space remaining in the driveway. I took it. The tires crunched on the crushed gravel drive with the sound of small bones being broken. As we climbed out of the car, we could see that almost every light in the house was on and the music could be heard from the driveway. The house to the left of Julie's looked like there was no one living there. It was probably a secondary home for some doctor or lawyer in Knoxville.

Larry and I climbed out of the car and opened the trunk to unload the beer. The cans were not as cold as they were twenty minutes ago, so we began to stack the cases of beer out of the trunk onto the ground as fast as we could. Julie must have seen us pull into the driveway because she came out to the small front porch and turned on a spotlight on the side of the house. Waving enthusiastically, she yelled, "Come on up, boys. We got more women than we do men."

Larry and I looked at each other and grinned.

"This is gonna be better than I thought," smiled Larry.

"That's the spirit. Now you're getting into the groove, pardner," I responded.

As we started carrying our load up the driveway to the house, I got a closer look at Julie's place after she turned on the spotlight. The gravel under our feet caused us to slip a few times as it gave way under the pressure of our weight. The house itself was a small white bungalow in bad need of another coat of white paint. I guess Julie's husband was gone too much to spend any time on home improvement. From the back, I heard the baleful barking of a dog. As we got closer, I could see a large, sad-eyed hound lunging fruitlessly against the rope that tethered him to a large tree. The yellow ski rope would stretch but not break, causing the dog to be yanked backwards with every lunge in our direction. I couldn't tell if it wanted to lick us or bite us, but I was grateful for the rope. I had been deathly afraid of dogs since the age of three, when I was bitten pretty badly by a neighbor's collie. I paused to watch the dog's efforts for a second, just to make sure that he wasn't going to get loose.

There was a side entrance to the house with five narrow steps leading to small deck, which in turn led to the kitchen through a screen door. Larry paused on the steps and looked back at me.

"You comin' or not, dumb ass. You thinkin' about that dog as your date?"

"At least mine would be alive. You need to fill your date with a bicycle pump," I said, tauntingly.

Julie pushed the screen door open almost losing her balance in the process. There was no spring attached to the door to make it shut so it swung against the side of the house with a loud whack. Watching her bounce on her toes to keep from falling was a vision made in heaven. She had one of her famed "cigar" dresses on, only this one was hemmed so far above the knees, it looked more like a nightgown. As she leaned over, she put one hand on the doorframe and the other on the top of her dress to keep the eighth and ninth wonders of the world from getting loose. When she saw both of us stock-still and gaping at her with our jaws hanging open to our chests, she winked at us and laughed wildly. Her laughter always made me think of the type of woman who would kick off her shoes, hop on the nearest table and dance frantically to whatever music was playing. I think she got as much pleasure out of torturing guys as we did in seeing the show. It was a kind of unspoken mutual interchange. She flirted, and men got goofy.

"Just look at the two of you. What they hell did you boys do to your hair?"

Larry and I just looked at each other and grinned.

We crowded ourselves into a small kitchen that resembled a booze warehouse in miniature. On top of the table were several bottles of different wines along with chips and other finger foods. The sink was filled with ice and cold bottles of beer. The kitchen counters held almost every conceivable type of liquor that was made. Gin, vodka, bourbon, tequila and other stuff I'd never heard of before.

"Load all that beer into the bathtub," she said pointing down a hallway out of the kitchen. "I got Roy to go git a big bunch of ice. Woooweeee."

She had obviously started the party before we arrived.

After we unloaded the beer into the tub, we went back to the kitchen to get a beer. Terry was in there mixing herself a bourbon and coke. I smiled at her and leaned over to kiss her. She merely pecked me on my lips and went back to her drink. She looked gorgeous in skin-tight jeans, a bright red tee shirt and no shoes. She looked at me with those beautiful green eyes and asked, "You want one of these?"

"No thanks. I'll stick to beer."

"Oh, so beer isn't really drinking?" she asked.

"Well, not like the stuff Martha drinks."

She laughed and said, "It ain't the kind of booze; it's the amount of the hard stuff she swills. Besides, I heard she wasn't really in Knoxville. I heard she was in some godforsaken place in Georgia where they dry you out. Pour bourbon on mashed potatoes and make you eat it. Stuff like that."

"What if she comes home hating mashed potatoes instead?"

Terry had just begun taking a sip of her drink when I asked that, and she spewed bourbon and coke all over the kitchen counter. Leaning over and holding the back of her hand against her mouth, she grabbed the kitchen towel I held out for her.

"Goddamn, boy. You sure got a funny way about you. I just hope you keep your sense of humor tonight."

"Why? What's happening tonight?"

"You never can tell at one of Julie's parties. Somebody said she'd invited a lot of those fag actors from that touring group that's been at the civic center for the last two weeks. And anyway, when people git to drinkin' too hard, almost anything can happen," she said while taking another sip of her drink and peering at me over the edge of her glass.

At that moment, I was sure she was giving me the green light. When I tried to kiss her, she pulled away.

"Don't be so pushy, dammit," she snapped. "There's a time and place for everything. What the fuck did you do to your hair?"

I was confused. One minute she's in heat, and the next minute she's like an old maid. I really think women are naturally illogical and booze makes it worse. I could see my plans for the evening starting to fall apart. I didn't know at the time that I was like the guy who jumped from the Empire State Building. As he fell through the air, people in the offices could hear him yelling, "So far, so good." I hadn't fallen yet, but I was on the ledge. I just didn't know it.

Chapter Seventeen

By ten o'clock, the party was in full swing and the night crew hadn't even gotten there yet. Julie had invited some people I didn't know, but everyone was really loose and friendly. I got Terry to dance with me a few times, but she still seemed a little distant. Also, I noticed Roy looking in our direction a few times and he didn't look particularly happy. I noticed he'd been drinking shot glasses full of tequila and following that with beer. I couldn't figure out how he kept it all down. I had been warned never to mix liquor and beer. If you followed that rule, you wouldn't get sick. Maybe those rules didn't apply to an ugly bastard like Roy.

There was so much smoke in the house you didn't really need to light up. Just take a deep breath and save your smokes for later. I decided to go out on the deck and get some air. As I stood there, several cars pulled up to the side of the road and began to unload. I figured it must be the night crew from the restaurant. There were some other guys in a car I'd never seen before, but I couldn't see in the darkness. I could hear their girlish laughter. Must be the fags Terry was talking about.

Paul was walking up the driveway with the night-side crew. He had recently quit both his other day job and the fudge shop job to work as a waiter at our place. He said he was making better money now with the one job without killing himself.

"Hey, Paul. How you doin'?" I asked as he made his way up the driveway.

"Great, Blondie. Get any on you yet?"

"Nope. But the night's still young," I laughed.

A tall guy just behind Paul was looking at me with a bemused grin on his face. This guy had to be an actor. He had perfectly tousled blonde hair, ice blue eyes, an athletic build and what appeared to be sixty four bright teeth when he smiled.

"My God, are you old enough to drink?"

Fag. This stand-in for Tarzan talked just like a woman. I just stood there letting flies buzz in and out of my open mouth.

"Do you speak, young man?" he asked as he held out his hand for me to shake. "My name's Darren. What's yours?"

"Uhhh...Doug," I sputtered. I had never heard a voice like that come out of a guy who looked like a professional athlete.

"That's a lovely name, Doug. What do you do?"

"I'm a busboy at the M&S," I replied in my deepest voice. "Oh, and I'm also a chauffeur for the owner's wife."

"Pretty opportunistic, aren't you?" asked Darren.

I wondered what the hell he meant by that?

"My girlfriend is inside waiting on me," I said, hoping this would protect me. Protect me from what, I wasn't sure. But I did know that I wanted him to know that I wasn't a queer.

"Wonderful. I'd love to meet her."

"Jesus Christ," I thought to myself.

When Darren and I walked in, I expected everyone to turn and stare at us like we'd been in the bushes or something. However, no one seemed to take notice, much to my relief. I looked around the kitchen and living room for Terry, but I couldn't find her. Darren was still hot on my heels.

"I'll bet she's stepped into the little girl's room to freshen up," said Darren with a smile.

"Yeah," I thought. That or puke.

"I just can't wait for you to meet some of my gang. I think you'll be awfully intrigued by them. They're so smart and all," he said as he flashed those neon teeth of his.

"Is there any wine at the bar? I just love a good cabernet. Don't you?" he asked.

"Yeah, sure. I guess," I responded. I had no idea what in the hell he was talking about. All I knew about wine was from communion at church.

"You find your little girlfriend and I'll fetch a glass of wine. Okay?"

"Yeah…uh…I'll…uh…do that."

With that I turned and headed for the other side of the room in a meandering fashion, between the bodies gyrating to the music.

"Jeez," I thought, "where the hell is Terry? Has she left the party?"

No sooner did these questions pop up, than I got the answer.

"Best damn fuck I ever got," yelled Terry as she came stumbling out of the bedroom with Roy in tow. She was pulling on her shirt with one hand, and her hair looked like she had been in a wind tunnel.

"Somebody fix me a damn drink," she yelled.

Her eyes were glassy and her lipstick was smeared horribly across her face. When her eyes focused on me, she began laughing drunkenly.

I started making my way back toward the kitchen to really pound some Budweiser when I passed Darren and one of his actor buddies who in a highly animated conversation and having a great time. When I finally did get into the kitchen, it was pretty well packed as well with Julie in the center of the group trying to tell some joke that her husband had told her the last time he was home. The floor was sopping with spilled booze and beer, but no one cared. I saw Paul leaning next to the refrigerator sipping on a beer. He wasn't much of a drinker but enjoyed being at parties. When he saw me he waved for me to come over in his direction.

"What's wrong with you? You about to be sick?" he asked.

"No, man. You know that girl that I told you about that was supposed to be my date tonight? She's the one that just balled that ugly cretin over there," I told him jerking my thumb in Roy's direction.

"Shit, man. That's pretty rotten. She dumped you in front of everybody like you were a greasy bag of shit. I don't believe I've ever seen a guy go down in flames as bad as you. That's one for the record books," he said, staring at me.

I looked at him.

"You really know how to cheer a guy up, Paul."

"No, I'm serious, man. You really got the shaft."

"WILL YOU SHUT THE FUCK UP?"

The room suddenly became as quiet as a grave. If it hadn't been for the music, I believe that there wouldn't have been the slightest sound. Finally, Darren walked up with a beer in his hand.

"You seem a bit edgy," he said as he handed me the bottle.

With the silence broken, the din of the party began to build to its former decibel level.

"Thanks, Darren," I said gratefully.

"I watched the whole thing. Didn't need to hear a word. Actors are trained in body language, and I could tell that you were having a terrible letdown," he explained sympathetically.

He turned to his friend who happened to be equally as handsome in a darker, more Hispanic sort of way.

"I'd like for you to meet Dom. It's short for Dominick. He's Italian of course."

We shook hands, and I got my hand enclosed in an iron grip. I figured this guy had to be normal. Firm handshake. Another build of an athlete, but not as muscular as Darren. He looked more like a track and field guy. Wiry muscles. About six feet and one seventy-five. Black hair combed straight back to his collar. His jet black eyes almost burned a hole in you.

"Dom is my lover. And he's a beautiful dancer," Darren whispered proudly as he nodded in Dom's direction. "For God's sake, don't tell anyone. I hear that down here in the south you'll be hanged or shot for being gay. You just gave me a feeling of being someone I could trust. Julie knows but she thinks we're so smart being from New York and in the theatre. My God, she even tried to get me in bed so she could 'cure' me. I told her I was comfortable with who I was, but that if I ever wanted to get cured, she'd be the one that could probably do it."

His lover. Jesus H. Christ. I had absolutely no idea how to respond. My first instinct was to yell something like "holy shit." The image of these two guys going at it was almost more than my imagination could bear. What the hell was I supposed to say? Nice looking boyfriend, Darren? Where did a nice couple like you meet? So, I reacted in the only way I knew how to in this situation. I drank off half of the beer. Then I turned to Paul for some support.

"Uh…Paul? This is Darren…and his…er…ah…friend, Dom," I stuttered.

"Nice to meet both of you," Paul said as he stuck out his hand.

His composure was impressive. At least I was impressed. I thought for sure that Paul would try to jump out of the nearest window or something. Anything to escape the clutches of admitted homosexuals.

They all shook hands and Paul looked at me with a smile.

"These guys know we're not gay. There's not a problem. Right, guys?" he asked looking from one actor to the other.

"Of course not, silly," responded Darren. "Who in your family is gay?"

"My Uncle Carl. He's my mom's brother. Lives in New Orleans and makes a living as an artist."

Paul then looked at me as if to say, don't you say a damn word about it.

Darren went on, "Well then you know that being gay isn't a terrible crime in New York. You also know we aren't into trying to make straight people gay, either. It's simply a difference in the way we were born. I didn't even realize I was gay until I was in my junior year at Yale while majoring in drama. Dom and I met in school and have been together in a purely monogamous relationship. Isn't that right, Dom?"

Dom merely nodded in agreement and winked.

I felt Julie's breasts touch my back before her arms went around me.

"Are you being nice to my Yankee actor friends or are you acting like white trash?" she whispered to me.

She had me in an almost painful hug so I could only move my head to my right shoulder and say, "I'm being nice. What are you talking about?"

"You know damn well what I'm talking about. You know how redneck mountain people act when they get wind of people like Darren and his friend."

I turned and faced Julie as she released me from her grasp. She didn't slur her words like a drunk usually does, but her eyes were glassy and a light film of sweat lay upon her upper lip. With her blonde hair damp from dancing and one thin strap slipped down on one arm, she was the picture of sex. As I stared into her eyes, they suddenly seemed to come into focus.

"Honey," she said, "don't let this evening's goin's-on disturb you none. Besides, you belong to me, now."

I grinned at her attempts to cheer me up and muttered a "thanks" as I looked down at the floor. She tilted my head up with her hand on my chin and kissed me quickly on the lips. Then just as quickly, she spun away, pulled her strap up and went back into the living room, leaving me gaping at her as she was swallowed by the crowd.

"Julie's just a jewel. Don't you agree?"

I turned to look at Darren who had just made that observation.

"Yep," I replied, "one in a million."

Dom finally entered into the conversation by asking in a slightly accented voice, "Has anyone here ever experienced…ah…the moonshine drink?"

"OH, what an absolutely fabulous idea," cried Darren. "Where can we buy some?"

"I know a place," answered Paul. "But we've got to drive to Newport to get it."

"Forget it, man," I said. "We don't need to be any closer to Newport than we are right now. Especially those two." I pointed my head in the direction of Darren and Dom.

"We promise not to utter a word. Can we go? How far is it?"

Darren was daring, I thought to myself. But Newport? Even the highway patrol called ahead before they went into the city limits. It was one bad place.

Paul said, "I know a guy who can call somebody he knows up there. All we have to do is tell him what our purpose is and what kind of car we will be driving."

"Be sure to tell him it's Martha Ronson's car. Everybody knows Sam and Martha," I offered.

"I'll drive," said Paul. "You look kind of tired."

Rather than argue, I just nodded in agreement. In truth, I was tired and just a little bit woozy. Little wonder with all the beer I'd had in the last eight hours. I handed over the keys to his outstretched hand.

"You're up, batter."

Darren laughed and patted Paul on the back as we all made our way out to the car. Darren and Dom climbed into the back while I sat in the passenger side next to Paul.

"Please don't let anything happen to this car, Paul. I'd get killed for sure."

"Don't worry. I was her driver last summer. I know the drill."

With that, Paul started the car and backed slowly out of the driveway, being careful not to hit any of the cars parked on the road in front of Julie's house. The night air was cool and crisp so there was no need for the air conditioner. I rolled down my window and lit a cigarette. I finished off the beer that I had with me and tossed the empty out the window. The hollow sound of the empty can as it hit the street rang once before landing in the tall grass at the side of the road.

Paul drove in silence while the two actors whispered to each other in the back seat. For a moment I began to get annoyed by them, but decided to let it pass. Paul maneuvered the car skillfully through the night traffic and finally pulled into a filling station at the edge of town.

"The guy that works the night shift will make the call to Newport for us. But it'll cost five dollars, so somebody needs to cough up some money. I'm just the driver," said Paul.

From the back, Darren immediately waved a five-dollar bill on Paul's right shoulder.

"By all means, I'll gladly cover the price of admission," laughed Darren.

Paul took the money and slid out of the car, closing the door behind him. Inside the garishly lit gas station sat a heavy-set man in a filthy pair of dark blue coveralls. He stood up slowly as Paul walked into the station and pulled a greasy rag from his back pocket and began smearing the dirt around on his chunky hands. Laborers hands. Darkened and cracked from years of toiling under the hoods of thousands of cars. His black hair was cut short on the sides, almost a military cut and a dirty baseball cap with a Gulf logo on the front sat on his head.

I couldn't hear what they were saying, but Darren said that everything was going according to plan and that the guy agreed to call. In a moment, Paul handed over the five, which the guy quickly shoved into one of the front pockets of his coveralls. He then picked up the phone and dialed a number. As he waited for someone to answer, he gave the car a good look and said something to Paul. Before Paul could answer, someone apparently started talking on the other end of the line. A few words were spoken, a question was asked of Paul, Paul answered, the man nodded into the phone as he spoke and then hung up. Paul nodded to the guy and came out of the station.

"We're in," Darren chirped from the backseat.

"Gotta go to the first goofy golf place on the left about a quarter of a mile after we pass the city limits. The guy who runs the place will be looking for us," Paul stated.

"How much for a quart?" I asked.

"Five for the good stuff. Four for the cheap run."

"Oh, let's get the good stuff. I'm treating, anyway," said Darren.

Treating, I thought. If this rot gut stuff doesn't poison us or blind us, we'll be lucky. Great. We drive all the way to what is possibly the most dangerous place on the planet just to buy something that has a better than fifty percent chance of causing either permanent damage or killing us all in the name of adventure. I guess I must be insane. We were all insane.

The drive up to Newport was very pretty during the day, but at night, the steep hills and narrow curves of the mountains hid everything. Trees canopied over the road as if they were trying to protect you from some overhead danger. With the absence of tourist traffic, the long, winding road seemed more like a path through a cave. A cave that had form and life, but a life trapped. Trapped by uncertainty and coldness without love or caring or simple human contact. It was merely a void that held us at a steady and unrelenting speed with no change in direction. Only the car lights parted the blackness in front of us. As I look back, I can compare this trip as a microcosm of my own journey through life.

Paul began to slow the car as we saw a few lights shining from Newport.

"Where are we supposed to go?" I asked.

"The first putt-putt course on the left. Guy said he'd be looking for our car," replied Paul.

I could sense an anxiety between us as I listened to the two actors gush about what a big adventure this was. I thought, the big adventure would be getting out of here without stirring up some kind of trouble among the locals. I was pretty sure that inbreeding was not only allowed in Cocke County, but encouraged as well. Gave me the creeps.

"There it is," I said pointing to a neon sign that read " utt-P tt Golf."

Paul wheeled the big Pontiac into the gravel parking lot. A tall, skinny guy wearing bib overalls, a filthy tee shirt and a greasy ball cap advertising Red Man Chewing Tobacco sat on the small fence surrounding the course.

Spitting tobacco juice in a stringy line in front of him, he scratched the side of his pimply face and asked, "You'ins the ones Harvey called about?"

Paul got slowly out of the car and nodded affirmatively.

"Got the goddamn money fer it?"

"Yep." Replied Paul without flinching. He wasn't about to be cowed by this country piece of trash.

Country boy stared at Paul for a second then pushed off the fence and stood in front of Paul. "Let's go git it then," said Country.

He led Paul to a small stand where people paid, picked out a putter and got a golf ball. There was a large white box in the back of the shed that was padlocked shut. After fishing out a large ring of keys from his front pocket, he began searching for the key to open the lock. After studying a few different keys for a minute, he tried his choice and the lock snapped open. As he raised the lid, I could see the expression never wavered on Paul's face. Country handed Paul two mason jars that were filled with a clear liquid that could have passed for water. Paul nestled both jars in the crook of his arm as he fished out the ten dollars and handed it over to our new friend. The lanky hillbilly then shoved the money into his pocket, slammed the box shut, locked it and followed Paul back to the car.

"You boys is real lucky with this last batch. Smooth as silk and don't have no horseshit in to age it none. Ain't been run through no car radiator neither. My daddy has one hell of a fine still jest like his daddy afore him," he said proudly beaming at us.

We just looked at him without comment. I remember being so fascinated with the freaks at the county fair that I could stand and stare at them for hours. It was the same feeling I got with this idiot. I hoped he would keep talking just for the entertainment of it all. I felt pretty sure that he had probably lost his virginity with either his sister or a barnyard animal. In a perverse way, I hoped it was an animal.

Darren and Dom were speechless and pale. They gave the impression of seeing someone from another planet. As far as they were concerned, Country Boy was from another planet.

Country placed his hands on the roof of the car after Paul climbed inside and shut the door. From where I was sitting, I could smell the rank mustiness of a man who had probably never bathed in his life. He looked from me to the backseat back to Paul and asked, "Where yawl from? Gatlinburg?"

We all nodded in unison as Paul started the car. Country stepped away from the car and told us to have a good time and for us "not to get no bad pussy, you hear?"

As we pulled out on the road leading us back to Gatlinburg, we could hear his high-pitched laugh follow us as Paul began to press on the accelerator.

"Man," Paul breathed, "that was one weird son-of-a-bitch."

"Excellent example of inbreeding," I said trying to lighten the atmosphere in the car.

"My God," exclaimed Darren. "He was frightening. How could you tell that person was the result of inbreeding?"

"It's a gift," answered Paul. "Most of Doug's relatives are like that, so he's good at picking them out."

With that, I punched Paul on the shoulder and called him an asshole. The ride back to Gatlinburg seemed to take half as long as the ride up. Soon we were turning on to Julie's road and parking in front of the house.

When our foursome piled into the kitchen, everything was still in full swing. Many had given up trying to dance and were content to concentrate on getting blasted. Big Bill and Laura were on their way out as we were setting the mason jars on the table.

"Better be careful with that stuff. It'll blind you for sure," he said nodding his head at the jars. "I seen my daddy drink hisself blind, so I know what can happen."

"Stick around won't you?" I asked. "It's too early to leave."

"Laura's had a couple of drinks and that's about all she can hold before she gets to throwin' up all over everything."

I shrugged as they turned to leave. Julie waved bye and told them to come over on Sunday night for spaghetti. They waved back and went out the door. Julie then turned to me with a devilish look on her face.

"Come slow dance with me, Doug. Okay?"

"Sure, Julie."

She then put on an album by Ray Charles that started with "I Can't Stop Lovin' You." Then she turned to me and I took her into my arms. We weren't really dancing as much as we were clutching each other tightly and swaying to the music. Her large breasts were pressed firmly into my chest, and I could smell the remains of her perfume mixing with the musk odor from her body. As she felt my erection growing, she ground her pelvis against me. I was in a state of excitement that nearly swept me away. Finally, she raised her face to mine and began kissing me with a deep urgency, and I responded in kind. When the music stopped, we remained that way for what seemed to be several minutes. Others began to notice us and started hooting about throwing a pail of water on us. We were generating too much heat in the room.

As we broke free from each other, we looked at each other with surprised looks on our faces. The intensity of the moment caught us both off guard. Julie took me by the hands, looked down at the floor, and then back up at me.

"We better cool down a bit," she whispered.

I don't know if, at that second, I had fallen in love or in lust. Whatever it was, it was powerful. I couldn't take my eyes off of her. What in the hell was I doing getting mixed up with a twenty-two-year-old married woman? I was gonna get killed, that's what.

"Well, my goodness. You two better find yourselves a room or something," Darren giggled.

He then raised his glass as if to toast us and said, "Go fix yourselves one of these moonshine cocktails. They're wonderful."

We walked hand in hand into the kitchen and someone put a large glass of what appeared to be a very watery coke in my hand. I took a large gulp and felt my chest and stomach catch fire. I was jolted by the lethal concoction in my glass.

"Holy God," I gasped. "What the hell is this stuff?"

Larry, who had been non-existent all evening, suddenly appeared in front of me and said, "Take it slow, man. It starts going down easier."

I could tell he was smashed by the way he teetered back in forth in front of me. He also had the shit-eating grin of someone who was ten feet tall and bulletproof. The man was gone.

"Go slow with that, sweetie. It'll reach up and knock you into the middle of next week," Julie warned me.

I took another sip and noticed that the second one did go down a little bit easier. Paul looked at me and simply shook his head. I raised my glass to him with one hand and told him to keep the car keys for the rest of the night. He nodded his head in return and gave me a thumbs-up sign with his hand.

Julie lightly scratched my back and told me she would be right back. When she left, I joined Darren and Dom who were now mixing their second or third drink.

Darren looked at my glass and said, "I can see you're ready for a fresh one, too."

I was amazed when I checked the glass in my hand to find it nearly empty. How the hell did that happen? As I handed my glass to Darren, I could feel a slight shifting movement in the kitchen floor. Fearing some kind of landslide, I gripped the counter ledge tightly with a panic-stricken look on my face. Then I realized that the moonshine was kicking into high gear. I told myself that one more would do me for the night. Besides, I still had some unfinished business with Julie, or so I thought.

I began to circulate through the room, shaking hands with every guy I saw and hugging every woman within reach. I felt good-looking, popular, intelligent, hysterically funny and any other desirable trait I could think of. A few more hits from my drink and the feeling grew. At last, I was ten feet tall and bulletproof myself. Unfortunately, it didn't last too long. My stomach began to tumble and knot all at the same time. Sweat broke out all over and I was barely moving. Then the nausea swelled, and I lurched for the bathroom. Luckily it was empty because I barely made it to the commode before the projectile vomiting took over. A few people barely paused by the door and quickly turned away. I was doing my best to hold on to the sink, the commode, anything I could to stop the room from spinning. Finally, I heard someone come in and close the door. They turned on the faucet to the sink and then put a cold cloth on my forehead, wiping away the sweat.

"Thanks, honey," I said, thinking it was Julie to my rescue.

"Not a problem," giggled a familiar male voice.

Darren. Damn. But I was in no condition to protest. I heaved mightily into the bowl and thought my ribs were going to start breaking any second. My whole body seemed to contort with each spasm. Darren continued his ministrations until it appeared that I had thrown up everything I had eaten for a week plus a few bodily organs.

Gently he sat me on the edge of the tub and wiped my face with the damp cloth.

"You okay, now?" he asked.

I looked at him and nodded weakly.

"You know, this is the best I've ever felt about myself in my whole entire life. Have I lost my mind?"

"No. You're just really, really drunk. You'll be okay," answered Darren.

I didn't respond because another massive seizure gripped me like a vice as I leaned over the toilet bowl fearing that my entire head would burst open any second. I was held in a long agonizing retch that produced nothing but spittle. I finally gasped for breath, positive that I would be unable to stand another contraction again. A few moments went by while Darren wiped my face and neck with the damp cloth. Here was a guy, a homosexual, taking care of me like I was his son or something. All the rest of my so-called friends could've cared less. I considered myself lucky to have met Darren; he made an impression on me that night that lasted forever.

"Do you think you can stand up? Paul's ready to take you home."

"Yeah, Darren. Thanks."

When I got to my feet, the world tilted about forty-five degrees and I grabbed the sink for support. Darren held on to my arm and guided me through the living room out to the car where Paul was waiting.

"Get him to bed and put a waste can next to his bed. I don't think he's through yet," Darren said to Paul.

I plopped down in the passenger seat. Paul looked over at me disgustedly and said, "You better not puke in Martha's car, man. Sam'll kill you for sure."

Then the lights went out.

I awoke in darkness, twisting with another long retch that produced only pain from the top of my head to the tips of my toes. My pitiful condition had improved enough for me to realize that I was in my own bed with absolutely no idea how I got there. I glanced at my clock and saw that it was four in the morning. Another hour and a half before I had to get up and go to work, and I was still drunk. Afraid of oversleeping, I sat up slowly and was stunned by the immediate pounding in my skull. I sat there holding my head for a good five minutes before trying to stand upright, fearing that I would fall down and hurt myself. When the hammering finally subsided from a kettledrum to only a snare drum, I slowly stood up. Holding my hands in front of me for balance, I located my shaving kit and started to make my way gingerly down the stairs. I was sure a long bath, a shave and four aspirin would make the world right again.

Downstairs, I felt my way into the bathroom, turned on the light switch for the single bare bulb that hung down a braided wire from the ceiling. Closing the door, I shielded my eyes against the blinding glare of the harsh light. I looked at myself in the mirror and saw someone I didn't really know. Red-eyed and pale, I appeared to be the victim of some horrible disease. The eyes were the most disturbing. Not only were they bloodshot, they had a depressing, haunting look. I had to look away.

I carefully turned on the hot water faucet in the tub so as not to wake the others in the house. I then got out my razor and shaving cream and ran the water in the sink to shave. As I lathered my face, I tried to avoid looking myself in the eye, concentrating more on hands rubbing my face. When I picked up my razor and ran it under the tap, I noticed my hand was shaking. It frightened me at first, then I just shrugged it off as part of the hangover. I decided that a light shave would have to suffice. Before putting away the shaving stuff, I pulled a bottle of aspirin from my kit and washed down four of them, using my hand under the water tap as a glass. No sooner had I raised my head than another wave of nausea clutched at my insides. I don't even think the aspirin had a chance to reach my stomach before I threw up the water and partially dissolved pills into the toilet.

"Great," I thought, "I can't even hold down water."

By now I had to turn on the cold water in the tub because the bathroom steaming up. After a few moments, I eased myself into the hot bath. Soon sweat began to ooze from every pore in my body that wasn't underwater. I had never sweat this much at football practice. Gradually, I began to cool off as the water temperature dropped. I stayed in the tub until the water was tepid, climbed out slowly to try to minimize the pounding in my head and began to dry off. I was still shaky but felt better than I had when I first awakened.

I leaned over the sink again this time to just rub some water on my parched lips. I was dying of thirst but didn't want to set off another spasm of heaves. I was able to give my teeth a real good brushing to try to rinse the foul, bitter taste from my mouth.

Re-packing my kit, I went back upstairs to my bed. The clock read five o'clock. I lay there trying to remember the events of the night before. I could get as far as watching Larry mix me a cocktail of moonshine and coke and hand it to me with a big smile. After that, nothing. I vaguely saw brief scenes of Julie's bathroom and Darren. Then I began to worry anew. What had happened with Darren? He was gay. I had to know. I began to shake all over from a fear deep within me and tried to harness my imagination. The harder I tried to avoid bringing up horrific images, the harder my imagination worked. I got out of bed and got dressed for work.

"Go through the routine," I told myself. Calm down. Maybe nothing at all happened. I was drunk. Apparently I got sick and nothing else went on between Darren and me. Shit.

It also occurred to me that being that drunk was the best I'd ever felt about myself in my whole life. I didn't realize it at the time but I would come to regret that many years later.

I crept silently down the stairs, out of the house, and headed in the direction of the restaurant. The cool morning air made me feel a little better physically, but my mind was still racing, almost causing me to hyperventilate. Suddenly, another spasm of nausea hit me, and I leaned over in the middle of the road and gagged. Nothing but air. Jesus. How damn long was this going to go on? Maybe I damaged my stomach with that moonshine and would never be able to hold down food or water for the rest of my life. Good. I wanted to die anyway. My whole world was turning to shit and there was nothing I could do to stop it.

Chapter Eighteen

The morning sun had just started to lighten the sky as I got to the restaurant. I knew I was earlier than normal for my shift, but I just couldn't lie around with my thoughts as company. I needed some activity to focus my mind on the present.

As soon as I reached the back steps, the smell of frying sausage and bacon hit me. It didn't just hit my sense of smell; it hit my whole body. For more times than I could count, my stomach seized up, and I bent at the waist to heave more air. The blacksmith who had taken up residence in my brain was hammering angrily again. As I stood upright, I wondered how in the hell I was supposed to work today? What if I had one of these spells in the dining room? That would make a big impression on the tourists. I could hear them relating the story to their friends and relatives back home.

"Yeah, this kid was coming apart trying to vomit in a gray tub he was carrying. Ruined our whole breakfast. Left without paying for being subjected to that kind of shit. That bastard was either sick as hell or had one bad hangover."

I tried not to breathe as I forced myself through the door and on in to the kitchen. Roy was there whistling some happy tune and sweating into the grease.

"Goddamn, boy. You look worser 'n shit," he said laughing.

"What's so damn funny, Roy?"

He just laughed harder as he walked over in my direction. He came around the warming counter and went to a cabinet where he pulled down some Alka-Seltzer.

"You got the dry heaves?" he asked.

"If that's what you call it, yeah."

"Keep takin' some of these here in a glass of water till it stays down. Either that or drink a few beers. I advise this though. You too damn young to be hittin' the sauce in the mornin'."

I mumbled "thanks" and went to get a glass of water. I took it to the back room where there was a large tub sink used to wash the bulk vegetables. I dropped two of the tablets in the water and watched them fizz. Finally, I held my nose and turned the glass up. The mixture stopped for a brief visit in my stomach and shot right back out again.

I went back in to the kitchen and told Roy that it was no use.

"I tole you to keep a doin' it till you can hold it down. Now, don't argue with me about this. I been there afore. Wait about a half-hour and try it again. You ain't gonna die, you jest think you are," he said laughing again.

Bastard.

All the employee in the place looked like they had been hit by a truck. They all moved listlessly as if they were trudging through mud. Their faces were pale and their eyes were as red as Georgia road maps. Terry looked particularly bad. When she came in an hour late this morning, she looked as if she and Roy had gone at it all night.

The rest of my day was just a blur of cleaning tables and running back to the sink to heave some more air. Finally, about one o'clock, I was able to hold down some ginger ale and some crackers, and I started to feel human again. By quitting time, I was drinking ice water, one glassful right after another. My headache was gone, and I actually started to feel good in comparison that is to the wreck that I was when I showed up that morning.

When Julie showed up for her shift, she looked as radiant as ever. I just stared at her for a moment until she saw me looking at her. She winked and, with her head, motioned for me to go back to the kitchen. When I got back there with my tray, she told me to set it down and come out back.

The sun still hurt my eyes.

"How are you holding up today, sweetheart?" She asked.

"Barely. Last night almost killed me. How about you?"

"Oh, I feel great. I slept like a baby last night and dreamed about us." She winked at me as her mouth slowly widened into big smile.

Did she say us? Was I imagining that? "Uh…what was your dream about?"

She leaned over and wet my right ear with her tongue as she whispered, "We'll talk about it later, honey."

With that, she went back into the kitchen and left me standing there with my heart pounding away and my imagination going haywire. "God," I thought, "this woman is coming on to me. **To me**."

I went back into the kitchen and Larry came up to me at quitting time.

"How you feelin'?"

"Better than I was. How about you?"

"I feel good, but then I didn't drink a half a quart of shine last night," he responded.

"How did I get home last night?" I asked.

"Paul drove you home in Martha's car. I caught a ride with Darren and Dom. They're not too bad for a couple of fags. That one guy, Darren? If he hadn't helped you in the bathroom, you'd have drowned in the toilet."

"What did he do?" I asked nervously.

"Nothing. He just treated you like he was your mama or something. Wiping your face and holding your head. I kept an eye on him just in case he tried something with you while you were out of it," Larry explained.

I breathed a sigh of relief but said nothing.

"Wanna grab six and head for the house?" He asked me.

"Head for the house yeah, but don't even mention drinking. My drinking days are over for a while. I almost killed myself last night."

"Aw, shit, man. Give it twenty-four hours and you'll be good as new."

He grabbed a six-pack out of the cooler, and we headed back to the house. When we got back, I changed into shorts and a tee shirt and collapsed on the bed. In a matter of seconds, I was asleep.

Paul, shaking me roughly, roused me out of my stupor to tell me I had visitors.

"Wha...who?"

"Your family is here to visit you. They're downstairs on the front porch. Get your shit together, man."

I sat up on the side of the bed and rubbed my face. My parents? Did somebody call them out about last night? What the hell were they doing up here? I didn't even know what day it was. I pulled on my tennis shoes and looked at myself in the mirror. Not too bad. I could probably pull off feeling good.

When I got outside, I greeted my parents as cheerfully as I could. My mother took one look at me and asked me if I felt all right. She said I looked sort of pale.

"Well...er...I had some bad hamburger last night and got kind of sick," I explained lamely.

"Where in the world did you eat? We don't want to risk going there," she said.

I mumbled the name of some restaurant that came to my head and changed the subject.

The she started in on my hair. I had actually forgotten about it until I saw her ice-blue eyes zeroed in on the top of my head.

"Hiya, Dad. Rob. How are you guys?"

"Not so damn fast. I want to know what the hell you've done with your hair? Have you looked at yourself in the mirror? You look like shit. You look worse than shit. I'm going to do something about that before school starts. Everybody will be laughing at you. You must be crazy."

Mother had gotten progressively louder as her comments continued and I could here laughter coming from upstairs. Shit. This was awful. Plus, I'd just gotten over the dry heaves.

My dad was standing by the car smoking a cigarette. He and I were about the same height, five-ten or so, but he was a little on the paunchy side. He almost never exercised, and he sat at a linotype machine all day. His hair was still black with no traces of gray, but his posture made him look older than he was. Getting in shape was not high on his list of things to do. The story I had told my mother did not fool my dad for an instant. He just stood there with a small grin on his face and shook my hand. As we shook, he leaned over and whispered one question: "Hamburger come in a brown bottle?"

The look on my face gave him the answer. He laughed slightly and told me to be careful about my "eating" habits.

I tousled the hair on Rob's head. He jerked his head away and said, "Don't do that, you crud. I hate that."

"That's why I did it."

I could tell he was in a bad mood. Maybe mother had gotten on his case about something on the way to Gatlinburg. Could have been anything.

Mother then walked over to the car and pulled a plate covered with foil that she peeled back to reveal a huge chocolate cake. I winced as I stifled a gag.

"Oh, boy. I could really go for that right now," I said as enthusiastically as I could.

Some of the other guys were leaning out the window to applaud and cheer.

"How 'bout now, Doug? Will you share with us, Doug? Man, that looks good enough to sit down and eat with your hands."

I looked up at them and they all had these clever grins on their faces. Their actions served to confirm what my dad already knew. Mother, on the other hand, seemed genuinely pleased by the comments from those assholes. I took the cake from my mother and said I would put it upstairs to share with my friends.

I took the cake and ran it up to my room.

"Will you bastards just shut up?"

They responded my laughing and making vomit parodies.

When I got back to my parents, I asked them what they wanted to do.

"We packed a picnic lunch with fried chicken. I just know you're tired of restaurant food," my mother said.

Dad asked, "Do you feel like eating anything after your bad hamburger and all?"

I looked at him and said, "Yeah, I can eat."

He just grinned some more and nodded his head.

"Well, then, let's go find a place close to the river. It's hot here in town," offered mother.

We piled into the car. I showed them a back way to get on the "mountain side" of town. The "mountain side" was opposite from the direction of Pigeon Forge and Sevierville. That was the "Knoxville side" of town. I was in pretty good shape until we started hitting the curves that wound their way up towards Cherokee. I dug a coke from the cooler that sat between my brother and me. That seemed to help a little.

We finally found a spot and dad stopped the car. As I got out, I pulled the Coleman cooler from the back, while my brother grabbed the old army blanket we kept on hand just for picnics. After everything was all laid out, I saw there was potato salad, fruit salad, baked beans, a mound of fried chicken, and home baked rolls. Suddenly, I was starved. I guess everyone was because we all dug in hungrily.

After a few moments of serious eating, we all began to slow down. Dad wanted to know how I liked my job. Mother wanted to know about the people I worked with. As for Rob, he didn't give a hoot in hell. He was too hungry to care. I answered all the small talk questions with the exception of the most interesting job I had. Driving Martha around. For some reason, I don't think they would have understood. Within the hour, they were getting on my nerves so badly I wanted to scream. But I resisted.

Finally, mother stood up and announced that they better get back on the road so they could get home before dark. That's pretty much the way she liked to do things. Do it. Finish it. Move on to the next item on the list. The idea of savoring the present moment was completely foreign to her. I think she had a problem with knowing how to relax. Everything with her was full steam ahead and don't stop for the wounded or injured. In a previous life, she probably rode a horse for the Pony Express.

On the ride back, I tried to concentrate on the beauty of the tumbling water as it ran its course through the mountains. But my mind kept wandering back to some of the answers I had given my parents about work, the people I'd met, what I did with my free time and all of that kind of stuff. Rather than treating them like interested parents, I felt as if I was being interrogated. So, I lied. I told them all of the things that I thought that they would want to hear rather then telling them the truth. I told them I went on hikes with my friends, spent a lot of time reading, did a lot of tourist watching and a lot of other stuff that would make me look like a boy scout. I guess the thing that bothered me the most was I felt absolutely no remorse for my lying to them. Strange. I was concerned about being unconcerned. My primary goal was to appease them so they wouldn't make me come home. For me, going home would have been the ultimate disaster. The idea of going home had never really entered my mind until my parents came today to visit. With the exception of Rob, I had been able to completely shut them out of my mind. I thought of my parents as though they were some people I had known when I was a kid. Now things had changed. Maybe not so much "things" had changed, but I had definitely changed. I attributed this feeling to having had the opportunity to get away from home and pay my own bills. My parents never sent me any money, because they knew I could handle a budget and survive. Even if I had gotten into trouble, I would have never asked for help. For anything. From anybody. This feeling of being totally self-reliant completely altered the way I viewed my family and myself. Maybe this is what growing up was all about and I was just making a big deal out of it. As I looked around the car at dad, mother and my brother, I got the feeling that I no longer belonged to the "nest." The things I had seen and experienced made me feel older and wiser. I had no idea what the future held, but I did know that whatever choices I made, I was going to have to live with them. Whether they were good choices or bad choices.

By the time we got back to Gatlinburg, the early diners were out and about trying to decide on a place to eat. The early birds were made up of two kinds of people—old people and people with screaming toddlers. The old and the young needed early feeding and early bedtimes. The waiters and waitresses usually complained that they were the worst tippers, too. The old folks were picky as hell, and the young parents were watching every penny or just plain didn't know any better. The latter was probably closer to the truth.

My dad drove right back to the Cummins' house without a word of direction from me. My mother provided all of that. Rob had fallen asleep on the ride back home, so when the car came to a stop, he woke up with a scowl on his face.

"Where are we?"

"We're back at your brother's summer home," answered my dad, smiling.

We all piled out of the car, and gathered in a loose little group to say our good-byes. I glanced over at the porch and gave Mr. Cummins a brief wave as he sat in his rocker, leering at my mother. He grinned revealing his tobacco stained teeth, and gave me a small salute. I turned my attention back to my family. Mother held her cigarette behind her and gave me a big hug, telling me to take care of myself. She also pointed out that I had lost some weight, but that was probably a good thing. I shook Rob's hand and refrained from tousling his hair. He grinned back at me as if to say "thanks for not doing that."

"Stay out of my room while I'm gone," I said to him as I acted as if I were about to punch him.

He danced out of the way laughing and saying, "I'm going back and tear it up."

I looked at my dad and he nodded his head over to the side to let me know he wanted to speak to me privately.

"Keeping secrets, are you?" asked my mother as we strode away.

"Just a little man-to-man talk," my dad responded to her with a weary smile.

After we got out of earshot from mother, Dad asked me, "Are you taking good care of yourself? I hope you're not getting up with a hangover on a regular basis."

"Naw, Dad. It was just this one time at a party."

"What were you drinking?"

"I'd just had two beers the whole evening until somebody started fixing cokes and moonshine. I had one of those and it about killed me."

Dad looked down at the ground and shook his head before speaking.

"Just two beers, huh? How many times have I said that? Well, just be careful. I know you want to sow some wild oats and all of that kind of stuff. Believe it or not, I was sixteen once. Just be sure you watch out for yourself. Okay?"

He was looking at me with both pride and concern etched on his face. He treated me just like another man. Didn't bust my balls or anything. Treated me as an equal. I felt a strange swelling in my chest as I reached over and hugged him.

"Thanks, Dad," I said as he hugged me back.

We locked eye to eye, and no further words needed to be said.

He turned to mother and said, "Well, let's get on the road and get back to the house before dark."

With that, they got into the old Ford and drove away waving as they left.

As I stood and watched the car disappear, I thought to myself, "I'm glad that's over with."

I felt a little guilty for thinking that way as I turned toward the house but I was glad they were gone.

"You tell 'em what a good boy you been?" cackled Mr. Cummins.

I must have turned about three shades of red before I said, "Mind your own damn business, you old bastard."

He responded by howling that much louder and slapping his hand against his knee. In a second or two, we were both laughing like a couple of loons. That old bastard didn't miss a trick. In fact, I had begun to develop a liking for the old guy because he fooled a lot of people. Most thought of him as nothing more than a booze soaked old geezer who didn't know where in the world he was half the time. He just sat and drank and watched and listened and learned and kept to himself. By my way of thinking, that was a pretty good way to live your life. Be a cautious observer while still taking part. It seemed that people who tried to interfere in other people's business started a lot of arguments. I probably hated arguments more than anybody did because I had heard my parents argue enough to last me a lifetime. If the best way to avoid arguments or confrontation was by staying away from people, then so be it. My favorite book as a kid was the one about Robinson Crusoe being stranded on that island in the middle of nowhere. I always figured he had a pretty good thing going there until that guy, Friday, showed up. Then the whole story started going sour. I think some people were meant to live alone, and I was one of those people.

Chapter Nineteen

I left Mr. Cummins chuckling to himself and his booze. When I got to the top of the steps, Paul, Lonnie and Larry were all in the room Paul and I shared. All three held bottles of beer in their hands, and Larry held one out to me.

"No way, man. I've heaved enough for one day."

Larry looked at me and said, "The hair of the dog that bit you is just the cure you need."

The other two nodded their heads in agreement and raised their bottles as a salute. I thought about Larry's recommendation for a cure, reasoned that it was logical, accepted the beer and sat down. Unknowingly, that philosophy about drinking would stick with me for years to follow. Taking a tiny, cautious sip, I sat back to make sure I wasn't going to paint the wall with fried chicken.

Lonnie said, "I heard Money Dick and a couple of his snotty friends up in his room this afternoon planning a beer party for the night of the fourth of July. One of 'em asked Money if he was going to invite any of his roommates and he said 'no way because they were all a bunch of trashy rednecks.'"

"Who the hell does that son-of-a-bitch think he is, anyway?" Asked Paul.

"Thinks he's better than we are because his parents are rich," said Larry.

The Fourth of July, I thought. Was it here already? That meant the summer was about half gone by Tuesday when the great independence celebration hit. I was going to have to go back to school for the start of fall football practice the second week of August. I had just a little over a month to take advantage of my freedom. I could only imagine how bad it was going to be to have to go back home. Curfews, no job, no drinking or smoking. The pits. I took a large sip of beer.

"Fuck him, and the horse he rode in on," I said. "Let's have our own damn party."

"Yeah," everyone cried in unison. We clashed our bottles together so hard, it was a wonder we didn't end up clutching four broken bottlenecks.

"Trashy rednecks. I ought to stomp that little bastard's pampered ass," said Lonnie.

We all took his threat seriously because Lonnie hardly ever spoke unless he had something of extreme importance to say. I looked at Lonnie and grinned. His dark eyes lit up and a wolf-like smile stretched across his narrow face. Lonnie, who was repeating his senior year in high school, was not only two to three years older than the rest of us, he looked and acted a lot older. He never took part in any of the horseplay and ragging that the rest of us engaged in on a regular basis. He also had that lanky, rangy build that was so common to guys who worked at jobs like construction or gas stations. Although he did pretty well in tips at the place where he worked, he just didn't fit the mold of a waiter. Larry said that women went wild over him and that his brother had to beat them off with a stick. But you never heard Lonnie bragging about any sexual conquests. I guess that's the way really cool guys acted. He used the four-F system: find 'em, finger 'em, fuck 'em and forget 'em. His attitude justified serious consideration.

Paul offered, "It's set then. Tuesday after work, we go find a good swimming spot and have a party."

Lonnie looked at his brother wryly and asked, "You gonna steal enough beer for this deal or do I have to steal some, too?"

"You steal some this time. I just got through robbing the cooler for Julie's party. Somebody's gonna notice pretty soon."

"Then we're set," I said

"Yep," said Paul, "we're set."

I wasn't in the mood for dinner so I asked Larry if he wanted to hang out in front of the Greystone and watch all the goofballs go by. He said he was going to go to a movie with Lonnie. When I asked Paul what his plans were, he said he was going to go over to the amusement park and hang out and try to meet the girl that worked the concession booth.

I put on a clean tee shirt and left the house, heading for Main Street and all the brightly-lit activity it offered.

I made my way among the throngs of people like a halfback weaving his path through opposing players. I didn't have any place to go, but I didn't want to look like a gawking tourist. Finally, I came to a crowd of people stopped in front of a large glass window at Kauffman's Fudge Shoppe. They were watching a team of guys beating the hell out of a large copper bowl of fudge. Their damp tee shirts were stretched tightly across their muscular arms and chests as each guy took a turn with a large wooden paddle. As one of them pounded away at the candy, the other took a breather. After about two minutes, the one at rest stood close to the guy at work and placed his hands next to his partner's hands to get the rhythm of the motion. When the relief guy barked something at the sweaty beater, the relief guy took over as the other guy stepped out of the way. Perfect timing and coordination. It was almost like watching two people functioning as a perfectly tuned machine.

I knew when Paul worked there they had two teams of guys working. Paul had gotten in great shape working in this place, so I began to think about football practice in August. It would be here before I knew it, and

I was in terrible shape from the lifestyle I had been leading all summer. Smoking, drinking, goofing off. Basically doing nothing other than shovel dishes from tables to the kitchen. That and drive around a sloppy drunken woman. That brought another question to mind. When was Martha coming back? I really missed the extra twenty dollars a night of tax-free income. Unless she came back soon, I might have to get a real job like those two poor bastards beating the shit out of that fudge.

As I wormed my way around the crowd, I began pondering the possibility of seeing old man Kauffman and seeing if he needed any help. I could get in some pretty decent conditioning and make some money at the same time. Besides, much of the crowd in front of the big window was made up of some pretty good-looking girls who looked as if their mouths were watering over something other than candy. I decided to stop by the candy store and speak to the old kraut who ran the place to see if I could work a few hours after work.

Braced with a plan, I dodged my way between the cars inching their slow path down Main Street. There were three or four empty lounge chairs close to the sidewalk where I could lay back and make up stories about the people as they wandered by. Each either eating something or holding a bag containing some kind of lame souvenir of their trip to the Great Smoky Mountains.

I grabbed a chair and lay back to watch my answer to television. Sometimes I felt like I was invisible on my perch. No one even glanced my way as they strolled by. They, too, seemed to be lost in their own thoughts. Some, however, gestured excitedly at different things (these were the new tourists) while many of the parents were trying to calm their whining kids. Poor little bastards were probably exhausted from being dragged all over so their parents could tire them out by the time they got back to their hotel room. Not a bad idea. Then mom and dad could crack out a bottle of Jack Daniels and have a couple before turning in themselves.

Combined with my blood-sugar free-fall and the cool breeze that wafted through the night air, I began to doze lightly. Only the cars passing by with radios playing kept me from falling into a deep sleep, so I just drifted along in a state of semi-consciousness. My thoughts swooped and rose like a kite in a strong wind, carrying various inner visions across the landscape of my brain.

"You drunk again, dumb ass?" somebody shouted at me, jerking me to full alertness.

I looked in front of me and saw Paul and a tall blonde grinning and licking on huge ice cream cones. The blonde ran her tongue around the head of the cone, bring the ice cream to a delicate point.

"Drunk on chocolate cake and coke," I answered. "What about you?"

"Chocolate ice cream," he replied, laughing.

"Meet my friend, Kathy. Kathy, this is Doug, my roommate," he said by way of introduction.

"Hi," she said, smiling.

"Hi. Like the ice cream?" I asked.

She swirled her tongue around the cone and answered, "I love it."

Her large green eyes were unblinking as they locked onto mine. Two words came to my head — cock-teaser. She had the sexy babe thing going pretty well. Paul had lost about forty points of his IQ, and she knew it.

"I just bet you do," I said as I stared back her.

After Paul and his new friend strolled away, I was getting cranky. I got up from the lounge chair and started back home. My head was full of odd thoughts and perceptions that seemed to be in conflict with each other. Rather than coming up with answers, I was just coming up with more questions.

I took a back street close to the restaurant and noticed that the lights on the run-down garage were on. I remember meeting the old guy who owned the place, but I couldn't remember his name. Hands in my pockets, I sauntered into one of the bays in his shop. He looked up when he heard me come in and nodded his head in my direction.

"What can I do fer you, buddy?"

"I noticed your lights were on and decided to stop in and say hello. I'm sorry I don't remember your name. I met you about a month ago. My name's Doug. I live over at Mr. Cummins' place."

"Everett," he said as he stuck out a greasy hand to shake.

I ignored the grime and shook his hand.

"You one a them summer workers?" he asked.

"Yessir, I am."

"Sir? Goddamn, I ain't been called 'sir' since I was in the navy. You seem to be a nice enough fella. Here, have yourself a bracer," he said as he held out a pint bottle of gin in my direction.

Muttering a thanks, I turned the bottle up and took a long swallow. When I handed the bottle back to him, I resisted the urge to cough. The stuff tasted like pine oil. I didn't know how in the hell somebody could drink enough of that stuff to get drunk.

"Thanks," I involuntarily gasped as I handed the gin back to him.

He smiled widely showing what remained of his tobacco-stained teeth.

"Me and Dudley used to run together when we wuz young'ins. He and I drove shine fer Alvin Carpentar till Dudley joined up with the Army. He said them gov'mint cars wuz getting too damn fast. Time to get out. I agreed with him and I joined up with the Navy."

"Why the Navy?" I asked.

"Never seen the goddamn ocean before. Figured I'd get a chance if I wuz a sailor," he said as he grinned his horrible grin. "They made me a airplane mechanic, since I told 'em I wuz purty good at a-tinkerin' on automobiles. Served on a aircraft carrier. Weren't too bad."

He shook his head, took another swig from the bottle and handed it back to me. I took the bottle from his hand and took another drink. This time it went down much easier. I took one more hit from the gin and handed it back to him.

"Thanks for the drink," I said.

"Come back any time, boy."

"Yeah, I will," I said as I gave him a wave.

As I walked back to the house, I was thinking about how people never turn out to be what they seem to be. Just about everybody I had gotten to know was much different from my initial opinion of him or her. Some turned out better and some turned out worse. Most of the men were better, and most of the women worse. Except for two people, Julie and Money Dick. Julie turned out to be beyond wonderful, but Money Dick was getting more despicable by the day. Something needed to be done with that snobby bastard.

I rose early the next day to go to work. It was Sunday. I knew we were going to be overrun with customers. Good. Made the day go by faster. Besides the waiters and waitresses were usually in a good mood on a day that promised good tips. The only thing was they sometimes wanted the table bussed as soon as the people started getting up out of their seats. Kinda pissed me off, but I'd bust my ass. Wide open was the only way I knew how to work, and I guess that I got that from my mother. If you're gonna do a job, give it everything you've got.

It was a pretty busy but otherwise uneventful day. Before I knew it, I had worked a half-hour overtime. With the other two busboys in, I left. Instead of lifting some beer with Larry, I headed downtown toward Kauffman's Fudge Shoppe. Nobody knew when Martha was coming back, and I got tired of wasting time when I could be making money.

There were a few people out in front of the store, but most people were trying to do something other than stand around in the hot sun. Must've been ninety-five degrees. I opened the front door to the shop and was hit squarely in the face with a strong smell of dark rich chocolate. It was a smell that would stay with me for a lifetime. A heavy-set woman with a ruddy complexion stood behind the candy case and smiled at me.

"Can I help you, young man?" she asked. Had to be Mrs. Kauffman with that heavy German accent.

"Yes, ma'am. I was wondering if you were hiring any part-time help?"

"Oh, ja. We always need good help. Nobody wants to work hard anymore. Mr. Kauffman, he has such a hard time with some of these boys. You not afraid of hard work, are you?

"No, ma am. I like hard work."

"Goot. I call Mr. Kauffman. You stay there," she said as she pointed with a finger the size of a polish sausage.

"Klaus, come quickly. A young man wants to work hard. You should talk to him," she yelled toward the back.

I was a little embarrassed as some of the customers looked in my direction and smiled. I hoped they were glad to see a "hard worker" rather than some goof in a bow tie and a red plaid vest. I took off the bow tie and stuck it into my shirt pocket.

Soon, Mr. Kauffman came trundling from the back of the store with a scowl on his face. He looked like he had been interrupted from a good nap. He looked at Mrs. Kauffman, and she pointed to me. Kauffman was a large heavy-set man with a shiny, bald head. Although he was fat, you could tell that most of his bulk was composed of massive muscles. He was, to say the least, intimidating.

Turning his scowl in my direction, he asked, "You work hard?"

"Yessir," I replied nervously.

"Goot. You start tomorrow at four o'clock. Work four to eight. Three dollars and fifty-cents and hour to start. Goot pay. Work real hard and I maybe raise your pay Okay?"

"Yes…yeah…okay."

"Goot. Come in a little early and get a uniform. I provide. Is good benefit for working here. Okay?"

"Yes sir, that's great," I answered.

"Goot."

With that, he grasped my hand in his meaty grip and we shook. Signed, sealed and delivered. Tomorrow I was going to be a candyman.

When I got back to the house, Larry was in his room sucking on a beer. I could hear Jungle Jim snoring like a log in his room so I asked Larry why Jim was home at this time of day.

"He worked some kind of banquet last night at the civic center so his boss let him off a couple of hours early. They were having a slow day anyway. Besides, if Jungle Boy can get a job there as a waiter, the place must really be bad. Would you want someone who looks more ape than human serving you food?"

"If I liked hair in my food I would," I laughed. "Hey, I got a part-time job today."

"Doing what? Working in a blow job booth?"

"No, you bastard. I'm gonna be working at Kauffman's Fudge Shoppe as a candyman."

"Beating-off fudge, huh? You'll be a natural at that," said Larry, laughing at his own pathetic attempt at humor. In a more serious tone he warned, "That old man Kauffman is a real brutal guy to work for. You'll have to work your ass off. How many hours a day are you gonna work?"

"From four to eight on Thursday, Friday, Saturday and Sunday," I answered.

"You're gonna be so sore, you won't be able to feed yourself. Much less jerk off," he said, smirking.

"You sound like the one with the masturbation obsession. Hell, I bet you crank it while you think about Money Dick."

"Fuck you," he yelled as he threw his pillow at me.

"I guess I stuck a nerve, huh?"

"Get outta my room, you bastard," he said, glaring at me.

I just laughed and kicked his pillow back in his direction. When I walked over to my bed and flopped down, I started thinking about what Julie had said at the party the other night. I had almost forgotten about it until the remaining cobwebs cleared out of my brain. I'm sure she was coming on to me, but I wondered if it was just drunk-talk. I needed to figure out a way to see if she wanted to pursue this line of friendship any further before I messed everything up. Besides, I sure as hell didn't want her old man coming after me with a gun. However, if she could keep a secret…hell…maybe. Damn you, you idiot. What the hell are you thinking? She's a lot older at twenty-two compared to your sixteen years of total inexperience. On the other hand, maybe she would make the perfect teacher. Yeah. She could tutor me in sex. So, looking at it that way, it would be more like an educational relationship. It wouldn't be like she was cheating on her husband or anything; she would be functioning as a teacher. And a very able teacher at that. I'm so glad I was able to use sound judgment in solving this problem. Proudly, I realized that I was using adult rationale, rather than some goofy teen-age daydreaming. With the help of the proper perspective, a whole fresh look at my world was now possible. As I let out a huge sigh of relief, I folded my hands behind my head and began to think of how I could approach Julie with my idea. As I thought about my approach, I nodded off to a dreamless sleep. Much later in life, I had to ask myself, "What I was using for a brain?"

Chapter Twenty

"Wake up, Doug. Martha's back. Get up, you lazy bastard."

Larry was shaking me and blowing his beer-breath right into my face.

As I turned away my head, I asked him, "What the hell are you talking about? And back off, before I have to puke on you."

"Martha's back from the dry-out place. I went down to the restaurant, and she was there visiting with everybody. Man, she looked good, being stone sober for a change."

"Martha's back? Sober?"

"Yeah, man. I was as surprised as anyone was. I thought sure she'd stay a bottle-baby," Larry said shaking his head.

I didn't say anything to Larry, but I was sort of angry. If she were off the sauce, that would mean the end of my chauffeuring job. She could drive herself around now. Shit. Now I was stuck with the candy shop where I'll really be working for money.

"She asked about you, hotshot. Wanted to know how you were getting along. Told me to tell you to come by for a visit when you had the time," Larry said grinning.

"What the hell are you grinning at, bastard?"

"The older ones get hot for you, don't they? They think you're cute," he continued with a snicker.

"Get outta here, you stupid bastard. You don't know what the hell you're talking about. Get the fuck away from me," I yelled as I kicked at him from my bed.

Larry jumped out of harm's way spilling some beer on the floor and laughing like a loon.

"Maybe they want to NURSE YOU, shithead," he cried as he started holding the catch in his side from laughing so hard.

I jumped out of bed, but he was too quick, expecting me to come at him. He ran to his room and slammed the door so hard the entire house shook. I could still hear him howling.

From downstairs, Mrs. Cummins hollered, "What you boys a-doin' up there? Tearin' up my house? Settle down, now."

I walked back to my bed and sat on the edge thinking. What if he was right? What if they saw me as some child that needed mothering? Hell. He was just jealous, the stupid shit. Damn women just mess with a guy's head. No wonder people got divorced. A man could only stand so much crap before he bailed. I decided right then that marriage was an institution that I needed to avoid at all costs. Besides, why buy the cow, if you could get the milk for free?

Angrily, I jerked on some shorts and a tee shirt and went down the steps to get away for a while. I needed some time to walk off whatever was clinging to my head. I didn't know what was bothering me, but I knew something just wasn't right.

I avoided the main drag, glad that it was only Wednesday so I didn't have to show up at the fucking candy store. In the mood I was in, I would have probably tried to assault people with a chocolate stained wooden paddle. I could see the headlines now: "Crazed Fudge Beater Goes After Stunned Crowd." I'd be booked in jail as a loony who tried to commit murder with a candy paddle. My parents would kill me. I'd lose my job, for sure. I'd go to jail and end up in the loving arms of some guy covered in tattoos and a taste for teenagers. All of this misery over women. The best bet was to be on your guard when it came to the opposite sex because they really couldn't be trusted. And it took decades for me to change my opinion.

I don't know how long I walked, but I looked up and found myself in front of Sam and Martha's house. Not wanting to be seen by Martha, I started to jog toward Main Street when I heard a woman's voice call my name.

"Doug, wait. I need to see you," Martha shouted from her front porch.

Shit. A couple of steps too slow, as usual. I turned around and, with a fake smile on my face, waved to her. She walked quickly down the front yard in my direction. I noticed she was wearing the white slacks and red blouse I'd seen her in before. The time I told her she looked beautiful.

"How have you been, Doug? I missed you while I was away," she said to me her eyes shining brightly. "I like what you've done to your hair. What made you decide to do that?"

I just mumbled and looked at her eyes again. This time there was a clear shine to them rather than the watery sheen of boozy eyes. I noticed her smile was sincere, not like the half-hearted sneer she had when she was drunk. I was really impressed with the improvement in her appearance and I guess it was reflected in my expression.

"I've doing fine, Martha. You really look great."

She blushed faintly and looked down at her hands, twisting them nervously.

"Well, I feel pretty good. I guess everybody in this town knows where I've been. There's no such thing as a secret in this town. Everybody knows everybody else's business," she said ruefully.

"When people asked me about it, I just told them you were visiting friends for a while."

She smiled at me and patted me lightly on my arm.

"You're so sweet," she said. "What have you been up to while I was away? Why don't you come inside for some lemonade? I've got a huge pitcher already made. We can catch up on things. Okay?"

"Sure, Martha, we can do that," I said as she hooked her right arm around my left to walk her back to the house. I looked down at her, and I could smell a delicate perfume instead the rank stink of gin. She not only looked at lot better, she smelled better, too.

Together, we climbed the porch steps and went into the living room. Once inside, she told me to make myself comfortable on the couch while she went to fetch the drinks. As I watched her walk away toward the kitchen, I noticed a new bounce in her step that I had never seen before. She was obviously much happier now than before she went to the clinic.

When she returned with tall glasses of lemonade in each hand, I noticed a slight tremble in her hand as she handed me the glass. I decided not to comment on the tremor. Maybe she was wired from being back home.

"Yes, I've still got a little bit of the shakes," she said, looking directly in my eyes. "The doctor said it would take a while for me to get used to not being drunk."

"Do you want to tell me about your stay or would you rather talk about something else?"

"Let's talk about you first. Then I'll tell you about my trip. What's been going on in your life while you weren't driving an old woman around?"

"Come on, Martha, you're not old. Heck, you had Kat when you were only sixteen. Now you two look more like sisters than mother and daughter," I said with a wink.

She blushed again, this time covering her mouth to stifle a giggle.

"You, Doug, have become a silver-tongued devil while I was away. Have you been sweeping young girls off their feet?" she asked.

It was my turn to blush. "No. Mainly just sweeping floors. I'm having enough trouble figuring out the opposite sex."

"Well, take it from me, you won't have any trouble at all," she said as she sat her glass on a coaster on the coffee table in front of us.

"I guess you won't be needing a chauffeur any more, huh? Now that you're all better and everything," I said hoping she would not agree.

"Are you kidding? I had my license taken away from me by the magistrate last year. The reason Sam didn't take care of it was because he was afraid I was going to kill somebody. That's when he decided on this driver business for us both."

"Oh. Damn, I've taken a part time job at Kauffman's store as a candy guy. I'll be working from four until eight on Thursday through Sunday," I told her.

"Klaus Kauffman? That old bastard? He'll try to work you to death just like every one of the young men that go to work for him. Can't you quit?"

"I told him that I'd be at work tomorrow. I can't back out on my word. That wouldn't be right. My dad always told me that you have to keep your word. It's the right thing to do," I explained to her.

"Well, your father is right. You have to keep your word, but when you decide to leave, you can still be my driver. I'm not going anywhere for a while," she said with a smile.

"So, you want to tell me about the clinic? Did they teach you how to drink less?"

"The doctor told me that I shouldn't drink at all anymore. He said that alcohol in moderation is fine, but I was the kind of person who tended to overdo things. I can't recall all those medical terms they use. Something about compulsion or something. He even told me to see about going to Alcoholics Anonymous, but that's not for me. I don't want to be seen with those kinds of people. I didn't pull myself out of any gutter like most of them, I'm just a heavy drinker who needs to show a little more control."

Nodding my head in agreement, I asked, "What's Sam had to say about all of this? By the way, where is he?"

She turned and looked away from me before answering. "He's out with some of his drinking buddies. I don't know, but I get the impression that it makes him nervous when I'm not drinking. When he came to pick me up at the rehab center, that's what they call this place, he wasn't in a very talkative mood. I know that this has been real hard on him. Me being gone and all."

She looked up at me with the beginnings of sadness creeping into her eyes. I draped my right arm across the back of the couch, and she snuggled closer to me and leaned her head onto my chest. I placed my arm around her and patted her gently.

"Is there something wrong?" I asked.

"I don't know," she replied. "He just seems sort of distant. When he came to pick me up, I told you he acted kind of moody. Well, on the trip back home, he never said a word. Just kept sipping on his beer and looking straight ahead. He gets that way sometimes so I didn't pay too much attention."

"Has he asked you anything about what they did at the clinic?"

"No. He's been to it before about four years ago. For about a year after that, he was pretty careful about his drinking, but I guess, over time, he forgot what they told him. I kept a journal and took notes so I could remember some of the things they said."

I replied, "That's pretty smart of you, Martha. You ought to be proud."

She just laughed and looked up at me briefly before saying, "Now there's something nobody has ever said about me before."

"What's that?"

"Saying I was smart. Sam always said if he'd wanted a smart woman, he'd a married a schoolteacher or something."

I didn't respond, although I had the feeling that Sam wasn't too sharp for saying something like that to his wife.

"Anyway," she continued, "when we got back home, he gave me a present. I opened the package and saw that it was a beautiful cut glass goblet. I was just flabbergasted. Then he told me that it was my 'one-drink-a-day glass.' He said that I could have one gin-and tonic every night before dinner, and then I was to wash the glass and put it away. That way I could control my drinking. He's so thoughtful that way."

"That sounds like a pretty good plan to me," I responded.

"I told him how much I appreciated his thoughtfulness but that I'd better hold off on the sauce for a while until I got my land-legs back. After I said that, he told me he was going to see some of his buddies. Then he left. It was like he didn't want to be around me even though I'd been gone for almost a month."

We were both silent, hearing only the ticking of the clock on the mantle.

She looked up to me with tears welling up in her eyes. I hugged her a little closer, and she leaned up and kissed me. It wasn't a gentle 'thank you' kiss, but a kiss that was full of longing and desperation. I'd never been kissed with such fervor before, and I was getting very aroused. When we both finally came up for air, we stared directly into each other eyes as if to say to each other that this was going somewhere neither of us has been before.

She stood up from the couch and held out her hand to me. I looked at her face and saw that her lipstick was smeared like a badly made-up clown. Both of us breathing deeply, I stood, took her outstretched hand, and together we moved toward her bedroom.

Hearing a door slam in the kitchen, we both turned in the direction of the sound to see Kat staring at us with a look of anger and disappointment on her face. The three of us were motionless, frozen in time. Kat's arms hung limply at her sides, until she covered her face with her hands.

"Kat, honey, you don't..." Martha started to say when Kat let out a long pitiful cry and wheeled around, heading back out the kitchen door.

Martha stopped suddenly and hung her head slowly. Outside, we could Kat rev her engine loudly before tearing out of the driveway, showering the side of the house with gravel.

Martha turned to look at me with a sadness that I had never seen before.

"I'd better go," I said, wanting to awaken from this nightmare.

Martha simply nodded her head numbly, her eyes staring off to a point only she could see.

I turned, walked out of the house, jogged down her yard and onto the road leading to my place. As I jogged along the road, the sudden realization that Kat might tell Sam caused me to stop dead in my tracks. That drunken fool might find me and kill me. A chill ran down my spine, although my thoughts caused a feverish sweat to break out on my forehead. For a moment, I thought I was going to throw up. Things had gotten badly out of hand.

When I got back home, I ran into the house, up the stairs and sat down on the edge of my bed. Larry was in his room and came out when he heard me come in. He had a glass of coke in his hand and was studying me.

"What's going down, man? You look like you've seen a ghost," he said as he continued to stare at me. "Let me fix you a bourbon and coke. You look like a guy who needs a real, strong drink."

I didn't respond but took the glass from him when he returned from his room. I downed about half of the drink, shuddered and lit a cigarette.

"You want to tell me what happened?"

I looked up at him and told him to sit down for a minute. I poured the whole story out while Larry listened intently, never interrupting me once. When I was through, I finished off my drink and handed him my glass indicating that I wanted a refill. He quickly obliged and returned with my drink.

"What in the world are you gonna do, man?" he asked.

"Shit if I know."

"Maybe Kat won't tell her old man. Maybe she'll be too embarrassed or something," he offered in support.

I replied, "She hates me. She wants to see me dead."

"You know that for a fact? Maybe it's her mom that she's mad at. Maybe she thinks her mother seduced you or something. After all, Martha is old enough to be your mother."

"Just quit being so goddamn helpful, will you? I'm in fear of my life."

I lit another cigarette and hung my head. "This whole thing has gotten out of hand in the worst kind of way. Maybe I should call my parents and tell them to come and get me. Tell them the restaurant is closing or something. Shit. My mother would never believe that. I'm dead meat."

"You don't know that for sure," said Larry, trying to be helpful. "Besides, did anything really happen?"

"Well…no. But something was sure as hell about to happen. I mean, shit, the next step would have been to get naked."

"But you both had your clothes on didn't you?" Larry asked.

"Yeah…but…"

"But nothing, you dumb ass. For all that occurred, you both could have been working in a coloring book together."

"Yeah, that would explain the red smears all over our mouths," I replied sarcastically.

"Oh," Larry replied with a puzzled look on his face.

"See what I mean. Kat is going to run to Sam and tell him that Martha and I were getting ready to do it. I'm not gonna get laid, but I'm sure as hell gonna get fucked," I said miserably.

When I looked up at Larry, he was trying to control a spasm of laughter.

"What's so goddamn funny?"

The burst of his laughter burst forth like a cannon going off. Bending over at the waist, he attempted to say, "That… last… thing… you… said…about getting…FUCKED." Another volley of howling convulsed him causing him to spill some of his drink.

"You bastard," I said sullenly.

Finally, I couldn't help myself. His amusement was contagious. After I replayed my words in my head, I slowly began to chuckle, too.

Before long, I was bleating just like he was; each of us with tears rolling down our faces.

In minutes, we both fell silent.

"Look," Larry said, "I don't think you've got all that much to worry about. First, Kat has to be happy that her mother is back home from that dry-out place. Second, nothing really happened except that you and Martha obviously tried to swallow each other's faces. And third…well…I don't really think Sam gives a big shit about anything but his buddies and booze. He's already ignored her for some time. I bet that's why she started to drink so much."

"You know," I said, "that makes a lot of sense. That old bastard practically deserted poor old Martha. What the hell does he expect? He should be paying more attention to her instead of trying to drink the state dry. Screw him. Martha's too good for him anyway. The bastard deserves just what he gets. If he comes looking for me, I'll tell him that very thing, too."

Now I was morally outraged over Martha's situation. Even somebody like her deserves to get laid once in a while. I was just going to do her a favor. Sort of like physical therapy or something. Medicinal. Yeah, a medicinal fuck. I was simply offering my services like any doctor or psychiatrist would do.

Feeling much better now that I had applied some clear logic to my problem, I suggested to Larry that we go get a hamburger or something.

"Count me in man. I didn't want to get all plastered tonight anyway. Where do you want to go? I'm hungry enough to eat a dead dog's dick," Larry said as he started for the top of the stairs.

"You are so colorful in your descriptions. Where'd you hear that one?" I asked him.

"Old man Cummins. Where else?"

By the time we got to the main drag, we were too hungry to even discuss a choice of restaurants so we went into the first place we saw that didn't look like a tourist stop. Raymond's Sandwich Shop. Perfect. It was a small, cozy place that catered to the locals and where you could find the biggest ham sandwiches anywhere. Larry and I slid into a booth, and Raymond's only waitress, Lana, came over to take our order.

Temporarily bringing to a halt the powerful and determined effort she was putting into her chewing gum, she asked, "What yawl want?" She wasn't even looking at us.

"Well, Lana, aren't you a vision of beauty and warmth, this fair evening? I hope things are well on the home front," I said to her with a big smile on my face.

Larry was trying his best to keep a straight face.

She turned her face in my direction with a look that would stop a train. "Lissen, you little smart-ass bastard, my personal life ain't one damn bit of yore bidness. So, just tell me what you two little fags want to eat, and maybe I'll serve it to you without spittin' in it."

I loved this woman.

"Two ham sandwiches with fries and coleslaw, my good lady," I said in my most courteous manner.

"Anything to drink with that?" She asked sullenly.

"Two of your largest cokes, madam."

"Fuck both youins," she spat as she wheeled away with our order.

I looked at Larry. "How would you like to wake up next to that every morning?"

"Why the hell did you want to antagonize her for? She might really spit into our food," Larry said as he peeked in her direction. "If I've told you once, I've told you a hundred times, don't piss people off with your smart-ass mouth."

"I like going right up to the edge of the water, if you know what I mean." I countered smugly.

"Shit. One of these days you're gonna drowned," Larry said as he leaned back against the wall and stretched his legs out to the edge of the booth.

Lana returned with our cokes, some napkins and utensils. She wordlessly slung them in front of us, causing my fork to fall in my lap.

"Jesus, Lana, you almost castrated me," I announced dramatically.

"Good. I hope youins never breed," she replied and wheeled away.

I really, really loved this woman. No matter how bad you felt, you knew you had to feel better than that old bitch. She was at war with life.

Larry and I sat lost in our own thoughts until our food came. Lana, being Lana, slammed the plates down on the table and walked off without a word, chewing on her gum like it was a piece of leather that she was attempting to liquefy.

Between mouthfuls of food, Larry and I revisited my options about the recent domestic developments and concluded that the whole Ronson family was so screwed up that one more thing was nothing more than another gnat on a dog's ass. Larry was obviously fixated on canine privates.

We both finished eating at a pace that would have gotten us banned from the dinner table had we been at home. That was one of the nice things about being on your own. When you were eating in a cheap bucket of blood like Raymond's, you checked your manners at the door. We both belched loudly, adding to the ambiance of the establishment, and went to the register to pay our tabs. Again, Lana treated us with her typical hostility and never tried to charm us with the often-used southern expression, "yawl come back real soon, yah hear?"

When we reached the sidewalk, the tourists were doing their ritual march up and down Main Street. Because we were both exhausted, we agreed to head back to the house and call it a day. It had been a day for me, and I hoped I would never see one like this again.

Chapter Twenty One

When I arose the next morning, I felt better than I had in days. I suppose the previous days' activities, if they can be called that, were nothing more than a bad dream. Except for the fact that it all really happened.

While I was shaving, I began to think about all of the things that I had experienced in the past several weeks. When I went down the list, butterflies of excitement awoke in my stomach. Hell, a few weeks ago I was just another high school jerk from a small town in Tennessee with nothing better to do than drive around in an old Ford in a vain attempt to score with just about any female with a pulse. Not that I had enjoyed such luck so far, but I had opened a lot of doors in my life through which I had crawled, walked, stumbled or wandered, depending upon what was on the other side of the door. I felt older, and it was a good feeling. When I thought of my buddies back home, I sort of pitied them for some strange reason. They hadn't done what I had done so I was one up on them. Anyway, I sure had a better understanding about the true nature of people now than when I first arrived. Survival of the fittest was an apt description. If you weren't a predator, you were the prey. An important survival tactic that I had discovered meant never getting too close to anyone. That way, you'll never be the one who gets hurt.

When I got to work, I tried to read the faces of the people I worked with to see if I could tell if they knew anything about the incident at Martha's place yesterday. Nothing seemed out of the ordinary, which left me with a sigh of relief. In fact, most of the talk was about this weekend and the fact that the fourth of July came on Monday this year. The Fourth and Labor Day were the two biggest summer holidays for business, and everybody made money. Unless, of course, you were a busboy. You couldn't even get a piss break, much less time for something to eat, because the waiters and waitresses needed the tables cleaned as fast as the diners stood up. This was according to both Julie and Lois who had been reminding everybody of their duties for the last three days.

Today was my first day to report to work for old man Kauffman. Once again, I proved that my approach to earning money was becoming obsessive. Work at the restaurant like a Tasmanian devil and then report to the candy dungeon for more pain. I was in agony over the prospects for the weekend. The only bright spot was the plans for a beer bust on the evening of the Fourth. That's when we were going to fuck with old Money Dick and his prissy, asshole buddies. That was something to raise my spirits.

When I looked up from my coffee, I saw Lois heading my way with a frown creasing her brow. I glanced at my watch and saw that we would be open for another twenty minutes or so.

"What's wrong? You look sort of pissed about something," I volunteered.

"First, try to avoid using the word 'pissed' to describe irritation or anger. Secondly, that moron, Tubby, called in sick this morning. He did the very same thing on Memorial Day weekend. Somebody is telling him when to call in sick I guess. That's what happens when you have to hire the son of one of Sam's friends. You end up with a retard like that."

I feigned disbelief and asked, "How can you refer to a mentally handicapped person as a 'moron' and a 'retard' like that?"

Lois blushed while she stared at me for a moment. Finally, when I burst out laughing, she joined me, almost doubling over with spasms of giggling. A couple of minutes passed before we could carry on a reasonable conversation.

"Don't worry, Lois, I can pick up the pace. Everything will be alright," I said.

"I appreciate that, Doug, but you've never been here on the Fourth before. We get overrun from the time we open until the time we close. The restaurant will easily do twenty to thirty percent more business than we do on a normal summer weekend. Especially since the Fourth is on a Monday this year. It may even be twice as busy as usual."

"So? Ask everybody to pitch in a little," I replied.

Lois said, "I'll help you as much as I can. The next time you see your friend, Tubby, land a good one right on his nose."

I stubbed out my cigarette, picked up my empty coffee cup and went into the kitchen to gather my tools to go to work. I took a clean towel from the linen shelf and sprayed it with ammonia to use when I wiped down the tables. I grabbed an empty gray tub and headed out to the prep area to joke around with the morning crew before we met the first wave.

When we opened at six-thirty, it was like opening the floodgates. I guess people wanted to get an early start on the weekend, and a big breakfast was the first thing on their agenda. The next thing that I knew, the evening shift people were drifting in. The hours between six thirty and two thirty went by in a flash. I was soaked in sweat and my pants were wet from all of the wet dishes I had handled. I would have probably worked until dark had I not seen Paul walk into the dining room from the kitchen so he could view the chaos. The whole day had been a blur for me.

"Man, you look beat," observed Paul.

"Yeah, and I have to work at the fudge shop tonight," I responded.

"Christ, you ain't gonna make it. That fudge shop is nothing but hard labor."

"Thanks."

I left Paul and went to the back stockroom to rest and have a smoke. When I sat down on a case of canned goods and lit up, I realized just how tired I really was. My options were limited, too. I could just not show up for work, or I could suck it up and make the best of it. If I didn't show up…hell, that was no option.

I stood up and headed out the back door. I had just ground out my cigarette when I heard Martha call my name.

"Doug. Doug, come here. I need to talk to you for a minute," she said from her chair by the pool.

My blood turned to ice. Great. What was she going to do now? Tell me that Sam was looking for me with the biggest pistol in the county, probably. I marched over to her side like a man going to hear the final verdict on his life. Madam Foreman, the verdict please.

"You're not going to believe what happened?" She gushed.

"I probably won't, but don't let that stop you," I said morosely.

"After you left, I sat down on the couch for a good, long cry. I must have sat there for a couple of hours when I heard Kat's car pull into the driveway. When she came in, I started to apologize to her when she started off the conversation by telling me she understood. She said that I was probably starved for affection and was turning to the only person who had treated me with any kindness for the last several weeks."

"You mean she isn't going to tell Sam?" I asked incredulously.

"No, silly. She just told me not to tempt eligible guys her age. She even said I was robbing the cradle. We ended up talking almost all night in a real mother-daughter way. Actually, we even had a good laugh about the whole situation."

"Yeah, I guess, that's great."

I felt very awkward talking to Martha about that situation because I took the whole thing a little more seriously than she did. In a way, my feelings were a little bruised, but I didn't say anything.

"Well, it's been good talking to you, Martha, but I've got to run. I've got that part-time job a Kauffman's, and I don't want to be late on my first day."

"Kauffman," she spat. "Won't you reconsider that?"

"I needed the income, since I lost my job as your driver. And you obviously don't need one now. Besides, the work will do me good in August when football practice starts."

She stared at me for a minute before saying, "If it doesn't work out, you come and see me. Will you do that?"

"What about Kat? I bet she would like to see me dead," I said.

"Not on your life. Why, I think she was a little jealous. I think she's got a crush on you," she said with a wink.

Nothing like cutting a huge swath through Sam's whole family, I thought to myself. If Sam ever killed me, I'd deserve it. However, I had the feeling that those two girls were gonna keep secrets from old Sam. Man, I chuckled to myself, that was that old bastard's problem. It sure as hell wasn't mine.

When I got back to the house, I grabbed my toilet kit and ran back down to the bathroom. I figured even a short bath might rejuvenate me a little. After I had donned a pair of shorts and a tee shirt, I ran down the stairs and out the front porch.

"Where you goin' in such a all-fired hurry? Gonna get some pussy?"

Mr. Cummins was grinning at me and watching me closely with his watery eyes.

"Got a part-time job at Kauffman's. Can't be late," I said as I jumped off the porch onto the dusty ground that he called his yard.

"Hee-hee, boy. That old bastard's gonna work yore no-good ass off and that's a fact," Mr. Cummins said gleefully.

The opinion polls were definitely working against my survival.

"Good way to get into shape," I yelled back at him as I jogged away.

He said something else that I couldn't really hear, but it must have been a real bell-ringer. He was laughing so hard, I thought he'd fall off his rocking throne. Old drunken bastard.

I got to Kauffman's about the time one of the other guys was taking out a large bag of garbage. Under his cap was a head of blonde hair held beneath a white paper cap. The guy was about my height but was definitely in good shape. Now I remembered another reason for taking this job: to get in that kind of physical condition. He stopped for a minute after he had deposited the trash and grinned at me.

"You the new slave? Hi," he said as he stuck out his hand. "My name's Gene."

"Doug," I said as I shook his hand. "Good to meet you, Gene."

"You might be sorry you ever took this fuckin" job. Old man Kauffman's my uncle so I have to work for the old bastard. He's my old man's brother. Dad told me if I could work a whole summer at this place, he'd buy me a brand new car to drive to school. I may not live that long. What's your deal?"

"Need the money for college," I answered.

"Take my advice and go rob a gas station. Working on a chain gang couldn't be as bad as this," he said as he reached for a cigarette.

He held the pack in my direction, but I shook my head and told him thanks.

"Good luck and welcome to hell."

"It's been great talking to you," I replied sarcastically.

"Yeah. No problem."

I knew then that I was dealing with a real dim bulb. If that kind of sarcasm went over this loser's head, I hope his dad bought him a Nash Rambler. Jerk.

When I got inside, Kauffman walked over to me quickly and took me by my arm. At first I thought he was going to throw me out before I ever got started.

"Goot. You hurry and put on dem clothes I give to you. To wear. Not to keep. Change out of those clothes you got on and put dees on. Okay?"

"Sure, Mr. Kauffman."

I put on the stupid white pants, the white tee shirt, the white apron and finally the white paper cap. I was sure that I looked about as foolish as a person could look on any other day than Halloween. "Man," I thought, "the things we do for money."

I walked into the kitchen area and heard him yelling for Gene. There were two other guys toiling away in front of a large copper bowl that must have measured two feet across the top. Actually, there was one guy working and another guy watching. Sort of like those guys who work on roads and highways.

Gene came running in from the back and Mr. Kauffman yelled at him for being lazy. Gene looked at me with a see-what-I-mean look on his face.

"You show him what to do. And show him right with no fucks up. Okay?"

"Sure thing, Unc," replied Gene. "No fucks up."

Gene looked at me and winked.

"Don't call me Unc. You call me Mr. Kauffman at work," he said as he trundled away.

"Can you dance?" Gene asked me.

"What is that supposed to mean?" I responded.

"Have you got rhythm like the niggers do? You gotta have rhythm to do this job right."

"You're not in the Klan are you?" I asked Gene.

"No. Why do you ask?"

"No reason."

Just another redneck hillbilly. I was sure my mother was right about a Negro's work ethic. If we had more people that worked as hard as most of the Negroes I had met, this country would be in better shape. I hated hillbilly rednecks. They were the very reason that people up north made fun of people in the south. Saying we were stupid and inbred and God only knows what else. As long as people in the south had guys like Gene representing us, we would never receive the respect that real southern people deserved. Then again I was unaware of the kind of racism that went on in the North. I surely hoped guys like Gene were in a dwindling minority.

Gene introduced me to the two other guys who merely nodded their heads in my direction. One was using a large wooden paddle that looked like a small camp shovel. With one hand on the top of the handle and the other hand down near the handle's base, he was raking the fudge in the large cooper bowl in rapid continuous movement as if he were about to rake the fudge out of the bowl onto his mid-section. Dripping with sweat as he worked his arms like pistons, he seemed oblivious to his surroundings as he stirred what appeared to be about ten pounds of the thick, dark, chocolate goo. Meanwhile his partner stood closely to the left of the paddle man. Finally, the guy watching put his right hand on the top hand of his partner and his left at the base of the of the handle. When they were both moving a perfect unison, the relief guy hollered, "go." The sweating fudge-beater stepped aside, giving way to his partner.

"You see how they do that? We gotta do it the same way," Gene explained.

"How long does it take to finish a batch?" I asked.

"About fifteen to twenty minutes or until Mr. Lard Ass comes over and sticks one of his fat fingers into the fudge and tastes it. Then you scoop the whole mess out of the bowl onto a large tray. That's when Mrs. Lard Ass comes over and gets the tray to spread it out evenly for cutting. Without a break, the boss comes over with a new batch in one of those bowls, takes the old one away to wash it, and sets the new one down in front of you. Sounds like fun, huh?"

"What keeps the people outside from seeing all that sweat dripping into the fudge?"

"Those big windows have a special tint on them. It helps keep the sun from heating up the bowls and offers enough of a shadow to keep the tourists from gagging," Gene said with a giggle.

About that time, Kauffman came over carrying a large bowl and asked, "You got training now? You ready to make fudge? Okay, goot."

He the set the bowl down on the stand in front of us and told us to go to work. Gene started first, attacking the fudge with a vengeance. After a couple of minutes passed, he looked at me and waved his head in the direction of the paddle. I stepped in close and positioned my hands next to his as I had seen the other pair work. When we were in sync, Gene yelled, "Go." I grabbed the paddle and began working the fudge. I was slow and awkward at first, but the longer I paddled, the smoother my rhythm became. In no time at all, I could feel a burning sensation in my arms, shoulders and back, and the sweat started to gush from my pores. Soon, Gene appeared at my left side and began placing his hands over mine to match my rhythm. This repetitious dance continued for an hour, before Kauffman told us to take a five-minute break.

The four of us leaned against anything that would keep us standing while we waited for Kauffman to come over with another load of candy. I was too tired to talk and still had three hours to go. One of the other guys looked at me and asked me how I liked it.

"So far, so good," I answered with a nod.

"I'll ask you that again when you get off," he replied without looking at me.

In less than our allotted five minutes, Kauffman returned holding two more bowls of fudge in his arms looking like a woman carrying two infants in her arms.

"More goot candy," he fairly shouted with a broad smile and placed the bowls on their stands. "Now, get to work before candy starts to set." He wheeled away leaving a pair of twin bowls staring at us.

"Let's hit it guys," said Gene.

My next idea was intended to help us get motivated but ended with disastrous results.

"Why don't we race?" I asked as I looked at the other guys.

They looked at me for a few seconds before one of them asked, "What do you mean by race?"

"Let's have a contest to see who gets their fudge done first. Put old lady Kauffman into high gear for a change. What do you think?"

Gene shrugged and said, "Good idea. Losers have to buy the winners a six-pack."

"You're on," replied one of the other team members.

With that, we attacked the bowls. There was a crowd gathering out in front of the window, so that sort of spurred us one to greater efforts. Beating and switching. Beating and switching. Over and over and over. The people outside were fascinated by the choreographic dance in which we were so deeply involved, and I could see them applaud us. As the competitive juices began to flow, the beating came harder and faster.

At one point, I glanced over to the guy working the other bowl and saw that he was moving like a finely tuned machine. I took that as a challenge and began to go after my fudge pile with renewed effort. My strokes became longer and harder until I felt as though I had become more machine than human. Finally, I hit the accelerator and moved into high gear.

That was my downfall. With one strong stroke, I was able to empty the contents of the bowl by splattering myself from my chin to my knees in thick, dark chocolate. I momentarily froze while the crowd outside was convulsed in laughter. Gene brought me out of my shock by grabbing my shoulder and yelling for me to run. And run I did. I headed for the back for my clothes when I heard old man Kauffman screaming in both English and German. Without stopping to change, I grabbed my shorts and tee shirt and ran out the back.

My career in the candy business was over. Abruptly.

When I got back to the house, I took off my sweaty white clothes and stuffed them into a paper sack. I would drop them off tomorrow afternoon after work, maybe just walk by the front door and toss them in. Plus, there was no point in asking for whatever pay I had earned, because I had already destroyed about ten pounds of candy. Hell, he'd probably demand money from me for damages. No matter, I hated that fuckin' job anyway.

When I got back to the house, I decided to take a bath and stay in for the night. After I had cleaned up, I remembered that I hadn't eaten all day. So I set out for the downtown area to try to find something I could take back to my room. I found a small odds and ends store that carried film, postcards, and other junk and had a cooler in the back with cold drinks. As I reached into the cooler to pull out a coke I realized that my arms did not want to move any higher than my waist. The burning agony in my arms and shoulders was almost too much to bear. I finally succeeded in lifting my right arm with my left arm to try to reach to cokes. Since they were on a higher shelf, I had to settle for Pepsi's. After I got them out, I stuck one under each arm, hoping that I could manage to round up something to eat. I took my drinks over to the cashier, and with enormous effort, put them on the counter.

"I'll be right back," I told her as she looked at me in a funny way.

I got two packages of beef jerky, a bag of potato chips and three packages of Twinkies. Picking out items on the shelves that came to about waist-high, it took three trips to the counter to carry my stuff to be checked out. In my judgment, my selections rounded out a pretty sound meal of meat, vegetables and a light dessert.

"Is there sumpin' wrong with you, buddy?" The cashier asked me.

"I got hit by a car about an hour ago," I lied.

"Well why the hell didn't you go to the doctor?"

"It was a real small car."

"Oh," she said with a puzzled look on her face.

I paid for my stuff and waited as the cashier bagged it when my attention was drawn to a couple behind me who arguing over where they should go to eat dinner. I turned around and, trying to be helpful suggested the M&S restaurant up the street about four blocks. They both stopped and looked at me in utter silence. The woman, who appeared to be in her mid-forties, had a beehive hairdo, lots of bracelets and about a pound of lipstick on told me to "mind my own fuckin' business." The odor of gin she sprayed in my face reminded me of Martha. Although I was somewhat stunned by her rudeness, I just shrugged and turned around. I also noticed that the crowded shop was totally silent and staring at the woman behind me. I could see her reflection in the glass behind the cashier, and I watched her look around then grab her husband's arm and pull him out of the store. I hoped a truck would hit the stupid bitch. A large, fast-moving tractor-trailer rig. In front of her kids if she had any. Playing the scene in my head brought a grin to my face that was noticed by the cashier.

"You're not mad at that crazy, drunken bitch?" She asked in disbelief.

I just shrugged and replied, "Probably from Ohio. What are you gonna do?"

"Yeah," she said shaking her head. "Ohio."

She handed me my bag of goodies, and I headed back to the house. This food and a paperback book were the only companions I wanted tonight. I was pretty much burned out on people for one day.

Chapter Twenty Two

The days continued to roll on in a blur of tourists, late nights, flirting with Julie and work. More work than anything else.

I put in two consecutive ten-hour days on Saturday and Sunday because we were so slammed with customers. Tubby never showed up so I was pretty exhausted by the time I got off work in the late afternoon. My nights were comprised of eating a sandwich in bed and falling asleep with a book on my chest. It was boring, but I ended up getting some much-needed rest. Tubby finally showed up on Monday claiming he had had a stomach problem. He had a stomach problem all right. There was too damn much of it.

Larry and I had time to sit down and have a quick bite in the back stockroom and lay out our plans for the beer bust.

"Lonnie told me not to steal any beer for our deal. He said he knew a guy with a fake ID who would get it for us. Lonnie said to take up a collection and pay for the beer just like everyone else. I told him he was being a jerk, and he told me I was being a thief," Larry grumbled to me.

"Well, he's right you know," I countered.

"I know, I just hate to pay for something that's so ripe for the taking. Besides, the Ronsons have got plenty of money. They'd never miss it anyway. They're just rich people who don't give a damn anyway. People like that should share more with others who don't have as much."

"By that logic, you're saying that anybody that has worked their ass off to make a living should feel guilty and give some of their money to others?"

"Well...yeah," Larry countered defiantly.

"That kind of thinking will never fly in the good old US of A," I responded.

"Why the hell not? Don't you give a damn about the less fortunate in society?"

"What you're describing is already in practice in Russia. It's called the redistribution of wealth. In a word: Communism. I learned about it in history class."

Larry looked up at me for a second then grinned and lifted his middle finger as a salute to my observation.

"Up yours," he said.

We then ate our lunch quickly and went back to finish our shift.

When we got off work, we headed back home, jogging most of the way. By the time we got to the Cummins place, I was puffing like some old locomotive. I decided that I'd better start getting into some kind of shape before August or I was going to die at football practice. Maybe I should cut back on the smoking some, too. Hell, maybe I should just quit football. Who needs that shit?

We went upstairs to wait on Lonnie, as he did not get off work until four o'clock. Jungle Jim said he wanted to go with us because he didn't like Money Dick or his shitty friends once he got to know them. He said they were stuck-up as hell. We both welcomed him back into the fold and told him to ante-up some money for beer.

The four of us piled into Jim's '54 Ford, and Lonnie directed him to drive over to an Esso station just off Main on Pine Drive. When we pulled into the station, a skinny, rawboned guy with red hair ambled slowly toward the car, wiping his grease-covered hands with an equally grease-covered rag. Lonnie got out and approached him as the attendant shoved the rag into his back pocket and shifted his toothpick around in his mouth.

"How you doin', Red?"

"Fair. You want me to git you and your buddies some beer?"

"Yeah. You gonna charge me a fee for your services?" asked Lonnie.

"One six-pack is all," Red answered laconically.

"Well, I reckon that's a fair deal," said Lonnie, handing Red enough money for two cases of beer. He also gave him an extra two dollars to buy himself a six-pack.

Red took the money and said, "Be right back."

Jungle Jim had thought ahead and put some wax-lined boxes in the trunk of his car for the beer. The restaurant where he worked received frozen meat in them, so we stopped and took some out of the stockroom. He also got a package of hamburger buns and a package of hamburger patties all ready for grilling. We didn't have a grill, but he said we could go to Wilson's Grocery to get mustard, plates, charcoal and other stuff and he'd steal one from the forty or so they had on display out in front of the store. It sounded pretty foolproof, and it was. I guess anybody that saw him just figured that he'd already paid for it inside. At least anyone who saw him was half right. We'd bought several bags of ice that we dumped into the boxes that held the beer, the meat, and other stuff that needed to be kept cold.

After putting a couple of six-packs in the car, we headed off to what was called "The Sinks." It was supposed to be a sinkhole in the river that was over sixty feet deep. There was also plenty of parking in the area, and we'd heard Money Dick telling his buddies about what a great spot it was.

The drive to The Sinks only took about thirty minutes, enough time for the four of us to drink the twelve beers we had. When we got there, Money and his prissy friends had already set up a nice little area with a large charcoal grill, a huge cooler full of beer and enough fried chicken and fixins to feed a small country. Since they had gotten there ahead of us, they were feeling no pain and were pretty loud as well.

They quieted down momentarily when they saw us pull up. Lonnie got out of the car with a baleful look on his face and stared at them. It seemed to make them self-conscious for a minute, then they returned to their horseplay. They decided the best thing to do was ignore us. That was fine with the four of us because we'd had just enough beer to make us surly at the sight of Money and his friends.

Larry and I helped Jim take the food and beer out of the trunk and set it up on a picnic table not far from the other guys' table. Jim noticed that someone had previously built a fire within a small circle of rocks, so instead of putting the grill together, he simply laid the wire rack on top of the circle of rocks to see if it would fit.

"Ha," he yelled in discovery. "A perfect fit. We won't be needing this anymore."

He took the box containing the rest of the grill parts and dumped it into a large garbage can. He set about dumping charcoal into his rock pit, soaking each and every briquette with lighter fluid. As a matter of fact, he used almost all of the fluid in the can.

"Stand back, men. She's gonna blow," he warned dramatically.

Since I had been watching his fire-starting procedure, I took a position on the other side of his car, a good twenty feet from the pile of dripping charcoal. I had a pretty fair idea of what was about to happen, but I didn't say anything. I thought the result would be kind of funny.

It was.

When Jim gleefully tossed a lighted match into the charcoal, a huge burst of flames exploded upward with a loud "FOOMP." It was so loud that even Money and his friends looked over in our direction to see what happened. Jungle Jim, the fireman, turned around with a huge smile on his face, unaware that his eyebrows were smoldering. Money's group started laughing hysterically at the sight of Jim's predicament. The three of us were doubled over with laughter, as well.

Finally, Jim looked at us in a funny way and asked, "What?"

Lonnie ran over and led him to the edge of the mountain stream and told him to put out the eyebrow fire. Startled, Jim immediately began splashing the cold water on his face. This called for a new round of beers. With "Green Onions" by Booker T. & the MG's blaring on Jim's transistor radio, I figured that this was about as good as it gets.

While we waited for the coals to burn down, we decided to cool off in the water. Having little interest in freezing to death, I thought the addition of some more beer to my system would allow me to brave the frigid waters. I was amazed when I saw Jim pull off his shirt, climb up on a high rock and do a somersault into the deeper part of the water. When he broke to the surface, he let out a joyful yell.

"Come on in. You'll love it," he cried.

Following that, both Lonnie and Larry dove into the water and came up screaming from the cold. I finished the rest of my beer and stood at the edge of the water, trying to go in slowly rather than suffer the icy shock of the mountain stream. There were some things you just didn't want to dive into and this was one of them. When I got to a point about where the water level was up to my waist, I took a deep breath and completely submerged as fast as I could. When I stood up, I felt as if my heart was going to beat a path out of my chest. Of one thing I was certain: I lost my buzz from the beers I'd had. My whole nervous system was on red alert.

After a few minutes of horseplay, we saw our neighbors getting into the water. None of them dove in as my three partners had done, so Lonnie began asking them where they'd left their bathing caps and if they were going to use the buddy system like they did at camp. Money Dick glared in our direction without saying a word.

The four of us climbed out of the water and sat on large rocks close to the fire to warm up and dry off. We made fun of Jim because he looked like a bear that had just emerged from a fishing expedition. Lonnie tossed everyone a fresh beer and continued firing belittling remarks in the direction of the little rich boys. The words "fag" and "queer" were frequently used in Lonnie's arsenal of insults.

Finally, Money started wading rapidly out of the water and glaring at Lonnie. Thinking that he was going to come over and start something, Lonnie stood up in preparation to tear Dickie-boy a new asshole. Instead, Money began climbing some large rocks toward a point where some of the braver, crazier, drunker swimmers had dived into the water. I had stood up there once just to see what it looked like, staring down at the large sinkhole in the middle of the onrushing water. I suspected it was fairly similar to the view those nutty divers in Acapulco enjoyed. Only this perch was not but about twenty-five feet from the water.

Everyone had stopped what they were doing and riveted their eyes on Money Dick as he scaled the rocks toward the diving point. Once he had gotten to the top, he looked down at us with disdain in his eyes.

Larry and Jim yelled at Money, "Jump you chicken shit."

I didn't say anything, but I looked up at him with a smirk on my face.

Lonnie never said a word. He just looked back at him with a smile on his face and toasted him with his beer.

Money took one more look at the deep pool of water and dove. I guess his adrenaline was really pumping because he came close to overshooting the center of the sinkhole. He splashed headfirst into the water and surfaced very slowly. The expression on everyone's face turned to a look of concern—Money Dick came up in a dead man's float.

"Holy Christ," mumbled Lonnie as he sat straight up.

Dick was obviously unconscious. Being the closest, Lonnie ran into the water to see if Dick was dead or alive. Lonnie gently rolled him over onto his back and held his ear next to his chest. He then looked back at us with eyes as big as saucers, his face dripping water.

"**Goddamn,** somebody call an ambulance. **He's alive**," he screamed. "Somebody needs to get an ambulance even if you have to drive all the way back into town to get one."

"Get moving, for Christ's sake. I'm just gonna hold him in a floating position until the medics get here," the last words he said more to himself than to us.

One of Dick's friends jumped into his VW Beetle and sped away in the direction of town. The rest of us stood around quietly wondering if he was going to be all right. Saying somebody should drop dead and seeing them nearly do it was a harsh taste of reality. In about ten minutes, a forest ranger came tearing down the road with the VW not far behind. We quickly stashed any traces of beer into the trunk, hoping he wouldn't see it.

The ranger stopped his truck and told us he had radioed for an ambulance.

"Is he breathing?" He asked Lonnie.

"Yeah."

"Just keep him steady and try not to move him until the paramedics get here," he said.

The ranger then focused his attention on the rest of us and asked, "What happened here?"

Everybody looked around, mostly staring at the ground. Finally, Lonnie spoke up and said that Dick dove from up there, pointing with his head in the general direction of the ledge.

"I think he hit his head. There's a knot coming up on the top," Lonnie informed the ranger.

He looked around at the group again and asked, "You boys haven't been doing any drinking have you? I'd hate to have to call the sheriff and have him put the whole lot of you in the pokey."

We all responded in unison with a chorus of: "No, no sir."

He looked at each of us again then shook his head.

"I hope that boy is gonna be okay but let this be a lesson to you bastards. Drinkin' will make a person do some real stupid things sometimes. Real stupid," he warned as he eyed us carefully.

We all stood staring at the ground, nervously shifting our weight from one foot to the other. Nobody wanted to say anything. Nobody knew what to say.

In a couple of minutes, an ambulance came roaring into the area with lights flashing and siren screaming. When the driver stopped, he turned off the siren and it wound down with a moan. He and his partner jumped out while the vehicle was still rocking and ran to the rear doors. They slid a stretcher out and grabbed something that looked like an ironing board.

"Hey, Tom," the driver said waving to the ranger. "Got a diver, here?"

"Yeah. Looks like it. Don't know what the damage is."

"Hey," screamed Lonnie, "his eyes are open."

"Don't let him move," yelled the driver's partner.

"Second one this summer," the driver said to no one in particular.

The two medics waded into the water with a small bag and the ironing board. When they got to Dick, Lonnie eased out of the way.

"Can you hear me son? What's your name?" asked the driver.

"RRRRichard," Dick answered shakily. "What happened? I can't feel anything. What's going on? Am I going to be all right? Somebody tell me something."

The driver and his friend looked at each other briefly before the driver told Dick, "Don't be alarmed, son. We're gonna take you to see a doctor and see what's up. We're gonna take real good care of you. Do your parents live in Gatlinburg?"

"No. Knoxville," he said as he rolled his eyes from one medic to the other.

"Well, if you can remember their phone number, we'll give 'em a call. Okay?"

"Yeah. Call my mom," he said trying to hold back the tears.

Jim finally took notice of the Beach Boys singing "Surfin' USA" and quickly turned off his radio. It seemed inappropriate under the circumstances.

Once the medics got Dick strapped onto the ironing board, or whatever it was, one of them went to the ambulance and brought the stretcher over to the edge of the water. He then turned to the group standing around watching and asked, "Can a couple of you guys give us a hand?"

Lonnie was the first one in, and I was second. Dick's "friends" looked like they wanted no part of anything so distasteful as an injury. I wanted to strangle each and every one of those stupid assholes and throw their worthless carcasses into the water.

Gently, following the directions of the paramedics, Lonnie, the ranger and I hoisted Dick out of the water and carried him to the stretcher on the shore. Dick looked at me with tears running down the sides of his face and said quietly, "Thanks."

I could only mouth the words back to him, "You'll be okay."

I had a lump in my throat the size of a grapefruit as they loaded him into the meat wagon, but I refused to allow myself to cry.

Once everything was strapped down, the ambulance crawled onto the highway as Tom held up traffic. The driver hit the accelerator, the siren and the lights as soon as he got on the pavement. In a second, we were left behind with our shock and disbelief. Seeing someone you'd shared a house with get carried away in a speeding ambulance was too much reality to handle. Especially when you felt that you had goaded that person to attempt something just to make a statement about his manhood. It was all such a damn shame, and I was part of it.

There was nothing for any of us to do now but clean up our mess and leave. We were all drawn into our own solitary world of concern and regrets. Jim and I gathered up everything while Lonnie doused the burning coals with water. For finality, he dumped a box of the ice on the coals and threw the box into the garbage. The four of us climbed wordlessly into Jim's car and drove back to town.

When we got back to the Cummins house, Mrs. Cummins had already heard the news from a neighbor who worked at the hospital.

The neighbor had called to say one of her boarders had been injured and the parents had been contacted.

Lonnie asked, "Did she say anything about his condition?"

Mrs. Cummins looked down at the floor and wrung her apron in her wrinkled hands. When she looked back up at us, there were tears in her eyes.

"His neck is broke. They don't know how bad it is though. The doctors is waitin' fer his parents to get there so they can tell them which hospital in Knoxville to take him to."

Without a word, we all turned and went upstairs. Guilt hung on to each of us like a heavy wool coat. It would be ours to wear for quite some time.

As I lay on my bed, I replayed the events of the day in my mind in a vain attempt to see if there was any way of going back and changing things. The problem with reality was that you were stuck with it. Reality wasn't like some football play that you could run four or five times until you got it right. What's done is done. Maybe that's what growing up is all about. The stuff you do as a child or an innocent teenager can be excused as youthful ignorance or "just being a kid." The older you get, the stupid stuff you do is not funny anymore. Then it becomes something you regret or have to carry around with you. Man, life was getting to be heavy. I was starting to think that growing up was not so much like a move upward to adulthood as much as it was a descent into adulthood. Hell, people even phrased it that way. You "travel on **down** the road to the future." I never really heard anybody say "you traveled **up** the road to your future." Maybe there was a reason for that, and you just had to learn it the hard way. If only I knew then what I know now....

There was no music, chatter or laughter up here tonight. I heard a beer being opened by either Larry or his brother but nothing else. I forced myself up into a sitting position and sat with my elbows on my knees for a long time. Thinking.

I finally pushed myself off the bed and padded on my bare feet to Dick's room. Now it was just Jim's room. Jim turned over and looked at me. His eyes were red from crying and he seemed embarrassed by it. I acted as if I hadn't noticed and stood awkwardly in the middle of the room, not wanting to sit on Dick's bed.

Since Jim didn't seem to want to say anything, I said, "Maybe we should check out his stuff before his parents get here. You know…see if he has any Playboys or fuck-books that we should dump. So his parents don't see."

Jim looked at me and let my words hang in the air for a few seconds.

"How thoughtful of you, you fucking ghoul. If you find any money, I guess you'll keep that too, huh?" he said as he looked at me disdainfully.

Blushing, I said, "You're missing my point, man. I'm not planning on stealing anything. It's not like I'm robbing a grave or something. I just don't want his parents to see that kind of stuff if he has any. That's all."

The silence hung in the air between us.

"Yeah," he finally said, "you're probably right. I'd want one of you guys to do the same thing if it were me, laying paralyzed and scared shitless."

We both began to sift slowly through his things to see if there was any damning evidence of wickedness, as the preachers would probably say. After a minute or two of searching, I lifted up his mattress and was startled by what I found. A Bible. He was hiding a damn Bible under his mattress. What the hell was that all about, I wondered?

Then I began to recall the way we acted most of the time. Drinking, smoking, tales of imaginary and real sex. Dirty books and magazines. If a guy was any kind of a Christian or something, he was surely surrounded by sinners. But he kept quiet about it. Never said jack shit to anybody. I guess he figured we'd react with outrage and derision and he would be right. For a moment, I was almost hesitant to pick up the book. For some reason, I felt like I was invading something holy. I finally grabbed it and threw it on the top of the bed covers.

"He used to read it at night by flashlight," said Jim quietly. "I told him he could turn the light on. I said I wouldn't tell any of you guys."

I started to get mad and say something to Jim, but I realized that he was exactly right. We **would** have made fun of him. Probably calling him Reverend Dick and picking on him for reading a sissy Bible. Jim was dead on, and I was stunned with shame. I just studied the boards of the floor, turned wordlessly and walked out of the room.

I walked to the door of Larry's room and looked in. Lonnie was asleep and snoring lightly. Larry was propped up in bed, reading a paperback and sipping from a bottle of Budweiser. He held up his beer and pointed to me with it. I nodded yes, and he retrieved one from the box he had brought in from Jim's car. We both went into my room and sat on the floor.

After taking a sip from my beer, I said, "I feel like shit."

"Why is that?" Larry asked.

"Where the fuck have you been today?" I shot back angrily.

"Whoa, man. Cool it a little," he said as he held his hands palms out in front of him.

I sat and fumed.

"Mind if I offer a little observation on this whole event? Did you see anybody with a gun pointed at his head? Did anyone force him to climb up on those rocks and dive in?" Larry waited for my reaction.

"Somebody should've tried to stop him."

"Are you kidding me? He was going to do what he wanted to do, come hell or high water. There wasn't a damn thing any of us could have done and that's a fact. It was his choice and he has to deal with the consequences," Larry stated firmly.

"That's cold, man."

I took another sip of beer and refused to look at him. I **had** said that, and it had come back to haunt me. He was right. My mother always told me that if you were gonna dance, you had to pay the band.

"I suggest you quit beating yourself up over something that was out of your control. If you live your life trying to control everything, you're in for a real rough ride, man. Think about it. My dad always told me that, and he's right," Larry asserted.

Funny. Now we were beginning to quote our parents. How'd that happen?

I took a long pull on my beer and looked around at my alarm clock to check the time. Ten o'clock. How the hell did it get that late? I suddenly realized that I hadn't eaten, but I was in no mood to go get anything. And I was beat.

I said to Larry, "I'm turning in, man. I'm dead."

"Me too," he said as he slowly stood up. "See you in the morning."

"Yeah. G'night."

"Night, man."

Chapter Twenty Three

When I got to work the next morning, the local radio station had already been broadcasting a story about Dick's accident at the Sinkhole. Lois and Terry were sitting in a booth having a cup of coffee and waved me over when they saw me. I walked over with a cup of coffee and slid in next to Lois. I didn't want to be close enough to Terry to touch her.

"That guy that got hurt, he lived in the house where you do, didn't he?"

I answered Terry while looking at Lois, "Lives. He's not dead, he just moved out."

I took a sip of my coffee.

"Well, excuse me," she said in her snotty way and slipped from the booth, leaving Lois and me sitting there.

"Bitch," I whispered.

Lois said nothing but patted my hand soothingly.

"Was he a good friend of yours?"

"Not good enough," I replied.

She wiped her eyes and blew her nose on her napkin.

"Let's get to work. Starving tourists will be descending upon us any time now," she said, trying to sound cheerful.

I stood up and let her out of the booth. She squeezed my hand once and walked toward the kitchen.

Man, I thought, life is turning into the pits.

The restaurant was still pretty busy several days after the Fourth. A lot of people had tacked on some vacation time to the long weekend in order to get a whole week off. Pretty smart since they only used four days out of whatever they were allotted. My weekend off was coming around again, but I doubted that I would be allowed to take it because we were so busy. I didn't really care. With no car, there was really not much to do anyway. Of course you couldn't tell that by the number of people who crowded the restaurants, motels and attractions. If you called a snake farm an attraction. Maybe they should turn the snake farm into a petting zoo and do permanent psychological damage to all the little no-neck monsters who infested Gatlinburg like a plague of locusts. I wouldn't mind taking a picture of that horror.

Although we were busy, there was enough time for a couple of us to take the time for a quick bite. Usually the waiters and waitresses would wait on customers between bites of food or puffs on a cigarette. I did the same with the table cleaning. Tubby, of course, would have Roy fix him a cheeseburger, and the not-so-stupid retard would take his lunch out back behind the restaurant. He would sit next to the garbage Dumpster and battle the flies for his food. I don't see how he did it. He probably had no sense of smell to go along with his lack of sense about everything else. Except, he did know when to call in sick.

Roy had fixed me steak and eggs. Since I rarely ate much for dinner, I usually had a huge lunch even if I had to stay after I got off work to eat it. Whether or not I got breakfast kind of depended on how I felt that morning because I had never been late for work. Most of the time, I just had coffee and cigarettes. The damn smoking was going to have to go pretty soon. I was dreading two-a-day football practices in the August heat. I bet I would probably look like a coal burning locomotive when I had to run sprints. The coaches would pick up on that real quickly and make me run even more. Sadistic bastards.

I had just finished when Terry walked up to me and asked if she could sit down for a minute.

"Sure. I was just about to leave," I said without looking at her.

"Don't go, Doug," she said plaintively, "I want to ask you something."

"What little surprises have you got up your sleeves now? Will I be able to stop the bleeding or what?"

"Please don't be mad at me. I didn't do it to hurt you," she explained.

"Yeah, yeah. So, what is it you want?"

"Me 'n Roy's gonna have a real small wedding at the Baptist church two weeks from Saturday, and we want you to be one of the ushers."

"Terry," I said quietly.

"Yes?" she asked hopefully.

"Please go fuck yourself."

Her face turned red as fire, and she headed straight for the kitchen.

I didn't really give a damn. I was so miserable from the events of the last week and a half nothing really mattered. This world would be a great place to live if it weren't for the people.

I never wore a watch to work so I never really knew what time it was. The day seemed to go faster if I didn't know the time, and the way I banged the dish tub around, I'd probably break it anyway. I was in the kitchen when Paul came in the back door, putting on his bow tie.

"Man. You should be glad you weren't at the house this morning," he said as he walked over to me.

"Why? What happened?"

He shook his head sadly and said, "Dick's parents came to pick up his stuff. It was real bad. Dick's dad was packing the stuff and his mother was just standing there bawling. I was sort of trapped up there with them so I asked them how he was."

"Yeah. What'd they say?"

"Paralyzed. From the neck down. Won't even be able to feed himself."

"Holy shit."

"Yeah, it's bad."

"Did they act mad or anything? Did they say anything?" I asked Paul.

"Not much. Apparently, Dick told them he was just horsing around with some friends. Didn't say anything about us."

I stared at the floor for a minute. Finally, I said to Paul, "He could have really made us look like the villains in this whole deal, you know. He must have been a better guy than we thought."

There we go again, I thought, talking about him in the past tense as if he were dead. He wasn't dead, damnit. Why couldn't we get it right?

"He's not dead. You are aware of that aren't you?"

"Yeah. Why do you ask?"

"Well, you keep talking about him in the past tense. Everybody is doing that. He is still alive. I just wish people would stop talking about him like some dead guy."

"I'll tell you something, Chief," said Paul as he squeezed one eye closed in a pained expression. "He might as well be dead. As a matter of fact, he'd be better off dead."

I didn't say anything, but I had to agree with him. I sure as hell wouldn't want to be a dead body with a live head. That was the worst kind of prison. A prisoner in your own body. There should be some kind of law that says if a person asks to be put to sleep because life wasn't worth living anymore, they should have their wish granted. Hell, when an animal is terribly sick or in unending pain, they kill it. The animals don't really know what's going on. They just know that they are living in a world of shit and want somebody to make the hurting stop. If you can treat animals that humanely, why couldn't you do people that way? Life is a fucked up way to live, man, cause there's not much help out there.

Julie came striding into the kitchen after making a grand entrance by coming in through the front door of the dining room. She had a solid red cigar dress on. She didn't just come in; she made an entrance. I just wish I could've been out there to watch all the wives watching their husbands watching Julie. I bet the whole room froze in a strange-looking tableau that would've made a great photograph. The Life Magazine people should send some photographer down here to get a few shots of people's reactions to seeing Julie for the first time. Julie knew what was happening and loved it. She reveled in it.

Roy looked over at her and sang out loudly, "**See the girl with the red dress on.**"

And Julie sang back, "**She can do it all night long.**"

Paul and I applauded and yelled, "ALL RIGHT."

With that, Julie took a deep bow, and the three of us took a deep breath. We were all probably thinking the same thing: Whose gonna be the lucky one to catch those babies? However, by some law of physics that I didn't understand, they remained tethered. But this time it was close.

She looked at us, one by one, with a big grin on her face.

"HA. One of these days, you horny bastards are gonna have a heart attack. And, Roy, I'm ashamed of you. You fixin' to get married and all. I'm telling Terry," she said with a wink.

Then she turned her attention to me.

"Dougy, you're as red as my dress. And close your mouth. Flies are gonna get in it," she laughed.

Then she leaned close to me and whispered, "I could just eat you up."

If it hadn't have been for my skin, I would have painted the kitchen walls with hormones. All four walls. Julie flirted with everybody, but I knew that she was singling me out. Even Paul, who heard what she said, was gaping at me with a look of surprise.

Julie then turned and flounced out of the kitchen to make another run on the dining room.

"Man," Paul gasped, "I think she's got the hots for you."

"Hey. She does that to everybody. I **couldn't** get that lucky."

"I don't know man. Maybe she thinks you're rich or something."

"Thanks."

Paul headed out the door laughing as I turned to head for home. About the time I reached the back stockroom, Julie ran up behind me and tapped me on the shoulder. When I turned around, she stuck a small piece of paper into my shirt pocket and held her finger to her lips to indicate that this was to be kept secret. She walked quickly away while I stood there trying to get my heart to stop pounding out of my chest. In a moment, I walked out of the restaurant.

As soon as I got outside and checked to see if anyone was looking, I pulled the scrap of paper from my shirt pocket. On it, Julie had written her phone number with instructions to call her as soon as I could. Now I was starting to think that a fantasy was about to drop into my lap. Literally. I shoved the paper into my pants pocket and headed for the drug store.

I was so engrossed in my daydreaming about Julie I had almost forgotten why I needed to come in here anyway. Thank goodness it wasn't for rubbers. I still had those from the Terry thing. What did I…toothpaste. That's what I came in for. I grabbed some toothpaste, a bottle of mouthwash and a bar of soap. I was getting low on the basics. As I walked by the magazine stand, I picked up the latest issue of Life Magazine. I loved the photography. It was every bit as good as in National Geographic and not just the African ladies, either. The cover of this issue had a picture of some ceremony that the Catholics were putting on for their head guy. Man. Now there was a religion that knew how to put on a show. Most of the preachers I knew were farmers who decided there must be a better way to make a living. I didn't know much about religion. I figured if you wanted to be a preacher, you just said, "I'm a preacher," and you could go get a job with a church somewhere. Or start your own. Either way, it was still better than farming. Except that you couldn't miss a Sunday because you'd been out too late. However, if you were a preacher, you wouldn't be out drinking and chasing women. You'd stay at home on Saturday nights and read the Bible. Super. I think I'd give the farming another shot before going to that kind of extreme.

I took all my stuff up to the register where I saw Jeff. He called me by my name and shook my hand, asking me how I was getting along. This guy was amazing. I hadn't seen him in several weeks, and he remembered my name. He even seemed sincere when he asked how I was doing. He was gonna be a big shot some day. Politics, law, hell, he might end up owning his own company.

The sidewalks weren't too crowded so I decided to head down Main Street and stop by Raymond's place to get a sandwich to go. When I went inside, I was surrounded by cool darkness. Going from the glare outside to the inside of Raymond's took time for your eyes to adjust. I stopped in my tracks to let my eyes adjust when I heard a voice from my right.

"You lost, asshole?"

Lana. The twisted love of my life was perched on a tall stool behind the cash register, chewing angrily at her gum and filing her nails. She never even looked up at me.

"Well, Lana, I see you're attending to the cash flow of this fine establishment today. And a lovely day it is, I might add."

"Fuck you, smartass. You couldn't add two plus two and come up with the right answer," she said as she worked rhythmically on her fingernails.

"You are such a kidder, Lana. Are you going to doing your toenails next?"

"Look, you little cocksucker, do you want something to eat or did you just come in here to make me miserable. I got better things to do than talk to the likes of youins."

"Trust me, I can see that. I am here, now that you mention it, to get one of Raymond's world famous cheeseburgers to go."

"Fries?"

"Yes, please."

"You fuckin' fag," she muttered under her breath as she turned away.

"Thank you, Lana," I said with a slight bow to her. "You do know how to make a person feel at home here."

Without a word or a look back, she gave me the finger. I just shook my head. She could cheer me up with just one of her icy glares. Anything else she did was a gift.

Once my order had been cooked and bagged, you could already see the grease starting to settle in the bottom of the bag. I'd have to carry it by the bottom if I didn't want it to fall through the sack. There was enough grease in that bag to cause cars to slide into one another if I dropped it in the street.

After Lana had taken my money and given me my change, she finally looked me in the eyes and said, "Choke on it."

"Thanks, Lana," I said as I gathered everything together. "It's been a pleasure."

She just turned and walked away without a response. What was not to love about a woman like that? She had to be one of the meanest women this side of the Mississippi River. And she dealt with the public. I think she was that way with everybody. It was possible that she, rather than the food, was the main attraction at this dive. Any other restaurant that had her as the only waitress would go out of business in a week.

Once I got back outside, I really wished that I had bought a pair of sunglasses at the drug store. The brightness of the sun was giving me a headache.

When I got back to the house, Mr. Cummins was at his usual position, rocking along and vainly trying to determine the differences in physical characteristics between his farm creatures and his grandchildren. After all, he looked at them both with equal amounts of affection.

When he noticed my approach, he yelled out, "Hey you no-good bastard. How you ah doin today?"

"Not bad for a no-good bastard. How about you, sir?"

"You a real smartass, ain't cha?" He asked while lifting his bottle to his mouth.

I guess everybody had me pegged as a smartass today. I looked down at my front to see if someone had placed a name tag on me with that written on it.

"I guess so," I replied with a smile.

He just laughed and went back to staring at his relatives.

I carried my stuff up to my room and noticed that Dick's bed was empty and his things were gone. It was kind of depressing to know that two days ago he was a happy athletic kid. Now he was a throw rug with a head.

I got a beer from Larry, who always had some, to help flush down the greasy food. I offered Larry half of my burger, but he declined saying he'd rather go hungry than eat Raymond's slop. I told him about Lana and he shook his head and laughed.

"I think it's some kind of act she has going on with you or something. The two of you have an unwritten script of some kind that you both follow by instinct," he offered.

"Must be, man. Sometimes it's hard as hell to keep a straight face. She tickles me to death with that attitude of hers," I said with a grin.

One of those awkward silences that happens when two people are talking about something that neither of them has any interest filled the room like a thick mist. Avoiding eye contact, Larry finally broke the silence by asking, "I wonder how Dick is doing? His empty bed makes me think of a coffin."

I wish he had used a better choice of words. My mind's eye made a sharp swivel to look back at my earlier thoughts about Dick being better off dead. My emotions rushed back to the moment when Lonnie looked up frantically screaming for help then moved forward to the tears in Dick's eyes. It seemed that he had been able look into the future to see nothing but years of bleakness. An involuntary shudder passed through my body, and I suddenly wanted to get out of Larry's stifling room, as it became hard to breathe. I turned without a word and left. Larry didn't say a word. We were both equally lost in our own guilt and sorrow.

I lay back on my bed and crossed my hands beneath my head. I wondered if I were truly sorry for Dick or was it something else? I had a dim thought that darted from spot to spot in my brain, never stopping long enough for me to identify it. Frustration needled me into forcing myself to deny any further thoughts about Dick or his parents or the accident or whatever the hell it was that was making me so restless. I sat up and drank down half of the beer and opened my sandwich. Now cold and soggy, I threw the whole thing into the trashcan. Fuck it. My stomach was already bothering me anyway. I finished the beer and dropped it on top of the mess in the can. I gotta get out of here, I thought.

I went downstairs and out on to the porch. I was surprised to see that the old geezer wasn't in his chair rocking back and forth as he killed more brain cells. That old bastard was a pretty good guy, I said to myself. Compared to me, he was a real good guy.

I hopped off the porch and broke into a slow trot down the side of the road. A little workout is what I needed instead of sitting around trying to suck the bottom out of a bottle of Budweiser. In a little over four weeks, I would be dying in the blistering August heat while coaches screamed vile names at me and the other players all in the name of character building. So far, I'd seen plenty of characters up here, and I don't think a damn one of them played any fuckin high school football.

As I ran parallel to Main Street, I could see the lights shining brightly from all of the businesses lined along the way. The "locals" with their thick, southern accents and slow ways of moving and talking were actually carefully calculated acts fashioned to delude the tourists. Delude them into thinking that these poor mountain people were so quaint with their mountain fashions and curiosities. The real truth was that several families in Gatlinburg were obscenely wealthy. Some of the wealthiest people in the whole state of Tennessee showed up for work every day in bib overalls and ragged shirts, or they had on cheap-looking calico print dresses that ended at their ankles just above a dirty pair of work-boots. These people were the artists of deception, and I found that a quality that should be developed and nourished. There's no telling how far you could go with the art of deception.

The road ended a few blocks later where it intersected with another large street running perpendicular to Main Street called Airport Road. I didn't even know if Gatlinburg had an airport or not. It was probably named that because they planned to build an airport someday. When they ran out of room on the main drag for shops, restaurants and attractions, the townsfolk just added some more of the same.

I was sweating heavily and bent deeply at the waist trying to catch my breath. I've got to quit with the smoking I thought. It was killing my wind. When I straightened up, I decided to head back to the house and call it a night.

I stuck my hand in my pocket to see if I had enough change to stop at a coke machine and found a scrap of paper in my hand. It was too dark to read, so I moved closer to the lights of the street. Damn. Julie's phone number. I had forgotten all about it.

I turned back toward airport road in search of a pay phone. I spotted one about a block up the road at a filling station. When I got there, I flipped open the coin return to see if some dumbass had left any change in there. No luck. I held the receiver next to my ear with my shoulder while I held Julie's number up against the glass of the booth. I dropped a dime in the slot and dialed the number. Before it rang, I slammed the phone back down and thought, "What if Julie's husband answered the phone? Ask for Dave? Oh, shit. What if her husband's name was Dave? Then he'd ask me who I was. What the fuck then? What was her husband's name? I'm sure I'd heard her say it. Damn. Try to think. Then I thought of something. Julie wasn't stupid. She wouldn't give me a piece of paper with her phone number and the words "Call Me" written on it. She had to be sure he was in California or Montana or someplace far, far away. But then again, what if he came home unexpectedly? What then?

I just wasn't prepared to deal with all of the things that could possibly go wrong. Then I realized I didn't have a thing to worry about. If he answers, I'll just hang up. There. Problem solved.

Pleased with my ability the use simple reasoning, I dialed Julie's number. When she answered, I felt a funny rush in my stomach and chest.

"Hello? Is anybody there?"

I don't know how many times she had said hello so I almost yelled into the receiver, "Hello, Julie. It's Doug."

"Why are you yelling, Doug?"

"Uh…er…I thought we might have had a bad connection. Anyway…uh…how are you?"

"I'm fine, Doug. You're a real sweetie to call me. I didn't know if you would or not," she said with what sounded like little-girl shyness.

My heart started hammering in my chest and my breathing became difficult.

"Well, that's me, you know. Sweet Doug."

I sounded like the village idiot. Had I forgotten how to talk? Why in the fuck was I saying 'Sweet Doug'. I better get hold of myself before I did something really stupid. As if I hadn't done enough already.

"You sure are, honey. Where are you calling from?"

"A pay phone," I said quickly.

Good. I got that question right.

"I know that, silly. I can hear traffic in the background. **Where** is the pay phone then?" She asked.

If she had any doubts about my stupidity, I had certainly put them all to rest in less than one minute of conversation.

"Oh. Over on Airport. At a…uh…Texaco station," I said as I spun like a top in the phone booth, the cord almost cutting off my windpipe.

"I know just where you are. Aren't you gonna ask me why I wanted you to call me?"

"Well…uh…sure. Why did you ask me to call me? No. I mean why did I ask to call you?"

"Are you okay? Been doin some drinkin?"

Based on my performance thus far, I genuinely wanted to say I was drunk on my ass. Nobody could be this much of a jerk and be stone sober at the same time.

"Uh…no. Actually, I've been out running. Trying to get into shape. For football, you know. Starts pretty soon."

I really wanted this conversation to either end or take a whole new direction, because I was dying a slow death by humiliation. I wondered if the undertakers could get that kind of pained expression off a dead man's face?

"If you want my opinion, I like your shape just the way it is," she purred into the phone.

Trying to be as dashing as I could, I responded, "I…uh…like your shape, too."

I cringed and bent over as far as the booth would allow and rested my forehead on the cool glass. Did you ever want to just reach out and grab some words that popped out of your mouth from nowhere? I sincerely hoped my brain didn't create that remark. If it did, I should go shoot myself before things got worse.

"Oh, my. You're so sweet for saying that. As a matter of fact, I was gonna suggest we get our two shapes together. What do you think about that idea, honey?"

What did I think? Was she saying what I think she was saying? Not in my wildest dreams. I've already shown her that thinking and conversation were way beyond my meager social skills.

"You still there, Dougy?"

"YEAH. I mean…yeah. That's sounds like a good idea. I mean…what **do** you mean?"

Oh, that was good, I thought. I started pounding my forehead with my hand.

"What's that noise I hear, sugar?"

"Uh, must've been a car with a flat tire."

How awfully clever of me. I was beginning to sweat profusely, now.

"Oh. Well, what I had in mind was maybe a little moonlight picnic. By the river. Just you and me. Whatta you say to that, baby?"

I began to gnaw on my right index finger to keep from screaming. My legs were shaking so badly, people going by would think I was listening to Elvis songs over the phone.

As calmly as I could, I said, "Sounds like a winner to me."

Surely, by now, she would hang up on me.

"Goody. Earl's gonna be makin a west coast turn next week so we'll get together one night then," she said with some finality.

Earl. Damn. I knew that.

"That'll be great. By the way, where is old Earl tonight?"

"He's in the shower right now. I'm glad you called when you did. You must have some kind of radar in your head."

I almost fell to my knees. I thought to myself, HE'S HOME? You used my name? Maybe I should go kill myself now and save Earl the aggravation. Moreover, what I have in my head is absolutely nothing. No brain, no radar, a vacuum.

"You still there, honey?"

"Yeah. When do we do this? I mean get together and all?"

"I've got to go. I heard the water stop running. We'll talk later. Bye, sugar."

She said the last part so rapidly and hung up, I didn't even get to say good-bye. I looked at the receiver in my hand for a few seconds before hanging up. I think that I just made a date with a married woman. A married woman five or six years older than me. A woman with a real live husband. Thankfully, my infallible logic kicked in again. I said to myself, screw Earl. I'm about to have an unbelievable fantasy come true.

I ran back to the house with renewed energy. I was gonna get laid by an honest-to-God, grown-up, MARRIED woman. How the hell did I ever get here?

Chapter Twenty Four

When I got back to the house, I ran upstairs and grabbed my shaving kit. Not only did I need a bath, I needed to relax. I was way too hyper. I started to stick my head in Larry's room to see if he was awake so that I could tell him about Julie. Fortunately, I pulled up short, when common sense set off a rare warning in my head. What the hell was I thinking? Tell somebody? Great. Maybe I should put it in the newspapers so old Earl could read about it while he was eating his breakfast. **Busboy Screws Earl's Wife,** the headline would read. Maybe he could find out about it on the radio station. **This announcement just in: In a recent report from an anonymous, but reliable, source in Gatlinburg, we've just learned that a busboy named Doug Wallace has been porking a hostess named Julie. Reports say that they both work at the M&S Restaurant, and they laugh at Julie's husband, Earl, when he's on a trip. More on this story later.** Earl would hear that on his radio and run over school buses full of kids just so he could get to me and tear out my heart with his bare hands.

Nope, this one had to stay with me. Jesus, it was like getting a great present except I couldn't show it to anybody. There I go, making chicken shit out of chicken salad. I had to think positive about this turn

259

of events. Viewed from every possible angle, I couldn't foresee a single thing going awry if Julie and I played our cards right. We just had to be careful. I wasn't some dumb kid anymore. I was going to treat this like a real man would. A real man wouldn't go blabbing about running around with some married lady. If he did, he'd be a real dead man. I wondered if I could get a picture of Julie to take back home with me? I'd have to see about borrowing somebody's camera or something. You sure as hell couldn't buy a souvenir like that anywhere in town.

After I'd gotten cleaned up, I realized it was only nine thirty. This would be the earliest I'd gone to bed since I'd moved up here. I didn't want to go out, but I was too hyped up to go to sleep either. I'll read. That'll help me relax. I picked up a paperback I'd been reading for the last two weeks. Finally, I slept.

When I got up the next morning, I noticed that I had not used the alarm to awaken. I guess my body had become accustomed to getting up before dawn.

I got dressed as quickly as I could and headed out for the restaurant. I kept replaying in my mind the conversation I had the previous evening. Just to make sure I wasn't dreaming, I pulled Julie's phone number out of my shirt pocket and looked at it closely. Yep. I could see sweat smears on it. I don't know if I had been sweating from my run or from nerves. Either way, I knew that this whole thing was real. In fact, I felt butterflies in my stomach to the point of almost being sick.

When I got to the restaurant, the heavy odor of frying pork did nothing to help the condition of my stomach. When I got into the kitchen, I grabbed a glass and filled it with milk in hopes that it would make me feel better.

Roy watched me gulp down the milk and asked with a big grin on his face, "What's got into you, boy? Get some more 'shine' last night? You tryin to get yore stomach lined up?"

He had been teasing me unmercifully about moonshine ever since the party. I'm certainly glad I could bring a ray of sunshine and happiness into his life by nearly dying. I was really getting tired of his bullshit.

"No, Roy, I didn't drink any moonshine last night. As a matter of fact, I've had enough of that stuff to last me for the rest of my life. I was trying to coat my stomach a little before I tried to eat some of that shitty, yellow mess that you think passes as scrambled eggs."

I left the kitchen and went out to get some coffee. There was one pot brewing, so I put on another. We usually tried to keep four pots up all of the time. The employees would consume the first pot and a half and the rest would get us started for the early rush.

Because I was so anxious to see Julie when the night side came in to work, I thought the day would never end even though we were pretty busy. Finally, about two fifteen, I saw her come in the front door in one of her flowered cigarette dresses. My heart leaped to my throat, and it was all I could do to move. She saw me looking at her and gave me a sly wink. For a moment, I forgot where I was and what I was doing. I was on automatic pilot as I finished cleaning the table and took the tub back to the dishwasher.

Julie was back there being Julie. Teasing and flirting with everybody. For a moment, I was concerned that she might have just playing some game with me. As I was emptying out my tub, I felt someone come up next to me. When I turned, Julie was standing so close, her right breast was pushing against my left arm.

She stood on her tiptoes and whispered two words, "Soon honey."

When I looked at her again, she gave me a wink and mouthed the words, "call me."

If there were an odor to testosterone, mine would have drowned out all the different odors in that hot, steamy kitchen. I felt for an instant that I wasn't going to be able to breathe. Moreover, I was positive that I was in love with her.

It was all I could do to leave the restaurant that day. I just wanted to go sit in a booth and stare at her. Knowing that was impossible, I decided to head back to the house as quickly as possible. I needed to go work out or do something to burn off the adrenaline rush that was causing my heart to race wildly.

As I approached the house, I saw Mr. Cummins back at his usual post.

"How are you today, sir?" I asked cheerfully as I bounded onto the porch.

He gave me one of his sideways looks and asked, "What the hell you so fired up about?"

"I'm just so glad to see you," I responded with a big smile.

"Go on and git away from me, you lyin little bastard. You so fulla shit, yore eyes is brown," he said with his signature cackle.

Hmm. It just so happened, my eyes were brown so I good-naturedly gave him the finger and ran into the house. I was already at the top of the steps before he made any kind of response. I was so full of energy I told myself that I better put this drive to some good use. Since my laundry bag was about full, I decided to get the washing done. That would be a productive thing to do. Besides, I could probably find a pay phone somewhere and give Julie a call at work. The hostess on duty always answered the phone so I didn't have to worry about old Earl picking up the phone.

This time I got my laundry done without using the wrong machine. Since that first time, I would always check three times to see if the coin slot was connected to the machine. To the other people in the place, I guess I appeared to be from another country or something. In case anybody asked me if I needed help, I was going to speak to him by using a mixture of sounds that sounded vaguely German. I was afraid somebody might actually speak Spanish, and French sounded too much like some kind of fag language to me. To my ear, the German language always sounded like you were about to get clobbered even if you were being asked directions for the bathroom. That kind of aggressiveness would deter anybody from helping me, unless of course they turned out to be German. In which case, I was screwed. However, nobody seemed to pay any attention to me, but I was glad to have a plan in place in case I needed it.

After I had gotten the wash cycle going, I left to find a phone. Directly across the street, there was a wax museum where you could see mannequins made up to look like famous dead people. I'd been through it twice and found it to be simply terrible both times. I guess I went in twice because it was free to the locals. The only people that you could actually charge for something like that and get away with it were people you hoped you never saw again. I'm sure if anyone ever came back to this place for a second vacation, they would definitely avoid this crappy joint.

I pulled some change from my pockets and realized that I didn't know the phone number for the M&S. When I pulled out the phone book, I noticed that some asshole had torn out all of the pages that had the restaurant listings. I couldn't believe somebody could be so damn thoughtless. I hope whoever did tear out those pages died from food poisoning from their next meal. Served them right.

I went over to the glass booth where a bored-looking brunette, about my age, was chewing gum and reading a paperback novel.

Without looking up from her book, she asked, "How many?"

"Forty," I said.

That got her attention. When she looked at me and peered around trying to see the other thirty-nine people, I said, "Just kidding. I need to see your phone book. Okay?"

She pulled the small book from a shelf in front of her and slid it under the glass in the booth.

"Here, you smart bastard. Don't run off with it either," she said as she glared at me.

Man, if something that minor set her off, I'd say she had more problems than a rotten personality and acne on her chin. I was tempted to say "nice zit," but thought better of it.

I found the phone number, said it to myself five times and shoved the phone book back at Miss Congeniality.

"Thanks."

"Fuck you," she replied without looking up.

I thought about asking her if I could go get her some Midol, but I really didn't have time to waste aggravating this dumbass.

I went back to the phone booth and dialed the number of the restaurant. It rang about fifteen times before Julie picked up.

"M&S. May I help you?"

"Hey, Julie, it's me. At first I thought I'd dialed the wrong number. It rang so much."

"I was selling a cigar, sugar. You know how that is."

"Yeah."

"So what's going on?"

"Me and you, I hope."

"Where's Earl?"

"Somebody called him and asked him if he could make the California run in a few days. Said they'd pay him extra if he would. Naturally, I encouraged him to do it," she said with a giggle.

She continued, "You want to get together real soon? Go have a picnic? Do some skinny-dipping?"

Oh, God, I thought. She just came right out and said we were gonna get naked. That meant sex for sure. Oh, man. This was too good to be true.

"You still there, honey?"

"Uh, yeah."

"I'll bring some chicken and beer, and you bring yourself. You know where the Holiday Inn is out on Airport Road?"

"Yeah."

"There's a little market right next to it. I'll pick you up about dark. Say around eight o'clock. That sound good to you?"

"Yeah."

"Great. Then we got a date. I got to run, baby. I'm so glad you called. See you Thursday, darlin."

"Yeah."

She hung up and I stood there and thought to myself, she's sure not shy about taking control of the situation. It was a good thing, too. For all I contributed to the conversation, she could have been talking to a trained seal that barked on command.

I hung up the phone and started walking in the direction of the Cummins' house. I'd gone about a block when it suddenly occurred to me that about every stitch of clothes that I owned was back at the coin laundry. So I turned around and went back to finish that and start planning for Thursday. What did I need to plan? Hell, she was running this show with beautiful precision. I've seen coaches whose game plan wasn't as good as this was.

I finally got my laundry done and headed back home. By now, the tourists were out on the prowl for some place to eat. I figured I'd go dump my stuff and do the same thing. The walk back to the house would remain imprinted on my mind forever. Besides the relief of the cool mountain air, I felt as if I was floating along, my feet not even touching the ground. Everywhere I looked, I saw smiling, happy faces and heard pleasant, cheerful conversations. Children seemed to be happy and content. My whole world had changed again in a matter of twenty-four hours, and it seemed as though everyone else was touched by my good fortune.

When I got back to the house, Mr. Cummins had fallen asleep in his rocker. I slipped past him quietly and went upstairs. Lonnie and Larry were in their room drinking beer and talking about the Navy. When they saw me, they told me to come in and grab a beer.

"Lonnie's thinking about skipping the repeat of his last year in high school and going straight into the Navy," explained Larry.

I looked at him and asked, "What made you decide on that?"

"I met this guy today at work. He's here on his honeymoon, and he and I started talking about jobs and stuff. I asked him what he did, and he told me he was a midshipman in the Navy. I told him that I was going to enlist right after I finished high school. He told me not to waste my time with high school, that I could get my college diploma while I was in the Navy through some kind of program they have. He said it was a good deal, and I'd still be getting full pay and everything."

"What do you think your parents will have to say about it?" I asked him.

"They don't give a shit. Anyway, Larry is the scholar in the family. He's gonna go to college. Me, I want to get started on my career now. I've wanted to be in the Navy since I was a little kid. My dad was in the Navy during World War II, so I'll bet he'll be proud of me."

I looked over at Larry, and he was grinning and nodding his head.

"Sounds like you've got it all figured out," I replied.

Larry announced, "A toast to my brother, Popeye."

We touched our bottles together and laughed at Larry's joke.

"Why don't we go somewhere nice for a change and get a real meal? We could get a steak or something," Larry said with some excitement.

"Let's do it," Lonnie and I said in unison.

That night, we all went to the Open Hearth and ordered rare steaks with baked potatoes, salads and quarts of iced tea. Then we left the waitress a big tip and went over to the Graystone and sat down to watch all the people go by.

"Man, that was a great idea," I said as I plopped down in a lounge chair.

We all three lit up cigarettes and sat silently while we smoked.

For about an hour, we made small talk until we decided to head back to the house. The heavy meal had made us all a little sleepy. When I turned in that night, I sort of envied Lonnie for getting some direction in his life. That was better than not having any idea what you wanted to do. My goals were all very short-term, but I could live with that, too.

The next few days dragged by slowly. I spent my evenings working out and reading in order to try to make time move a little faster. I arrived to work early every day with the hopes that the day would zip by for me. Pleasantly surprised, I discovered that Julie had switched shifts with Lois so she could be off nights for the weekend. I tried my best to pretend that it was just another day at work, but every time Julie and I made eye contact, my heart would skip a few beats. Several times she winked at me discreetly, and I could feel myself blushing uncontrollably. I was nothing but a ball of nerves and hormones all wrapped up in a bag of skin.

The next day, she came up to me and whispered one word in my ear: "Sunday."

My legs started shaking.

By Sunday, I was fit to be tied. What in the world was I going to do until tonight? I made some plans. I would go for a long run, take a bath, grab a couple of beers and just rest. I had the feeling that extra energy was going to be part of what I brought to the picnic.

While I was making a pot of coffee, Julie stepped up next to me and breathed into my ear, "See you at eight. Okay?"

Before I could turn and answer her, she was striding away toward the door. She knew damn well I was going to be there.

I spent the longest afternoon in my young life trying to make time go by faster. I worked out. I read. I worked out, again. I went for a one-hour jog. I shaved, bathed and mooched a couple of beers off of Larry.

"What are you up to tonight?" Larry asked me.

"Nothing much, man. Thought maybe I'd go to the wax museum or something," I said, trying to sound casual.

"You gotta be shittin me. That's the worst damn thing in this whole town. Besides, I thought you'd been there before. I know you have. I remember you bitching about it."

Thinking fast, I replied, "Oh, you got the wrong idea, man. I'm gonna try to hit on the girl that works at the ticket booth. See if I can get anywhere. You know?"

"Good luck," he said with a smile.

"Yeah, thanks."

By seven, I left the house and headed for the Holiday Inn on Airport. It was only a half-hour walk but I couldn't stand hanging around any longer. Besides, maybe Julie would show up a little early.

I took my time getting there so I wouldn't have to stand around like an idiot. I was afraid that somebody might come up to me and ask me if I was meeting a married woman. Damned if I needed that grief. When I got to the hotel, I went inside and walked over to the brochure rack and flipped through those as if I was looking for something. After a few minutes, I noticed the desk clerk watching me. Probably thought I was going to take a bushel of his precious brochures. I nodded at him and left.

I went into the little market next door and bought a pack of Marlboros and a pack of gum. While the clerk rang up my stuff, I asked her what time it was. She looked at her watch and told me it was eight o'clock.

Suddenly I began to panic. Hurry up, I thought to myself.

"You want a bag for that?" She asked.

"NO. I mean, no thanks."

I left the store and looked around for Julie. After a few minutes, I went back into the store and asked the clerk for the time.

"It's about five minutes later than when you asked me before," she answered.

I didn't respond because I had started filling my head with all of the possible things that could go wrong. Earl came home. She had a car wreck. She was just playing a big joke on me. I finally decided that it was all of them. She had a wreck on the way to tell me it was a big joke, and somebody had called Earl. I stood there staring at the ground when I saw my feet light up by a pair of car headlights. I looked up. **Julie.** And she was smiling.

I went around to the passenger side of the '59 Ford and climbed in. Julie was wearing a tee shirt and some cut-off jeans. She was barefooted.

"Did you think I'd forgotten you, hon?"

"No. I knew you'd be here," I answered, trying to sound confident.

Then she leaned over and kissed me full on the mouth, darting her tongue in and out of my mouth. I was ready to consummate our relationship right there. In the front seat of the car. In the parking lot.

"You seem stiff. Are you okay?"

Only part of me was stiff. The rest was jello.

"Yeah. I'm fine."

"Goody. Reach back there and get us a couple of cold beers and we'll be on our way. I can hardly wait," she said as she looked over at me.

You can hardly wait? I've been waiting all my life for this moment, I thought.

I got two beers as she pulled out of the parking lot and headed out of town. We listened to the radio as we took the dark, winding road through the mountains, past The Sinks.

"Isn't that were your friend got hurt?"

"Yeah. Right there."

"Happens to somebody every year. They ought to rope that place off as being too dangerous," she said with some conviction.

In about five minutes, she pulled the car off to a wide place on the bank of the river. The spot was partially hidden by trees, so seeing a car parked there would be very difficult. From that spot, I looked down and saw a small clearing on the edge of the splashing water. There was a full moon that night, so it was easy to see the beauty of the rushing water as it tumbled and foamed its way down the mountain.

When Julie turned off the engine, the only sound we could hear came from beneath the hood as the motor cooled down. That and the river. Finally, we looked at each other and fell into a long, lingering kiss. This time, there was more passion and heat than I could have imagined. We broke apart and looked into each other's eyes.

"Let's get down to the river," she said huskily.

We got out of the car and I pulled the cooler and picnic basket from the back seat. Julie had opened the trunk and took out a huge, multi-colored quilt to spread on the ground. We both carefully negotiated the path down to the river and set everything down in the middle of the small bank. Then we stood up and looked at each other.

"I'll start first, but don't waste a lot of time yourself," she said with a big grin, her teeth illuminated by the moonlight.

She pulled her tee shirt over her head and threw it on the ground. Then she dropped her cut-off shorts to the ground and kicked them away. I, too, had taken off my shirt and shorts and pulled off my tennis shoes. Now came the moment of truth. She quickly slid off her panties and leaned over to remove her bra. Her beauty in the moonlight was breathtaking. I shoved off my underwear, and when I stood up she was wading into the water and gasping from the chill.

"Come on in, sugar. I need to be warmed up."

God, how I hated cold water. But this time was different. I started for the water with long purposeful strides, determined to get in as quickly as I could.

I ignored the first shock of the frigid water as I strode in up to my knees. I wanted to scream, but I wanted to get to her even if it was painful.

Suddenly, Julie said urgently, "Be careful. There's a drop-off right as you..."

My momentum was too much for me to react. My right foot went forward and touched nothing. I went down quickly, wedged my foot between two rocks, twisting my body to the left as I got stuck. The knee joint was not meant for that type of motion and a level of pain ran up to my brain that almost caused me to faint.

Julie swam quickly to my aid and helped me back on shore, our bodies wet and slick against each other. This would have been exciting had I not been in severe pain. I felt my knee beginning to swell. I'd seen this before in football. My knee was wasted.

Julie helped me over to the quilt and kneeled next to me.

"Does it hurt bad, Doug?" She asked nervously.

"Yeah. It's real bad."

She helped me get into my clothes, then dressed herself. Once she had put everything back into the car, she came back and helped me stand up on my left leg.

"Can you make it up the hill, if I help you?"

"I think," I said as I fought back tears.

Julie was much stronger than she looked. She helped me up the hill by nearly carrying me most of the way. After she got me into the car, she backed quickly out of the parking spot and headed back for town. Then I passed out.

When I came to, the car was parked in front of a clinic and a nurse was trying to help me into a wheel chair. The pain from my knee was now a white hot agony that caused my breath to come in short gasps.

"Can you make it, son?" The nurse asked me as I collapsed into the chair.

"I think so," I whispered.

I noticed Julie standing next to the nurse with a look of fearful concern on her face. She held the door open while the nurse wheeled me into a small waiting area. A doctor came out of a room on the right and looked down at my knee.

"Son, I think you're going to need some surgery. Let me get that knee X-rayed, and we'll take a look at what we got here. You a local?"

"He works at the M&S with me," said Julie. "Summer worker."

"Where you from, son?"

"Maryville," I said. "Have you got anything for pain?"

"Linda," he said to his nurse, "fix this young man up with a shot of morphine, while I get things set up in X-ray."

"We better call your parents so they can take you to see your family doctor. I think I know what the x-rays are going to show. I got a son plays for UT's football team."

I wanted to ask him about his son, but I was in too much agony to care. By now I was sweating profusely from the pain.

Julie asked, "Is there anything I can do doctor?"

"Just stay with him while the shot takes effect. You might give his parents a call. I'll talk to them as soon as you get them on the line," he said as he walked into the next room.

"How you doin, sweetheart?"

"I'll be okay," I said, trying to be tough.

She kissed me on the cheek and stepped out of the way as the nurse walked up with the syringe.

"This'll do the trick. The doctor said to give you a pretty healthy dose."

She then turned to Julie and asked her, "Got his home phone number, yet?"

She shook her head and the nurse told her to get it pretty fast before the drug kicked in. After that, she said I wasn't going to be much of a conversationalist.

Julie got a pen and paper from the counter and wrote down my phone number.

The nurse looked at Julie and asked, "You his girlfriend?"

Julie looked at me and said, "Yes. I am."

"Well then, when you call his folks, be sure to start by telling them that he's okay. Then call for me and I'll get Doc on the phone. Understand?"

Julie nodded and left to call my parents.

She told them I was her boyfriend. That felt almost as good as the rush I was beginning to get from the morphine. Soon, I began to float.

"Can you hear me, son? Hey, young fella. I talked to your dad. They said they'd be up here in about an hour and a half. I told them that you had some torn ligament and possibly a dislocated kneecap. They said they'd call their family doctor and have him meet them at the hospital back in your hometown. You understand all that?"

I nodded weakly at him.

I tried to ask where Julie was, but I guess he read my mind.

"I'll send your girlfriend in here to see you. You're a lucky bastard, you know that?"

He said this last comment with a wink and walked off to get Julie. First time I ever been called a bastard by a doctor, but I wasn't really surprised. This was Gatlinburg.

Julie walked in clutching her hands together and took a chair next to me.

"You okay, sweetie?"

"Yeah," I said as I licked at my parched lips.

"You want some water? I'll get you some," she said and walked over to the sink.

When she lifted my head and gave me a drink, I started to thank her. I may have. I don't really remember because my world went blank.

When I awoke, I was in the back seat of my parent's car. My leg was bandaged and stretched out on the seat. My mother heard me stir and turned to face me.

"You okay back there?"

"Yeah. I'm just real groggy. Where are we?"

"Dr. Morton said to take you to Baptist Hospital. He said he'd meet us there with an orthopedic surgeon that he knows. They want to get you worked on as quickly as possible."

I dropped my head back against the seat and pondered my rotten luck. The last ten hours had to be the worst of my life. No, change that. I went from being the happiest I'd ever been to the lowest I'd ever been.

"That is a real nice friend you got there, son. What's her name again?" My Dad asked.

"Julie," my mother answered for me.

"While we were on our way up here, she went by your place and packed up all your stuff. She had it with her when we got there. She said she'd call and check on you."

I smiled to myself and thought, my summer adventure is over. I then fell into a deep sleep.

Chapter Twenty Five

The emergency room at the hospital was all a blur to me. I do know that they gave me another shot for pain. I did awaken briefly to see an orderly shaving my right leg, but before I could tell him to stop, I passed out again.

I awoke in a hospital bed, my mouth stuck shut from dryness. My mother was sitting in a chair at the foot of my bed, half asleep. I reached down to touch my right leg and felt the cast. Straining my neck forward, I could see that the cast ran from my toes to my hip and was elevated on some pillows. I dropped my head back on the pillow and felt tears start to run down both sides of my face. I don't really know why I was crying, because I wasn't in any pain. I guess I just feeling depressed over all the recent turn of events.

My mother got up and walked over to me.

"Are you in pain, honey?"

"No. Yes. Hell if I know. Can you get me a drink of water?"

I normally didn't curse in front of my mother without incurring her wrath, but she let that one slide.

She raised the head of the bed slightly so that I could drink a little more easily.

"Your friend, Julie, called last night to check on you. She said she'd be up to visit you in a couple of days since you were going to be here for the next five days or so."

I nodded and took another sip of water.

"I asked her about how you got hurt, and she told me you slipped on some slick rocks in the river. What were you two doing swimming at night?"

She was prying, and I wasn't opening.

"Because we work days," I said and pretended to fall asleep.

I heard her walk away and sit back down in the chair. "Mother," I thought to myself, "there are some things that are your business and some things that are my business. That was my business." Eventually, I drifted off to sleep.

I woke up when the nurse came in at around ten to take my blood pressure and temperature and, mainly, be a pest.

"How are we feeling this morning?" She asked

We?

I wanted to say that I didn't give a rat's ass about her morning, but mine was pretty shitty. So would she please just go get me some more morphine?

Rough was all I said.

"Any pain?" She asked as she checked my pulse.

"It's killing me," I said, exaggerating.

"Don't try to be a hero. The doctor said you could have something for pain as long as you needed it. I'll be right back with a shot for you."

Good, I thought. Morphine was the only good thing about this whole gig.

Just before lunch, the doctor who operated on me came in to see how I was doing. After he took one look at my glassy eyes, he knew I was in another world. I did hear bits and pieces of what he was telling my mother. Six weeks...cast comes off...weeks of rehab...watch for infection...and on and on. None of it sounded too good, so I let the morphine do its work so I could leave the room or the planet, whichever came first.

For the next two and a half days, I was in and out of a fuzzy world of utopia. I found I could control my universe by pressing on a little button that connected to the nurse's station. When they came in, I complained about needing something for pain. Sunday afternoon, the joy ride came to a halt when the nurse brought back two little tablets in a plastic cup.

"What's that?" I asked. "I need something for pain."

"The doctor changed your prescription from morphine to Tylenol," she said.

"Is it as good as the other stuff?"

"Almost," she answered.

Like a pound is almost like a ton. Whatever the hell Tylenol was, it wasn't morphine. I guess I'd just have to grin and bear it. Bastards.

On Monday, my dad and Rob came in to see me. They brought me some hot rod books and a science fiction paperback but no Playboy. I started to point out the mistake, then decided to leave well enough alone. It really was good to see them. Rob looked like he had grown about three inches since the first of June. They sat around until my lunch came, then left me to enjoy my food. Calling it food was tantamount to lying. If I'd had any money, I'd have asked an orderly to bring me a cheeseburger and a lot of fries. And a six-pack of cold Bud would be nice with that, too. I really was beginning to hate this place.

I spent the afternoon dozing when I felt a hand shaking my shoulder.

"Dougie? You awake, honey?"

I looked up and saw Julie standing over me. For an instant, I thought I'd just had a bad dream, until I tried to raise myself from the bed. Reality set back in quickly.

She smiled at me and said, "I could just eat you up, sugar."

Then she kissed me gently on the lips. From behind her, I heard Paul's familiar voice saying, "Who's up for a party?"

Julie moved to the side, and there stood Paul, Kat and Larry with big grins on their faces.

"How does pizza and beer sound, man?" Larry asked as he held a paper bag up.

"Who has a smoke?" I asked.

Julie lit one up and gave it to me.

"We thought you might need some cheering up."

"Man, it's really good to see you. All of you. How's your mom, Kat?"

"She's doing great. I'll tell her you were asking about her," Kat said with a smile.

"Hey, Larry, did Lonnie tell your parents about wanting to join the Navy?"

"Yep," he replied. "They even said it sounded like a good deal when he told them all of the details. He even quit his job and went back home to sign up."

The pizza was being passed around and beers were being downed at a frenetic pace. This was great. We talked about people we knew and what all was going on. All the time, Julie stood right next to me with her hand caressing my shoulder. Every time I looked at her, she was smiling at me.

"Good to see that sexy smile of yours. You didn't look too good the last time I saw you," she said as her eyes twinkled. "I spoke to both Martha and Sam. They said to tell you to figure on a job as a waiter next summer. You will come back, won't you?"

My eyes welled up with tears, and I said, "Thanks, Julie."

All the fun ended when the nurse came in on her regular rounds. Shocked by seeing the room filled with empty beer cans and pizza boxes, she demanded that everyone get out before she called security.

My friends came over to me to give me a hug or a handshake before they left. They left the room leaving Julie and me alone.

"I've got something to tell you, Doug," she said.

For some reason, I knew I wasn't going to be thrilled with what she had to say.

"Earl and I renewed our marriage vows and now we're tryin' to have a baby. I been knowin' all along that what I been doin' was wrong, and I've felt real bad about it. You understand what I'm sayin', sugar?"

She grasped my hand and I simply nodded yes.

With that, she turned and left me with my thoughts and my sadness. The sadness only lasted for a while because I really felt, deep down inside that the fantasy I was living had to come to an end pretty soon. If it's too good to be true, then it probably is too good to be true.

Man, I thought to myself, I'd come pretty close, and I'd still come away with a lot of knowledge over the summer. Some of it good and some of it bad.

Epilogue

I was going with the flow. High school began that fall with me on crutches and not in a football uniform. Not that I really cared. The cheerleaders appeared to be silly, loud puppets being jerked about by unseen strings. My buddies talked about goofy things that now seemed childish and trivial. I even found a different group of friends who more closely shared my perspective on life. High school seemed to be two more years of stuff to get out of the way, a necessary evil in a way, to advance to college.

The music I enjoyed moved from the Beach Boys to the Beatles to the Rolling Stones. The Stones definitely had the harder, blues edge that I liked. The music was just a microcosm of the changes that were going on in the world that lay beyond the halls of school and the town where I lived.

The Dodgers, in four games, swept the Yankees in the World Series. The Supreme Court outlawed prayer in school. And there was a march on Washington D.C. by over 200,000 blacks and whites over the civil rights issue. Only the last of those three items meant something to me; people who'd been stepped on were getting pissed. It was about time.

Something happened to me that summer that I look back on with both pride and disappointment. I was proud to think I had been exposed to a side of life I never thought existed. I was disappointed that having all the freedom you wanted was a big load to carry. I'll leave it up to you to be the judge of which resulted in pride and which caused the disappointment in your own summer of growth. You've probably traveled a similar path in your life and have your own choices to make, but I guess that gives you the two main ingredients of life.

As the years went by, things got even more complex and so did I.

I now find that nothing was ever as bad as it seemed or as fun as you thought it might be. I used to go to the edge of the cold mountain streams and stop dead in my tracks. But that summer, I didn't stop at the edge. I crossed it and never looked back. Sometimes you get to go over the edge again and breathe life anew. It took me almost thirty years to learn about growing up, and starting at the age of forty-five, I have spent the last eight or so years trying to pick up from that summer of 1963. I'm actually glad I didn't know then what I know now. I'd have missed a wild ride.

+ The End +

About the Author

Mike McNabb is currently a language arts teacher for the Greenville, South Carolina school system. He started writing this novel in 1998, has finished another titled **Out of Focus** and has begun a third novel. He has a short story, **The Exit Interview**, published in the summer 2000 issue of **The Storyteller.** Prior to teaching, Mike worked as a freelance writer and previous to that, spent seventeen years in sales management with Michelin North America.

He has been married to his wife, Kay, for thirty years. The have one son, Chris, who is practicing law in New Orleans and another son, Jon, who is a professional musician and photographer.

The Edge of the Water is his first novel.